Long, Hot
Texas Summer

Long, Hot Texas Summer

Carolyn Brown

Montlake
Romance

Text copyright © 2014 Carolyn Brown

Published by Montlake Romance, Seattle

www.apub.com

Amazon, the Amazon logo, and Montlake are trademarks of Amazon.com, Inc., or its affiliates.

ISBN-13: 9781477823897
ISBN-10: 1477823891

Cover design: Mumtaz Mustafa
Interior design and composition: Greg Johnson/Textbook Perfect

Library of Congress Control Number: 2014901935

Printed in the United States of America

To Jerry and Marian Goshorn
With much love.

Chapter One

*L*IVING IN THE SAME HOUSE with her ex-husband would be pure, unadulterated hell. But Loretta would face off with the devil on his worst day if it made her daughter decide to go back to Oklahoma with her at the end of the long, hot Texas summer. That was the endgame; hopefully it wouldn't take all summer to convince Nona.

The way the light of the big lovers' moon practically made the silver van glow under the twinkling stars, no one would ever guess that anger, determination, and anxiety filled the interior. The air conditioner put out all the cold air it could, but Loretta was still sweating. It had been four years since she'd laid eyes on Jackson Bailey, her ex-husband, and she had no doubt that he hadn't changed a bit.

"We have a request for Randy Travis's 'Deeper Than the Holler.' It dates back more than twenty years, folks. I remember listening to this when I was in high school," the DJ said.

"Oh, honey, I remember that song probably better than anyone in this whole part of Texas," Loretta whispered.

It was the very song that had been playing when she got pregnant with Nona. She and Jackson had gone parking out by the creek and Jackson had spread their old quilt under the big oak tree like they'd done dozens of other times. He'd held her afterward and sang that part of the song to her that said that his love was deeper than the holler and stronger than the river.

The sun had long since slipped over the western edge of the canyon, its last red rays sliding down to the bottom of the big hole called Palo Duro Canyon. The land was flatter than the old proverbial pancake in the Texas Panhandle. But story had it that God needed dirt to make the mountains in the eastern part of the state, so he scooped out a hole to get it. But he saved the most beautiful sunsets in the whole world for that desolate place of crazy formations and red dirt roads.

She made a hard right, leaving the paved road and turning onto one of those very red dirt roads that would have her van looking like shit by the time she reached Lonesome Canyon Ranch. The last time she'd seen a cloud of red dust boiling up behind her had been when she was leaving Lonesome Canyon, not going toward it. Nona had just turned four years old that week and had had no idea her whole world was about to change. She had played with her favorite stuffed Black Angus toy, Bossy, while Loretta alternately cussed and cried.

The old feelings from that night came flooding back and Loretta braked hard right there in the middle of the road, a cloud of red dust enveloping her van. She inhaled deeply, tears running down her cheeks, as the gut-wrenching pain she'd known seventeen years ago returned to tie her insides into knots. She leaned her head on the steering wheel, a broken woman for the second time in her life. She had no choice but to go on, so she took her foot off the brake and put it on the gas pedal.

The windows were up, but she could almost hear the squeak of the Lonesome Canyon Ranch sign as it swung back and forth on rusty chains. There was a time when Loretta had called this place home, when she'd thought she and Jackson were meant to be together, but that all changed in the blink of an eye one Sunday afternoon when Nona lost that damned Black Angus stuffed animal and refused to go to sleep without it.

The moon lit up the two-story white house with six columns holding up the second-floor porch. She and Jackson had had sex out on that porch the night before she left. Everything had been wonderful in their life. They had been young. They had a beautiful daughter they both doted on. They had finally gotten the debts all paid and Lonesome Canyon was showing a sizable profit on the books.

"And now from your all-country, all-night radio station, here's Brooks and Dunn with 'Red Dirt Road,'" the DJ said.

Even after she parked the van in the empty bay, she sat still until the song ended, the lead singer talking about being raised out past where the blacktop ended. She nodded when the lyrics said that's where she drank her first beer, where she found Jesus and wrecked her first car, because it was the story of her life up until she was twenty-two years old. She'd been raised in Claude, up at the top of the canyon, but they'd lived at the end of the blacktop and she'd found Jesus in the old church down in the canyon. She'd wrecked her first car coming up the incline out of the canyon into Claude when she was seventeen and she'd drunk her first beer sitting on a quilt out beside the creek with Jackson right beside her.

She shook her head from side to side when they sang that when they were back on dirt roads it felt as if they had come home. "I'm not home. I'm here to kick some sense into my daughter. And then I'll go back to Oklahoma and Jackson can have this canyon," she said as the song ended.

She hadn't seen Jackson since Nona had turned sixteen and been allowed to drive alone to visit Jackson every other weekend and for at least a month in the summer. But it would take a hell of a lot more than five years, or even one lifetime, for Jackson Bailey to lose his appeal or his power. The appeal she could skirt around; the power, well, she'd meet it head-on.

Their meeting would be like two bull elephants coming at each other from opposite ends of the ranch, and the old house might not even be standing at the end of the long, hot summer with the pressure of Loretta and Jackson across the hall from each other for weeks on end. She would be ecstatic if Nona listened to her arguments and decided to go home in a few days, but Loretta didn't fool herself into believing that could really happen.

Did the idea cross your mind that he might throw you out or tell you to go to a hotel in Amarillo? the voice in her head yelled as she turned off the radio.

"He won't, because that would mean I've got the ability to get under his skin. He'll let me stay to try to prove me wrong. I know him," she argued aloud.

Rosie, the housekeeper/cook/woman who ran the household, opened the door and stepped out into the garage when Loretta set her feet on the concrete floor. "Well, mercy sakes, is that you, Loretta? What are you doing here this time of night? Did Nona forget something?"

"Hello, Rosie. How are you? You haven't changed a bit." Loretta stiffened her backbone and straightened up to her full five feet ten inches in her bare feet. God, she hated being so tall that she dwarfed everyone around her.

Loretta's prayers had been answered when Nona showed signs at an early age of looking like her maternal grandmother—blonde haired, blue eyed, and small of build. She had almost danced with glee when Nona brought home her kindergarten picture with her in the front row. Loretta had always stood with the boys on the back row and the other girls had never let her forget how tall, gangly, and ugly she was with her red hair and long legs.

"Well?" Rosie crossed her arms over her chest. "You going to answer me or not?"

Loretta had always suspected that Rosie had already been there when the first strand of barbed wire went up around Lonesome Canyon Ranch, and no one had had balls big enough to run her off. As housekeeper, cook, and the only really stable person Jackson had ever known, Rosie ran the place with a steel hand and a soft heart. She'd tried her damnedest to talk Loretta out of leaving, but nothing, not even Rosie, could stop her.

Dark brown eyebrows drew down over eyes that were almost black and set into a bed of wrinkles. A sprinkling of gray frosted her dark hair.

"I'm still waiting on answers to my questions. Are you stayin' here and what's going on?" Rosie asked. "I'm gettin' older and bitchier every day. And my patience ain't what it used to be, especially since you left and Sam died and I had to keep Jackson from . . . Hell, you don't need a history lesson. You know that Jackson's daddy died the year after you left and that I never did have any patience," Rosie said.

"I'm here to stay a few days, Rosie. Where is everyone?" Loretta picked up the first of two suitcases, set it on the ground, and reached for the next one.

Rosie stood to one side and held the door for Loretta. "Nona is out on a date with Travis and Jackson is out to dinner with . . . hell, I can't remember her name. You're really plannin' on stayin' here?"

"I am." Loretta popped up the handles on the suitcases and rolled them toward the door. "Is there a problem with that?"

Rosie shook her head. "Not from me there ain't. I don't even like this woman he's out with tonight. She's wishy-washy and too damn quiet for Jackson. Does he know you're coming?"

"No, and I'm glad he's out to dinner with whoever it is. I can get settled in before he even knows I'm here," Loretta said.

"Need some help?" Rosie asked.

"No, but thank you. Is he still in our old bedroom?" Loretta asked.

"You can have that one. It's still like it was when you left it. He never slept in that room again after you run off instead of stickin' around and fightin' it out. Why in the hell haven't you called me all these years? If you was still a kid, I'd take a switch to your backside." Rosie talked all the way through the kitchen, the dining room, the foyer, and to the bottom of the curved staircase. "I expect you are here because Nona has decided to stay on at the ranch and not go back to school, right? Well, there will be fireworks. They should have happened back when Nona was a baby, but later is better than never. I'm not carryin' no luggage up there so you'll have to make two trips and if you bump the walls, you'll be cleanin' the marks off before you even look cross-eyed at that bathtub."

Loretta carefully maneuvered one suitcase upstairs. "You remembered."

"Of course I remembered. I was surprised you left it behind when you ran off like a crazy mule with a burr under its saddle."

"I still love that old tub and that's where I'm headed soon as I get unpacked," Loretta said.

"I reckon you've got two hours until they both get home. I don't even want to be here when that happens. So why now, Loretta?" Rosie asked.

Loretta stopped on the third step. "I'm not sure, but my heart said I had to try to change her mind about school, so here I am."

"It's good to have you back home. I'll see you at breakfast."

"Rosie, I'm not home. I'm here for one reason and that's to take my daughter back where she belongs. I hope it only takes a few days," Loretta said with as serious a tone as she could muster.

Rosie had hit the nail on the head when she'd asked if Loretta had thought about what she was doing, because she hadn't, not for a minute. Loretta had done two impulsive things in her life. One was leaving the ranch without giving Jackson a chance to explain jack shit before she filed for divorce; the other was coming back to stay at least a month without asking or telling Jackson jack shit.

She opened her first suitcase and her cell phone rang before she could remove a single item. Hoping that it was Nona, she flipped it open and answered without even looking at the caller ID.

"What in the hell are you doing? I swear to God, you never learn. Mama gave you a job when you came home with a baby and needin' a place to live, so why the devil would you ever go back there with Nona grown? Haven't you caused enough trouble and heartache for the family?" Emmy Lou, the oldest of her younger sisters, ranted.

"Well, thank you so much for the vote of confidence."

"You never did have a lick of common sense." Emmy Lou always was the bossiest of the four sisters.

"Tell you what, I'll lay the phone down and you go on and tell me how I ruined your life because I got pregnant and Mama couldn't bear the shame so she moved y'all to Oklahoma. I reckon by the time you get through with your bitchfest I should have my suitcase unpacked."

"Don't you dare!" she yelled. "I was just a kid when I said that."

"You might have been a kid the first time you said it but not the last time you brought it up, right?" Loretta reminded her.

Emmy Lou changed the subject: "Daddy is disappointed in you."

"That won't work either. I'm here on a mission. When it's completed, I'll go home. I suppose I can expect calls from Dolly and Tammy tonight too? I'm going to put you on hold. Mama is beeping in," Loretta said.

"Don't bother. I'll hang up. This is the biggest mistake you've ever made. Good-bye!"

Loretta punched a button and said, "Hello, Mama. I'm here and the trip went just fine. I'm unpacking now and Emmy Lou just called. I'm still happy to be the black sheep, so don't give Dolly or Tammy my dunce hat."

"You have six weeks of vacation time built up. I don't have to like the way that you choose to use it, but you remember things can change in six weeks," her mother, Katy, said coldly.

"Is that an ultimatum?" Loretta asked.

"I don't issue threats or ultimatums. I state facts. We'll all talk again in a few days when the tempers have cooled down. Give Nona a hug from me," Katy said.

The line went dead.

Loretta threw herself back on the bed and stared at the ceiling. She was forty years old, not eighteen and pregnant. The past should be dead and buried, but leave it to family to keep digging up the dry old bones time and time again.

She needed a drink or a maybe a long talk with Heather and Maria. She picked up her phone and punched in the number for Heather, but all she got was a computerized message saying that the number had been disconnected.

"Well, dammit," she mumbled. "I just talked to them a few months ago."

Hell, no! that niggling voice inside her head said. *The last time you talked to your two old friends was Christmas before last and that was eighteen months ago.*

❋ ❋ ❋

Nona snuggled down into the crook of Travis Calhoun's arm and tried to catch her breath as the warmth of afterglow settled around them. He traced her full lips with a fingertip before he brushed a sweet kiss across them.

"We have a request for 'Deeper Than the Holler,' by Randy Travis. It dates back more than twenty years, folks. I remember listening to this when I was in high school," the DJ on the radio said.

"Listen to the words of this song, Nona. This is our song from now on. This is how deep my love is for you. We'll be dancing to this when we have grandchildren," he whispered.

"Honey, I hope when we are old we are listening to this song after a hot bout of sex, not dancing to it," she said.

Travis hugged her closer to his side and wrapped his fingers up in her long blonde tresses. "Do you realize this is our last night in the bunkhouse? The full summer crew is arriving by sundown tomorrow."

She snuggled up closer to him. "We'll find another place. Daddy goes out on Saturday night pretty often and we could go to my bedroom. Or there's always under that old oak tree by the creek. I'll put a quilt behind the seat of my truck."

"Not on your life. Jackson Bailey would shoot me if he caught me near your bedroom. It wouldn't be a question of firing me." He pushed her hair back and kissed the soft part of her neck. "He would tack my hide to the smokehouse door as an example. And that creek is too public, darlin'. I was thinkin' more of a hotel room in Amarillo."

Nona pulled his face toward hers for series of hot, steamy kisses that left them both panting. "He'd have to shoot *me* first, darlin'. I'll protect my big, handsome cowboy from now on. I'm never leaving again."

"Your mama isn't going to like that decision."

"No, she isn't, but at least she's in Oklahoma. I don't have to see her face-to-face every day."

With his black hair; deep, dark eyes; and hunky, sexy body, Travis had set Nona's heart into double time from the first time she'd met him. She hadn't looked at another man the same since that day last summer. She'd spent two miserable semesters in college, making good grades, but her heart was at Lonesome Canyon with Travis every day of that year. Even with the texting and daily phone calls, the only place she'd wanted to be was at the ranch. Now that she was here and in his arms, she'd be damned if she left him again. She was a rancher by birth, by heart, and by choice and there was nothing her mother could do about it. And by staying in Lonesome Canyon, she was doubly blessed. She got to do the job she loved right beside the man she loved.

"I missed you so much." Travis's drawl came through even more when he whispered. "But I don't want you to make this decision and then regret it."

She rolled up on an elbow. "I made this decision before you ever came into the picture. I didn't even want to go to college. I wanted to start living on the ranch right out of high school and every semester since I've wanted to drop out. But this time my mind is made up. If—and that's a big word no matter how small it sounds—I decide I need to finish, I'll go back later. I'm a rancher and I'm going to prove it this summer by showing Daddy how hard I can work. That means midnight is my curfew, because I've got to get up early in the morning for chores before church."

He chuckled. "You might think about online courses like I've been doing, princess."

"Honey, I'm not a princess. The cowboy boots setting beside this bed don't turn into glass slippers at midnight. That means we have three hours to take advantage of this bunkhouse." She rolled on top of him.

Travis wrapped his arms around her. "You sure those boots don't have magic in them? You sure look like one to me."

She laid a finger over his lips. "Darlin', a princess is interested in a prince. I'm in love with a cowboy."

Chapter Two

*J*ACKSON'S DARK BROWN HAIR curled up on his shirt collar. Black lashes and heavy brows framed his blue eyes. A few crow's-feet around his eyes were the only sign that he'd just passed his fortieth birthday and they were minimized in the dim restaurant lights. His jeans were creased and stacked up over his highly polished black boots just the right way. Waitresses stopped what they were doing and gazed at him over their shoulders as he passed.

Their waitress led them to a corner table at the back of the restaurant and Jackson pulled out a chair for his date, Amelia. A fat white candle in the middle of the table put off a personal glow—enough for them to see each other, but limiting their field of vision to the edges of their table. The waitress took their steak orders and reappeared a few minutes later with two tall, frosted mugs of beer.

"So tell me all about your week," Jackson said.

Amelia, a dark-haired schoolteacher with dark eyes and a bright smile, picked up her mug of beer. "Pretty routine. Spent the week doing inventory and today all of us teachers had a potluck lunch and then finally got checked out for the summer. I don't have to look at my classroom again until fall."

"What about the summer? Got plans?" He liked Amelia, enjoyed her company. She was comfortable and she didn't fuss when the conversation turned to Loretta, which it did pretty often. And she was very easy on the eyes, with her slightly tanned skin and curves in all the right places.

She set the beer down and dabbed at her mouth with an oversized white napkin. "Have to do about a week of in-service hours to keep my certificate current, but I'm getting that done next week. Then at the end of June I'm joining my two best friends for a trip to the beach for a couple of weeks, maybe longer if we don't start to get on each other's nerves. Other than that, I'm going to sleep late, watch movies all night, and take care of my garden. It's been a tough year with twenty-five fourth graders in my classroom. Biggest class I've ever had to teach. You wouldn't believe the difference that five rowdy ten-year-old boys can make. And I'm ready to get my hands in the dirt, do some canning, and forget about the classroom."

Jackson smiled. "Summer is my busiest season and I love it."

Amelia reached across the table and covered his big hand with her small one. "Nona came home for the summer, right? Happy to have her back on the ranch?"

Jackson pulled his hand away from hers and raked his fingers through his hair. "Loretta is going to shoot flames out her ears if Nona doesn't go back to college, but the girl wants to learn the ranching business and I can see her point. Besides, I've walked a mile in her shoes. My mama wanted me to go to college, but all I wanted to do was ranch. She's my only child, so she will inherit the whole shebang and if she doesn't even know how to run it, it'll all go to ruin."

Amelia took another long drink of her beer and smiled at him. "Nona could finish her education, make Loretta happy, and still learn ranchin' in the summer and during vacation time from college. It's only one more year, Jackson. She's got three behind her already and it would be a shame to drop out now. And, darlin', you aren't too old to have another child. Then the ranch would be split two ways, or maybe you'd even have a son who would carry on at Lonesome Canyon like you've done."

"Children are definitely not something in my future," he said.

"What would you do if you did find out you were going to be a father again? In this day and age lots of people don't even start a family until they are forty or older," Amelia said.

"I can't imagine diapers, colic, and teething in my life right now. Hell, I don't even want to think about that. I've got a daughter I adore who is willing to learn the business," he said.

The waitress set a bowl of salad in front of each of them and refilled their beer mugs. "Your steaks are on the grill. They'll be out in a few minutes. Anything else?"

Jackson shook his head. "Not right now."

For the first time the silence between them was uncomfortable. He felt as if there was a full-grown elephant in the restaurant with them. They could both see it and they could both smell it, but neither of them would acknowledge the critter.

It stayed that way all through the dinner and the whole way back to the ranch. Country music played on the radio, but Jackson didn't listen to the lyrics. He tried to think of something to say. Nothing came to mind.

"You've been quiet," Amelia said as they dropped down into the canyon south of Claude. "Is Nona at the house?"

"No, she's out on a date with her boyfriend. I like him, but Loretta thinks he's out to get a toehold on the ranch. He's a hardworkin' cowboy and Flint, my foreman, is training him up to take his place in the next ten years. Travis will make a damn fine foreman. He's got ranchin' in his blood the same way Nona does."

"What if you are wrong and Loretta is right?" Amelia asked.

"Are you trying to pick a fight?"

"No, I'm only askin' a question."

"I'm not wrong. Travis is a good man. I know the Calhouns—he comes from quality stock," Jackson said.

"I'm talking about Nona. What if this is nothing more than a fling and she throws her whole life away for it? What if in four years she leaves with your grandson or granddaughter in the backseat of an old car like Loretta did? That will break your heart all over again, Jackson. Maybe you should take a step back and rethink this whole thing of going to battle with Loretta," Amelia said.

"I'm not talking to Loretta about anything. She can stay in Oklahoma and I'll damn sure stay in Texas. We haven't even seen each other since Nona turned sixteen and started driving herself to the canyon for visits," Jackson said through clenched teeth.

"Okay. Mind if I come in for a drink? We really need to talk," Amelia asked.

"Sure, but I don't want to talk about this anymore," Jackson said.

"Not about Nona. We need to talk about us, Jackson," Amelia said.

He crawled out of the truck, rounded the tail end, and opened the door for her. Yes, they did need to talk, even if it wasn't anything more than agreeing to disagree about Nona.

Amelia led the way into the house. "One drink, one goodnight kiss, and then I'm going home."

She stopped in the wide foyer, turned around, and rolled up on her toes for a hard kiss.

The moment his lips touched hers, an enormous chandelier switched on right above them. Once Jackson's eyes adjusted from semidarkness to full-blown light, he thought he was seeing things. Surely to God that wasn't Loretta standing at the bottom of the staircase, wearing a flowing silk nightgown the same emerald green as her flashing eyes. Red hair flowed over her shoulders. She was even more gorgeous than she'd been the last time he'd seen her. His mouth felt as if he'd eaten a dirt sandwich and even when he blinked a dozen times, she was still there, so it wasn't an illusion.

"Good God, Jackson, our daughter is living in this house. You don't bring your bimbos home with her in the house, do you?" Loretta's voice got louder with each word.

That was definitely not a hallucination. What in the hell was his ex-wife doing at the ranch, and dressed like that? Just looking at her put him in semiarousal. A vision of throwing her over his shoulder and carrying her off to his bed flashed though his mind, but that wasn't about to happen.

He didn't even remember Amelia was there until she cleared her throat. *Dammit!*

How dare Loretta come to the ranch uninvited. Worse yet to stand there like the queen of Lonesome Canyon and tell him what he could and could not do in his own house. He took several long strides forward, right into Loretta's personal space, stopping so close that his icy blue eyes locked with her blazing green ones.

His heart raced. His pulse throbbed. There was a slight pressure behind his zipper. But he didn't blink. "I don't tell you who to bring home to your house in Oklahoma, so you don't get to come down here and tell me anything. Amelia is not a bimbo, so watch your mouth. And what the hell are you doing here anyway?"

She popped her hands on her hips, nipping in her small waist and accentuating a big bust and rounded hips. The pressure behind his zipper grew tighter. Jackson's father said she was built like Marilyn Monroe and had the temperament of Maureen O'Hara. The man was a prophet for sure. Four years—hell, seventeen years—hadn't done anything but enhance what had been there her whole life.

She jabbed a finger into his chest and it felt like a hot poker had drilled right into his heart. "Oh, honey, I'm here for the next six weeks at least, maybe all summer. I intend to see to it my daughter goes back to school this fall and stops talking nonsense about runnin' this godforsaken ranch."

"Lonesome Canyon is not godforsaken and I didn't invite you here. Neither did Nona," Jackson said.

"I'll be leaving now," Amelia said.

"No, you will not," Jackson bellowed. "She's not running you off."

Loretta's eyes never left Jackson's for a second. "Don't let the door hit you in the ass, darlin'."

"I said you are not going anywhere," Jackson said.

"And I was fixin' to tell you, before the lights came on, that I'm not dating you anymore, Jackson. I'm going home. The rest of this fight belongs to y'all and I don't want any part of it, so have at it. Don't leave blood on the carpet or Rosie will have both your hides," Amelia said.

"Well, shit!" Jackson looked from girlfriend to ex-wife.

"You made a wise choice," Loretta said to Amelia.

Neither Jackson nor Loretta saw her wave or heard the door close.

"Dammit! Loretta! You can't stay here all summer," Jackson said.

"Why not?"

"Why would you want to?"

"I don't want to. I have to. Nona is going home at the end of the summer. She is going to finish college if I have to chain her to my wrist and go to every class with her."

"Did I hear . . . Oh. My. God!" Nona said from the doorway. "What in the hell are you doing here? And who was that woman speeding out of here, Daddy?"

Jackson looked from his daughter back to his ex-wife, who was still shooting daggers at him. "*She* says she's here to make sure you don't get too comfortable here at the ranch. That she's going to make you go back to college come fall if she has to chain herself to you and go to classes with you."

"And *he* doesn't have the sense God gave a pissant," Loretta said.

Nona frowned. "Okay, you two. Call a truce. Mama, you can stay, and, Daddy, you are going to let her. We are all adults here. Besides, she'll be bored to tears in four days and itching to leave. She hates the canyon. I've made up my mind, Mama. I'm not going back to college. That's settled, so you can go home and not waste your time here."

"It's only one more year, Nona."

"I don't care if it's only one more week. And, Daddy, it's a great idea that she's here. She'll see that I mean business and it'll give you two some time to work through this thing that neither of you would ever talk about. Good night."

Loretta crossed her arms under her breasts. "It's that damn cowboy. He's got his eye on Lonesome Canyon. One more year and she'll have her education, Jackson. Help me convince her."

"She's too much like you to talk her into anything. Once you set your mind, Jesus, God, and angels with harps couldn't change it," he said.

Nona pushed past her, stopping long enough to kiss her on the cheek. "Welcome home, Mama. Travis has his eye on me, not this ranch, and I happen to love him. And even if you two join forces, I'm not going back to school."

"You love him?" Jackson and Loretta said in unison, their heads jerking around to look at Nona instead of each other.

"Well, at last you are in agreement about something. I'm going to bed. You two can tear down the place with your snappin', bitchin', and bitin' if you want to. But you'd best have it rebuilt before Rosie wakes up in the morning." She flipped her blonde hair over her shoulder as she headed up the stairs and the bright chandelier lit up a silver-dollar-sized hickey right there on her neck.

"Did you see that?" Jackson's eyes settled on Loretta's gorgeous full lips.

"I saw it. Did you hear what she said?" Loretta gasped.

"I'll tear that boy limb from limb."

"Over a hickey on her neck? It's your fault, so you can't be judging her or him," Loretta said. "If you didn't bring women in here with expectations of taking them up to your bedroom, then by damn, she wouldn't have a hickey on her neck. How old is this Travis anyway?"

He backed up a step. "Twenty-three."

She followed. "Where in the hell was your mind at twenty-three? Think about that before you go runnin' off with your bimbo and leaving Nona to do whatever she damn well pleases!"

"I was a father and we were married when I was twenty-three, if you will do the math, woman." Jackson's tone was pure ice.

Loretta moved a few more inches into his personal space, but he didn't back up an inch. "You were a father and we were divorced by the time we were that age. And don't call me *woman*. You surely haven't gotten so senile you've forgotten how much I hate it when you call me that."

"We still are divorced, so don't be giving me any shit about dating other women." He rubbed a hand across his forehead. "Surely, they aren't sleeping—"

She shook her finger at him. "I don't imagine she got that hickey from holding his hand, do you? And I'm pretty sure she lost her virginity right here on this damn ranch at sixteen like I did."

"I damn sure don't like it," Jackson said.

"Well, you liked it back then," Loretta chuckled.

"I'm not talkin' about that. You know what I mean."

Loretta spun around with all the grace of a green butterfly about to take flight. "Yes, I do, and I'm not leaving her here to make the same mistakes we did. She is not going to get married at her age, and that's what'll happen next. Good night, Jackson."

He took a step toward her. "Where are you sleeping?"

"In our old bedroom. Rosie said that you don't use it anymore. Don't worry, I won't get in the way of your social life." She swept up the stairs in a fluff of emerald.

Jackson poured a stiff drink of Jack Daniel's and downed it like a cowboy in an old Western movie. He stared at the empty staircase and poured another finger of whiskey, turned off the lights, and carried the whiskey with him up to his bedroom. He slumped into an oversized leather recliner and kicked back.

It was going to be one long, hot summer. If they named tornadoes like they did hurricanes, this one would be named Tornado Loretta, and there wasn't a shelter in the world that could protect anyone or anything from that storm.

Chapter Three

"WELL, THAT DAMN SURE DID NOT GO WELL." Loretta threw herself across the four-poster bed and shut her eyes. "Why is it every time I drive down into this canyon I get the urge to fight with, cuss at, and screw around with Jackson? I thought I was over him, but seeing him kissing that woman—I wanted to yank all that pretty long black hair out and render the bitch bald-headed."

She tried to sit up, but the sheer green robe was tangled under her body. Finally, she stood up, jerked it off, and tossed it toward the rocking chair over beside the window. She paced the floor, trying to get ahead of the anger. Years ago they would have argued until the sun came up and then fallen into bed and had makeup sex.

"That's the problem," she sighed. "I've never fought with anyone like I have Jackson. Now it's time for the red-hot sex. And that ain't damn likely to happen."

She pulled the covers back and crawled into bed, beat her pillow into submission, and closed her eyes. Shut eyelids did not bring sleep, but rather produced a blank screen for memories to play across in living color. She thought she'd erased the ones that involved Jackson, but not so. Open eyes did not stop the memories from flooding through her mind.

"It's the room," she said. "The ghost of times past in this room but I can't ask for another one or he'll know. Be damned if I give him that satisfaction."

She tried to roll to her other side, but the tail of her nightgown wrapped itself around her long legs, binding them up like a calf rope. Finally, she threw back the covers, got out of bed, and whipped the green satin gown over her head. It flew through the air like a real butterfly, landing on the chair in a wad of liquid silk. Cussing under her breath, she riffled through her suitcase in search of something else, but she'd only brought the green silk and a crimson one very similar to it. Her mother had given her the lingerie when she caught Loretta sleeping in worn-out T-shirts, but Loretta had never worn either until that night.

The air conditioner clicked on and cold air flowed down on top of her from the ceiling vent. She crossed her arms over her naked breasts and wished for one of Jackson's T-shirts. No way was she parading across the hallway in nothing but a pair of lacy green underpants and asking him for a shirt, even if the look on his face would be totally priceless.

Instinctively, she pulled open the top drawer of the chest in case she'd left behind that old, faded nightshirt she used to wear. The drawer was empty. So were the second and the third, but the fourth was a gold mine. There was one of Jackson's shirts folded neatly beside half a dozen pairs of bikini underpants in white cotton, and an empty heart-shaped candy box.

She grabbed up Jackson's shirt and pulled it over her head and then picked up the candy box. Jackson had given it to her the Valentine's Day after they'd married. Inside were dozens of notes he'd given her from the time they were in fifth grade. She blinked back tears as she tucked the box back.

"Another night. I can't read those now," she whispered as she shut the drawer.

The scent of Jackson's cologne had long since faded from the shirt, but Loretta imagined it was still there when she crawled between the sheets a second time. This time when she closed her eyes, she drifted into a deep sleep where she dreamed that Nona was three again and toting around stuffed farm animals everywhere she went.

❀ ❀ ❀

Sunrays drifted into the bedroom, warming her face in spite of the cool air blowing down on her the next morning. She yawned and rolled over to snuggle up to Jackson's back, only to grab an armful of feather pillow instead of hard muscular chest. For a split second, she figured he'd gotten up before her and was in the kitchen with Rosie, and then all of the previous day's events came rushing back.

"Well, shit! I've got to get control of myself. I didn't come back here for walks down memory lane. I came to convince Nona that this is not where she belongs," she mumbled. "And the first thing I've got to stop doing is voicing my thoughts out loud. That could get me a hell of a lot of trouble. The second is to stop cussing."

Loretta felt the emptiness in the house when she peeked out into the landing. The doors were all shut and there was the faint aroma of coffee in the air, but it was otherwise eerily quiet that morning. She knocked on Nona's bedroom door. No answer. She opened it a crack and peeked in. Unmade bed, jeans and boots thrown in the direction of the hamper sitting beside the chest of drawers. A big four-poster bed that looked like the one they'd moved out of the bedroom when they'd decided to make it into a nursery had replaced the old crib. The same white chest and dresser that Loretta and Jackson had refinished while they waited on Nona's birth was still there.

"Anyone here?" Loretta called out before swinging the door wider.

That's when it dawned on her that it was Sunday. The clock on the nightstand said that it was ten o'clock, and everyone had probably gone to the little church a mile down the road.

Loretta hadn't slept this late in two decades. Forget about Sunday school or choir practice. She'd have to rush to get to church by eleven. She had to be there or Jackson would win the first round of the battle. He'd never say a word, but he'd be all smug about how he accompanied their daughter to church while she acted like royalty and slept until noon.

She rushed through a quick shower and gazed at the claw-footed tub longingly as she dried off on a big white fluffy towel that smelled like it had been hung out on the line. Then she darted naked across to her room and found a gauze skirt in flowing bright colors and a lime-green knit shirt and a pair of sandals in the same color. It took longer to tame her hair than to apply makeup, but the reflection in the mirror said that she was presentable in plenty of time.

Before she could close her makeup kit, the phone rang. This time it was her sister Dolly, who taught speech and drama at a local college close to Mustang. Loretta wondered which character she'd choose to play that morning. Would it be the smooth psychiatrist or the tearful daughter who couldn't bear to see her mother's heart broken by the actions of the irresponsible oldest sister?

"Make it fast. I'm on my way to church," Loretta said.

"I just talked to Mama. She's not even going to church this morning. You've given her a migraine, but then, it's not the first time," Dolly said.

Tearful daughter it was.

"I'll say a prayer for her. If they had candles at the little church here in the canyon, I'd light one. Is that all?"

"Dammit, Loretta! You've been good for so long. We were all talking at Easter about how that your wild streak was finally tamed. Why now?" Dolly's tone changed. She was a one-woman act, playing multiple parts.

"I'm here to talk Nona into going back to college in the fall. She's only got one year left." Loretta repeated the line for what seemed like the millionth time as she got into her van. "And I have six weeks' vacation time built up. If I can talk her into going back to school, it will be time well used."

"You never did have a lick of sense when it came to Jackson Bailey." Dolly's voice changed again. The many faces of Dolly now played the part of the doctor at the insane asylum.

"Is this the same sister who wouldn't talk to me for weeks because I left Jackson?"

"I was a kid back then," Dolly said bluntly.

"So was I. Talk to you later. I'm getting in the van and it's not safe to talk and drive." Loretta flipped the phone shut and tossed it over on the passenger seat. She checked the clock on the dashboard and there was plenty of time.

And then that damned cow stood right in the middle of the lane out to the road. No amount of honking, swearing, and even yelling would move the old girl until she located her calf, and then she did a jiggling jog that would have been funny if it hadn't been five minutes until the preacher would take his place behind the podium.

Dust followed her all the way to the highway and had barely settled when she whipped a hard right onto another dirt road that took her half a mile back into the canyon to a little white church. She braked and slung gravel everywhere in the parking lot, grabbed her purse, and bailed out of the van. Glad that she'd worn sandals instead of high heels, she figured she'd slip in the doors and sit in the back pew.

God had a sense of humor.

The preacher had already taken his place behind the podium. Not even a baby was whimpering. The church was packed full and the door squeaked like a cat with its tail caught under a rocking chair. Everyone physically able turned around in the pews.

"Well, who in the hell is coming to church late? I swear these teenagers ain't been raised right." Oliver Watson had gotten arthritis back when Loretta was in school, and evidently he'd since gotten hard of hearing. He probably thought he was whispering, but it carried all over the church.

Loretta took a couple of steps and started to sit down in the first available aisle seat. The little ladies on the pew shuffled toward the other end to make space.

"Loretta Sullivan Bailey. You are a sight for sore eyes," the preacher said in a loud, booming voice.

She'd know that voice anywhere. It was Bobby Lee Johnson, the wildest kid in the class with her and Jackson. The last time she'd seen him he was still hanging out at the Sugar Shack, getting drunk and trying to sing country music with the jukebox. When he started singing "Bubba Shot the Jukebox," they'd all known it was time for someone to sweet-talk him out of his keys and take him home. Too many times they'd sent Loretta to do the sweet talking.

"Darlin', you come on up here and sit with Jackson where you belong. There's plenty of room on the Bailey family pew." He motioned her forward. "We're about to have the Sunday school report and then Travis Calhoun, our new music director, is going to lead us in a hymn before I start my sermon. That's right, Loretta, right there. You haven't forgotten where you belong, have you?"

26

Bobby Lee read off hymn numbers and announcements, but Loretta didn't hear a word of it. She did feel every single eye boring into her back as she made her way up the center aisle and stopped at the end of the Bailey family pew. She bumped Jackson with her purse, and like a gentleman, he stood up, moved out, and let her sit down beside Rosie.

He had slapped her favorite aftershave on that morning, and when he sat down his whole left side was pressed against her. There wasn't a blessed thing she could do about it, not with Rosie and all her little elderly buddies packed into the pew as tight as sardines.

"Where is Nona?" she whispered.

"She sits in the choir with Travis. He's the one coming forward to lead the singing this morning," Jackson answered.

A handsome young cowboy came from the choir section and pulled a hymnbook from under the podium. "Good morning. Welcome to all our visitors this morning. If you will open your hymnal to page seventy-one, we will sing 'It's Not an Easy Road.'" He smiled brightly at the elderly lady playing the piano and started the song in a deep, rich voice.

Loretta reached for a book from the pocket on the back of the pew in front of her, but she wasn't quick enough. Rosie snatched it to share with the lady sitting to her left. Jackson nudged her with his shoulder and held the hymnal toward her.

"Surprised that our daughter is dating the music director?" Jackson whispered.

"More surprised that he knows how to put a hickey on her neck," Loretta answered.

Jackson sang along, but his body language said that he wasn't paying a bit of attention to the words. That was fine with Loretta. Neither was she. She wondered if God would really strike lightning through the church house ceiling if she stood up, cussed a blue streak, and then pulled her pistol from her purse and shot the youth director. God could have made Travis as ugly as a mud fence, but oh, no! He'd gone and made the boy almost as handsome as Jackson Bailey. His eyes were almost as black as his hair. His arms stretched at the rolled-up sleeves of his western-cut shirt and his jeans were snug on his thighs and butt.

She'd thought the war would be over in a couple of days. Now it looked like it was going to take at least a week. That should be enough time to put blisters on her daughter's delicate hands and dirt under her fingernails. Then, in a vulnerable moment when Nona was whining about being so tired she could drop from exhaustion, Loretta would offer her a summer in Paris, France.

All Loretta had to do was exercise a little patience. In a week she and Nona would drive away from cowboys, cattle, and ranching. By the next Sunday, she wouldn't be tingling from toenails to eyebrows sitting beside Jackson in church—of all places.

But then, from the time she'd realized that there was a boy as tall as she was in fifth grade in Claude, Texas, one who had beautiful blue eyes and dark hair, she'd flat-out been in love with him. He had broken her heart and she'd thought she could get over him in time. Evidently seventeen years hadn't been long enough.

She sighed as the song ended and Bobby Lee started his sermon. He began by reading a verse about God giving his people rain in due season and went on to talk about how sometimes people didn't even realize that God had a plan and he would work it out if people were patient and had faith in Him.

Loretta wasn't patient and her faith was threadbare, so her mind wandered and the preacher's voice soon faded away. Besides, for God's sake, that was Bobby Lee Johnson up there. How could she listen to him without skepticism?

She remembered sitting in the same church with Jackson years before, back when they were seniors in high school. It was that summer that all the hungry, hot teenage sex had finally caught up to them, and she'd told him after church on a Sunday morning in the middle of June that she was pregnant.

The next week they'd bought a marriage license and had gotten married in the county courthouse before they took the news home to their parents. Today was the twenty-second anniversary of that day. She wondered if Jackson even remembered.

Bobby Lee said something about, "in closing, remember," and she jerked her thoughts back to the present. There was a final verse to think about in connection to having faith in God during the tough times, one last hymn, and then Ezra Malloy gave the benediction.

Loretta leaned toward Rosie and whispered, "When did Ezra start coming to church?"

"About fifteen years ago. He always sits on the back row. Seldom ever talks to anyone after he shakes Bobby Lee's hand. He stays when we have a church social, but the only one he visits with is Jackson. We're having pot roast for dinner, so don't go hangin' around here talkin' all afternoon," Rosie said.

Jackson lost no time into getting to his feet and out into the aisle. Loretta followed him and said, "Rosie says that we're having pot roast for dinner. That much hasn't changed, has it?"

"Some of us like things the way they are and we don't want change," Jackson drawled.

"Loretta, darlin'!" Paula Dawson pushed past several people and wrapped her arms around Loretta, hugging her tightly. "I was so tickled to see you arrive this morning. You rascal, Jackson, why didn't you tell us she'd come home? This is the best news we've had in years."

"I'm only here for a little while, Paula. I didn't come back to stay," Loretta said, hopefully loud enough that all the gossipmongers who'd seen her sharing a songbook with Jackson wouldn't start making three-tiered cakes.

"Bullshit!" Paula whispered. "Oh, have you met Travis? He's a keeper. Come here, cowboy." She grabbed Travis by the arm and brought him to her side. "This is Travis Calhoun and Travis, this is Nona's mama, Loretta Bailey." Married to Flint, Lonesome Canyon's foreman, Paula had always been supersweet to Loretta.

"Right pleased to meet you, ma'am. I've heard a lot about you, but Nona didn't tell me you were a gorgeous redhead." Travis bent low over her hand and kissed her fingertips.

"Travis!" Nona rolled her eyes.

Jackson chuckled. "Travis, you've got a lot to learn. Pretty words and even a knight-in-shining-armor gesture like that won't pierce this woman's cold, hard heart," he said.

Loretta pulled her hand back and opened her mouth to say something, but Jackson butted in again. "Why don't you come to dinner with us, Travis? Rosie always makes enough to feed an army."

Jackson was testing her, trying to get her to make an excuse to keep Travis away that Sunday afternoon. This was only the beginning of a war that Jackson wouldn't win.

She laid a hand on Travis's shoulder and said, "Please say you will join us. I'd love to get to know you better. Which one of your parents is Scottish? I'd guess it would be your father, since your name is Calhoun. And don't let Jackson tell you stories about the Irish." She winked and whispered, "He's a Bailey and the Irish like to think they can outsmart the Scots. Don't let him intimidate you."

"Miz Loretta, you intimidate me a whole lot more than Jackson." Travis smiled.

"Good." Loretta patted his shoulder.

"Don't trust her. Any woman who brings a pistol to church is downright evil," Jackson whispered.

Nona grabbed her mother's purse and looked inside. "Why did you bring a gun to church?"

Jackson folded his arms over his chest. "It's a good thing Bobby Lee didn't preach on something that made her mad."

Nona handed the purse back to her mother.

Loretta cut her eyes at Jackson. "It was in my purse and I have had a permit since before Nona was born, so don't be givin' me no shit now. You are the one who took me to the classes to get a permit, if you will remember. You insisted. And when did Bobby Lee become a preacher?" She looked back at Nona.

"Which one did you have a mind to shoot? Jackson or Travis?" Rosie whispered as they moved toward the door with the rest of the congregation.

"Both," Loretta said.

"See, I told y'all that she's evil," Jackson said.

"Don't cross me or I'll prove that you are right," she said.

Jackson leaned forward and whispered, "Travis is a good man. Hardworking and he really does love Nona. Don't shoot him until you get to know him."

His warm breath on her neck sent shivers up dancing up and down her spine. She tried to tell herself that it was the way he looked all dressed up in his Sunday best, but her heart knew better than that.

"I don't care if he's got wings on his boots and a halo on his cowboy hat. She's not wasting her life in this canyon," Loretta said. "You know I don't give up easy, Jackson Bailey."

31

"You forget that I know your expressions even better than I know mine, and right now you don't believe that. You might be hoping for it, but you are fighting a losing battle, Loretta."

Three more inches and he would kiss that soft curve of her neck. In that moment she wanted to feel his lips on her skin so badly that it ached.

"What are you two arguing about?" Nona asked over her shoulder.

"We were discussing your mama's gun collection," Jackson answered.

Loretta shot a mean look his way, but he reached up and pretended to catch the look and shove it in his pocket. "I'll keep that one for later when I need to remember how mean you are."

She shrugged. "She's going to finish school."

Nona made the introductions when they reached the open door. "Pastor Bobby Lee, this is my mother, Loretta Bailey."

The preacher shook her hand. "Oh, Nona, I know your mother well. She and your dad and I all went to school together and graduated the same year. You've got to come out to my place in Silverton, Loretta. I married Susanna Wilson and we've got four kids. Oldest is ten and the youngest was born last week. I got a later start than you and Jackson but they're so much fun, I wonder why I didn't straighten up my act and start sooner."

"Well, congratulations! And tell Susanna that I'll try to give her a call before I leave." Loretta smiled and moved on.

Paula slung an arm around Loretta's shoulder and whispered, "Go home and play nice with Jackson. There's still time for you two, you know. You're not old by any means. Just look at Bobby Lee."

Loretta smiled and said softly. "That is not in the future by any means. I'm here to convince Nona that she is not a rancher, not take up residence."

Paula patted her on the shoulder. "But she is a rancher, has been since the day she was born, and there's still enough sparks between you and Jackson to rival a lightning storm. So don't be surprised if things don't come out the way you think they should."

"That storm you see hasn't got anything to do with attraction. It's got everything to do with the fight we're having about our daughter," Loretta said.

"We'll see." Paula moved on ahead to stand beside Flint.

"I heard that. You were always high tempered but you didn't used to be tacky," Jackson said.

"No fighting in church," Nona said.

"I can get real tacky, Jackson Bailey. If that don't work, then there are six bullets in the gun and a box of ammo in my dresser drawer," Loretta said.

"And I've got a gun safe brimming full, so you don't scare me. Besides, I could always outrun you, woman," Jackson said.

"I'll have your hide if either of you waste ammo," Nona said.

"Define *waste*," Loretta said.

Loretta hadn't had so much fun in years. She'd forgotten how much she loved to banter with Jackson, how much she'd missed taking it to the argument level and how fun it had been to take it to the bedroom for makeup sex.

Whoa, hoss! There might be bantering, but not sex.

Loretta was the first one back to the ranch that hot June afternoon. She went straight to the kitchen, kicked off her sandals and pulled a snow-white bibbed apron over her head. Rosie's fussing preceded her as she swung open the door and made her way across the kitchen floor.

She shook her forefinger up at Loretta. "I swear a woman can't linger behind long enough to tell the preacher that he speechified right good today without another woman don't try to steal her kitchen plumb away from her. You get that apron off and get on in there with your family, Loretta Bailey."

Loretta reached down and grabbed the finger. "I'm going to help. They don't want me in that den right now. It's not even safe for me to be in there. Did you know that Nona has a hickey on her neck? I do not want to be the room with the cowboy who put it there until I cool down. I played nice in church, but I need to cool down, so let me help," she whispered.

Rosie's brown eyes widened. "Are you sure? I can poison his tea. I've got the means and I'm so old I wouldn't mind spending the rest of my life in prison."

"I am very sure. Jackson lets her run wild when she's here. No rules or anything. No wonder she wants to live here permanently. But you can't poison Travis. Lonesome Canyon would shrivel up and blow away without you here to run the place." Loretta let go of Rosie's finger and tied the apron strings behind her back.

Rosie grabbed a second apron from a hook beside the door and whipped it over her head. "That girl has a mind of her own like her grandma Bailey had, and she won't be manipulated or bullshitted into doin' what either you or Jackson want. I'd tell her to follow her heart and to hell with both of you. But I'm of the old school and I don't like sucker marks on anyone's neck. I bet that's why she's wearing a scarf this morning in this damned hot weather, isn't it?"

Loretta nodded. "I'm surprised that Jackson hasn't shot him already."

"Me, too, or fired his sorry ass even if he does help out at the church. If she's got a hickey then by golly, there'll be a weddin' by the end of summer. Nona ain't a fast woman and Travis is a stand-up kind of cowboy. She's enough like her grandma to make it work, and I ain't never in my life seen no one, not even her grandma, take to ranchin' the way she does. Honey, she's better on the ranch than you were and you did the work to get out of the house and away from Jackson's mama. Never did see nobody dislike anyone like she did you. Roast is ready. You can slice it and I'll put the biscuits in the oven." The whole time Rosie fussed she was pulling a gorgeous salad from the refrigerator and browning strips of bacon in a saucepan before dumping in a quart of home-canned green beans.

"I can't believe you've mellowed this much," Loretta said. "You would have had a fit if I'd come in here with a hickey on my neck after church on Sunday."

Rose cackled with laughter. "Honey, you wouldn't have had the guts to walk into this house with a hickey on your neck, not in front of Jackson's mama. You tried to be a lady, I'll give you that much. But shit, woman, you didn't have a chance from day one. Eva Bailey wouldn't have liked an angel straight from heaven marryin' her precious only child, much less a girl who went and got herself pregnant."

"Ain't it the truth," Loretta sighed.

"Now quit your frettin'. At least Nona hasn't moved in with him. Just be careful you don't push her into that with all your highfalutin ways. Come down off that high horse you done crawled up on from livin' in the city and don't try to make her do something like go back to school this fall or you'll lose this war for damn sure." Rosie stirred the green beans.

"You haven't changed one bit," Loretta said.

"I'm too damned old to change."

Loretta smiled. "This roast is exactly like I remember. Nobody can make a beef roast as tender as you can."

Rosie shook a wooden spoon at her. "Don't try to butter me up. It won't work for you or Jackson. I like Travis Calhoun and I hope she's married before she moves in with him."

Loretta shivered. "She's not old enough to get married and face those responsibilities. She needs to experience life."

"Don't be spoutin' off that shit to me, girl. When you were her age, she was already two years old and talkin'. I remember how much fun it was to have a baby in the house. I still haven't forgiven you for takin' her away from us, Loretta. Just because I'm lettin' you cook in my kitchen, don't go thinkin' I've forgotten."

"It's complicated," Loretta said.

"I hate that damn word. You had your reasons and I'm sure Jackson had his that next year when he signed those papers. I swear to God all those times he went to Oklahoma, I thought he'd bring you back with him one of them," Rosie said.

"He came to Oklahoma?"

"At least once a month for that whole year. He didn't see you? He never did tell me why he finally let you have the divorce. Guess he had his reasons same as you had yours for leaving. And honey, if I remember right, it seems like your mama didn't want you movin' off down in this canyon, either, and Miz Eva damn sure didn't want you movin' to the ranch, but what was she to do? You was carryin' her grandbaby," Rosie said.

"What has that got to do with Nona?" Loretta asked.

"A hell of a lot. What your mama wanted and what Eva wanted was one thing. What you and Jackson wanted was another. Think about the way you felt about Jackson. That's the same way Nona is with Travis. Has been since the day they met," Rosie answered.

Nona poked her head in the door. "I've changed my clothes. What can I do to help?"

Rosie and Loretta turned at the same time. Nona wore jean shorts, a tank top, and cowboy boots.

"You know you're supposed to stay dressed until after dinner," Loretta said.

"Old rules. New ones say that I can get out of those fancy duds and put on what's comfortable. Travis and I are riding the four-wheelers over to look at a ranch across the road from Ezra Malloy's place this afternoon. Old Mr. Watson is ready to sell out and go live in Brownsville to be near his son. He ain't the same since his wife died last year."

"Travis plannin' on buyin' a ranch of his own?" Rosie asked.

"Dora died?" Loretta asked.

Nona shook her head and then nodded. "No, his cousin Waylon is lookin' to buy a place and yes, Miz Dora died."

"You can help put all this on the table and then call those two men to dinner. Biscuits will be browned by the time they wash up and get settled down," Rosie said.

"She gets to help and you give me a hard time?" Loretta asked.

Rosie shrugged. "She lives here. You're passin' through."

Chapter Four

TAYLOR SWIFT'S SONG "RED" PLAYED OVER AND OVER again in Loretta's mind that afternoon as she left the house and walked toward the creek. She agreed with the music. Loving Jackson had been more like driving an old pickup truck toward the creek on a Sunday afternoon with the red hues of the canyon all around than it had been like driving a Maserati, but the feeling was the same. Taylor was right. Red was the color of excitement, and there'd never been a dull moment with Jackson. Everything had been red: the canyon, the dirt roads, his hands on her body, their new love, the excitement of a new baby, the passion of their arguments and the makeup sex. It was all red.

The creek water appeared to be red as it flowed over the ocher-colored sands at the bottom of the canyon, but if no one stirred up the sand it was fairly clear. They'd skinny-dipped in it when they were teenagers, not caring what color the sand or the water were in those days. She sat down at the edge of the water, pulled her shoes and socks off, and eased her feet out into the coolness of the creek.

A school of minnows nibbled at the red polish on her toenails.

Taylor Swift had barely touched on the emotions of the rest of the song. Losing Jackson wasn't just blue; it was the darkest blue of a midnight with no stars in the sky. Nothing but pain and misery. Missing him wasn't gray; it was pure black, a void with no beginning and no end. But she was sure right about loving him: it was bright, exciting red.

She shook her head and thought of another song, one that would take her mind off Jackson, but everything that came to mind had some crazy line in it that looped her right back around to him. She bent forward to see the tiny fish better as she hummed "Red Dirt Road" and wondered if Brooks and Dunn had ever been to the canyon.

She'd had a mani-pedi the day before she found out that Nona had not enrolled in college for the fall. If the polish was going to last until she went home, she shouldn't be letting the fish chip away at it. But the water felt so good on her hot feet. Sitting there on the sandy bank with the shallow creek flowing gently around her ankles brought back memories that she could not delete by touching a button.

"Too bad, and I really do have to stop talking to myself. I wonder what he did when he came to Mustang. Did he spy on me or watch Nona play in the yard? Why didn't he at least call me?" she whispered.

She and Jackson had worked like plow horses, played like children, and had sex every time they could find a minute to be alone. Weatherwise, it had been the summer from hell, the heat even worse since she was pregnant with Nona. It was so hot that Jackson's dad said the lizards had started carrying canteens. But looking back, they'd been so in love they didn't even notice it most of the time.

She looked at the fish coming back for more nibbles. "Don't eat all the polish off. It doesn't taste like cherry snow cones."

She felt his presence long before she heard the dry grass and weeds crunching under his boots. Crazy, but everything seemed to take on a redder hue, even her toenail polish.

"Does to me." Jackson sat down beside her, pulled off his boots and socks, and rolled up the legs of his jeans. He'd changed from his Sunday clothing into boots that looked exactly like the ones he'd worn when Nona was little. His jeans were faded but snug. His T-shirt stretched over a muscular chest and biceps.

"Didn't think I'd find you here, not without a vehicle," he said. "And I disagree about your toenails. If they taste like your lips, then there's a good possibility they do taste like cherry snow cones, or maybe rainbow snow cones." He sank his toes into the water and lay back on the sand. "Does feel good, don't it? How did you get here?"

"Sweet-talking won't keep me from my mission, and to answer your question, I jogged. You were snoring in front of the television when I left."

His arm brushed against her bare leg when he stretched it up over his head. "I was stating facts as I remember them, not sweet talkin' you. My Sunday routine never varies—I eat Sunday dinner, I snore awhile, and then I walk to the creek and back every week. It's my meditation time. Now, tell me, Loretta, what brought you to this place?"

She wasn't surprised at the effect his touch had on her when a tiny shiver traveled from her head to toes. "I'll have to jog every day if I'm going to eat Rosie's cookin', and this is where I ended up."

"Then you better keep up the joggin'. It'd hurt her feelin's if you didn't set up to the table and eat," Jackson chuckled.

She'd gotten past that first initial shock, past the first fight, past her first appearance in public that morning. But still he made her heart do cartwheels and her pulse race; it could all be part of his plan to win her over to his side about letting Nona drop out of school.

"I can't believe Bobby Lee is a preacher. I remember when he brought me that note in fifth grade. Nona brought one home when she was in elementary school. I was amazed that kids still wrote those kind of notes in today's technical world." Loretta remembered her own note well. It had had a crudely drawn box beside the word *yes*. And another one right below it beside the word *no*. "Do you like me? Will you be my girlfriend? Check yes or no," was written above the boxes.

"I'm surprised you remembered that," Jackson said.

"I knew what the note was and I thought it was from Bobby Lee. Heather made me open it and take a second look. I'd already checked the no box and I had to erase it and check the other one before I handed it back to you." She pulled her feet out of the water, drew her long legs up, and wrapped her arms around them, resting her chin on her knees. "So what is Bobby Lee's story?"

"Drugs, alcohol, women, and then he figured out he was running from Jesus and Jesus wouldn't give up the chase. What he couldn't beat, he joined. Those are his words, not mine. Started preaching, settled down, does some ranchin' and is happy with his life. What other surprises have you found in the canyon?"

"I've only been here one day, but I was surprised to see Rosie still working. I figured she would have retired years ago. She's got to be pretty close to seventy."

"Bite your tongue. She's got ears like radar." Jackson lowered his voice to a seductive whisper. "And Rosie is probably closer to eighty, but we do not discuss her age or she gets bitchier than my mama ever was."

Loretta shrugged. "Lookin' back, I understand Eva a lot better. If my only son had come home at eighteen and said he had married his pregnant girlfriend, I would have been a worse bitch than she was. Add that to the personality change because of the brain tumor and it's a wonder she didn't get into your gun safe and do more than just cuss at me. Every time I looked across the table at Travis during lunch, I felt closer to her."

Jackson sat up and propped his elbows on his knees. "Dinner, darlin'. In the canyon the noon meal is dinner. The evening meal is supper. If you're going to stay with us all summer, you need to get it right. You used to know those things, but I guess all your fancy lawyer boyfriends in the big city taught you different."

"Don't call me *darlin'*," she said. How did he know she'd dated a couple of lawyers, anyway?

"Don't read more into it than it is. Crazy, ain't it, how we survived that first year and then the second with all the new baby stuff and two more before you got a burr up your ass and split? Are you ready to talk about it?"

She picked up her shoes and swallowed the lump in her throat. "Talkin' wouldn't have helped then and now it's too late."

She shoved her wet feet into her running shoes and stood. She tugged at the legs of her jean shorts and tucked a couple of stray strands of red hair back into the ponytail swinging on the back of her head.

"You leaving?" Jackson asked. "I didn't even get to taste your cherry toenails."

"That ain't likely to happen anytime now or in the future. Enjoy your meditation time," she threw over her shoulder as she took off in an easy jog toward the ranch house.

Twenty minutes later she collapsed on the porch in a sweaty heap, sitting on the steps and panting, glad that no one was home to see her in that condition. It wasn't fair that she was still attracted to Jackson after what had happened. But then, there hadn't been a fine-print paragraph in their marriage license guaranteeing that life would be fair or that she would never catch her husband kissing another woman in the barn.

When she could catch her breath, she headed into the empty house, up the stairs and toward that big, beautiful tub where she intended to let her mind go completely blank and not think of anything.

Chapter Five

$\mathcal{L}$ORETTA RAN WITH THE GRACE OF A WILD ANIMAL— all natural, nothing forced, and not a wasted movement. Jackson could have sat there in the dirt and watched her all afternoon, but in a few minutes she was completely out of sight. He had tried rationalizing what went wrong in their relationship; tried to shift the blame for that Sunday into her lap, but it still all came back around to him. If he hadn't been in the barn with Dina doing things a married man had no right to do, then Loretta wouldn't have left. Period.

He'd been given a second chance, though. What he did with it was totally up to him. When he was twenty-three, his mama's last words had echoed in his head every time he and Loretta walked into church, went to the Sugar Shack for a beer and to dance, or even went to the grocery store.

"She hasn't been faithful since before you married her. That baby isn't yours and she'll break your heart yet. Send her in here and leave us alone," Eva had said moments before she went into the coma.

Loretta's face had been ashen when she came out of the room a few minutes later, but she'd never answered when he asked what had happened in those last minutes of his mother's life. Six months later his mother's prophecy came true and his world fell apart.

Just to satisfy a niggling little seed of the doubt that his mother had planted, he'd paid for DNA testing to be done the first time he had Nona for weekend visitation.

She was definitely his daughter, just like his heart had told him all along. Loretta hadn't cheated on him and the flirting from the men had most likely been one-sided too. His mother had been wrong. He'd been wrong to listen to her and damn sure wrong to let things go as far as they had that Sunday with Dina, even if she was one insistent woman. He didn't deserve Loretta after the way he'd acted. It was his fault she was gone.

His father had still been living when the divorce papers arrived at the canyon. He could almost hear the whoosh of relief when Sam Bailey found out that all Loretta wanted was child support. She hadn't even asked for the rest of Nona's toys.

"She could have asked for half this ranch. I put it all in your name right after your mama passed on, as you know. It's always been an unwritten rule that Lonesome Canyon goes to the oldest child, but Loretta could have gotten a good lawyer and there wouldn't have been a ranch left," Sam had said.

Jackson pulled his feet up out of the water. Going back and reliving the days before and right after the separation didn't do a bit of good.

"Hello, the camp," Waylon Calhoun yelled from twenty yards away.

"Come right in and sit a spell. Don't have a campfire and beans to offer you, but there's plenty of water to cool your feet," Jackson hollered back.

Waylon sat down in the shade of the old oak tree a few feet away from Jackson.

He removed his hat, settled it on a knee, and combed back his light brown hair with his fingers. He sat silently, blue eyes brooding, for a few minutes before he spoke. "You know the Watson place, right?"

"Nona said you guys were going to look at that ranch this afternoon. What did you decide? Are you lookin' to buy the place on your own or are you and Travis both about to desert me?" Jackson asked.

"Travis isn't lookin' to leave his place on this ranch, sir. He knows Flint is grooming him to be the foreman here in the next ten years or so. And he's in love with Nona. He went along to offer his opinion and Nona went because Travis was going. You know the canyon better than anyone else. Do you think that spread would be a good starter place? I'll be thirty this next fall and I'd like to have my own spread."

"It'll make you a good livin' and you could raise a family on it. The Watsons had four sons and a daughter," Jackson answered.

A rare smile split Waylon's chiseled face. "Don't reckon I'd be worried about kids these first years. And I'm not real interested in getting rich overnight. I want a little place of my own and he's willin' to sell at a good price if I'm interested in buying what cattle he's got left. He'll even let the old yellow cow dog stay with the ranch. Someday I might be able to add on to it, but that's way on down the line in the future."

"It'll be a good start. You're not going into it blind and you're young and strong. You'll do fine," Jackson said.

"Thank you. I'll call my dad to come on down here and take a look then. Reckon I could have the afternoon off later in the week to go to the bank? I'll make up the hours next Saturday," Waylon asked.

"Sure and if you need a cosigner, let me know," Jackson said.

"My dad said the same thing, but I got enough saved from my rodeo days. Besides, I don't want to tie up all my capital and not have enough to run the ranch, so I'm going to ask to borrow one-third of the asking price."

Jackson nodded. "Sounds like a solid plan to me. And, Waylon, congratulations. You'll have a ranch that owns you."

A grin spread across Waylon's face. "That's what my dad said. Thanks for the advice, sir. I hear Nona's mama has moved in for the summer. Travis says that she's a force."

Jackson nodded. "There'll be fireworks for sure. We're at cross horns about Nona, but I'm sure you already know that."

"Womenfolks do like to have their own way, especially when it comes to their kids. And Nona is an only chicken. My mama is like that, only there was a whole houseful of us for her to fuss over," Waylon said.

Jackson's chuckle came from deep in his chest. "Never thought of Loretta as an old hen. I wouldn't say that too loud around her or the fireworks might really heat up."

"All women are protective of their children. It's just a natural thing, but it's worse when they've just got the one child. It's like they put all the love and energy and worry that should have been divided out into several offspring into the one," Waylon said.

"How'd you get so wise? You ain't nothing but a kid yourself," Jackson asked.

"I'm not wise. Those words come straight from my grandpa," Waylon admitted. "Nona is a wonderful woman and Travis is lucky to have her in his life. But believe me, ain't neither one of y'all got a whole lot of say-so when she sets her mind, because she's a force as powerful as her mama. Someday when I go lookin' for a wife, I want a woman like her. Canyon ain't no place for a weak woman. Only the strong survive this place."

"Be careful what you wish for, cowboy. You might get it and not know what to do with it," Jackson said.

Waylon chuckled. "Be fun to give it a try, though. It's my night to cook at the bunkhouse, so I'd best be on the way." He got to his feet. "And thanks for the advice about the ranch, sir."

"You are welcome, and good luck with the loan. It'll take a few weeks to get it all settled, I'm sure," Jackson said.

"I figure maybe I'll be ready to move by the first of August. This enough of a notice?"

Jackson nodded. "I'd love to keep you until then, but if things move quicker, then let me know. I'm glad a steady hand like you is settling in the canyon."

"See you tomorrow mornin'." Waylon waved over his shoulder as he headed back toward the bunkhouse.

The smile left Jackson's face. Waylon had put it all in a nutshell. Loretta and Jackson might fight, but the real war was going to be between mother and daughter. There might not be a whole lot left of the ranch by the end of the long, hot Texas summer.

※ ※ ※

Loretta sank down into enough water to cover her body all the way to her neck and blew the foamy bubbles away from her nose. She'd always felt like a giant, except in this tub. Here she was petite and she had blonde hair instead of flaming red. Here she spoke in sweet southern tones instead of a gravelly Texas twang that more than a decade in Oklahoma hadn't softened one bit.

Her neck rested on a rolled-up towel and her toes barely reached the end of the tub when she stretched out. She'd gladly pay to remodel the whole bathroom if Jackson would let her have the tub to take back to her house in Mustang. Legend had it that his great-grandpa had been a really tall man and had had the tub specially made. She knew for an absolute fact that a person could not buy one like it anywhere, because she'd checked.

She heard Jackson's boots on the wooden staircase, heard him pause by her bedroom door and then cross the landing to his own room and private bath. Those rooms had belonged to the nurse Sam hired to take care of Eva when she first came to the ranch. Before that a rotating number of nannies had lived in the room. Eva's sharp tongue sent most packing after a few weeks. One had managed to last six whole months before Jackson went to kindergarten. He always spoke of her as being older, with a gray bun on top of her head, and that he had put her in a grandmother role.

Loretta sat up in the tub and shook her head. The water had gone cold, so she stood up, slung a long leg over the edge of the tub, and stepped out onto a fluffy rug. She wrapped a towel around her body and all visions of petite blondness escaped when she saw her reflection in the long mirror on the back of the door.

A woman stared back at her with red hair sticking out like a punk rocker's, a towel wrapped around her that barely covered her ass, and long, lanky legs that belonged on a professional basketball player. She eased the door open and checked to make sure the coast was clear before she darted the few feet across to her room.

She sat down in the rocking chair and looked around. Nothing had changed. The chenille bedspread was the same and the old pair of cowboy boots she'd left in the closet didn't have a drop of dust on them. Pictures of her and Jackson smiling at the camera still sat in the same places on the dresser, along with a photograph taken of Nona not long before they'd left the ranch. She was a little blonde-haired beauty in her pink fluffy dress, hanging on tightly to a stuffed black-and-white bull toy.

"She cried every time we made her put Bossy away," Loretta mumbled. "That's why that damned animal is in the picture.

And that's why I caught Jackson with Dina. Eva said that he'd never be faithful and the only reason he married me was because I was pregnant."

She stood up and paced the floor, stopping to pick up each picture. Eva had been right all along. If Jackson had truly loved her, he wouldn't have moved from their room. He wouldn't have left all the pictures of them behind. But most importantly, he would have come to Oklahoma and fought to keep her.

She stopped by the tall poster bed and narrowed her eyes. If he closed the door to their room like he had to their life together when he and Dina made out in the barn, at least there hadn't been other women in her bed. That was comforting.

But how many women had been in his other bed since Jackson took over the nanny's space? She set her jaw and gritted her teeth. Dammit! A tear squeezed through her thick lashes and hung there for a few seconds before it dripped on her cheek. She swiped it away with the back of a wet hand. She flashed on that visual of Dina Mullins with her legs wrapped around Jackson's waist and her hands tangled up in his dark hair. They had been so involved with their kissing that they hadn't even seen her standing inside the door with Nona's stuffed bull, Bossy, in her hands.

"Water under the bridge," she mumbled.

History couldn't be changed no matter how much anger was applied. But that did not mean history had to be repeated—not even if a physical attraction would not die.

❈ ❈ ❈

Jackson heard the familiar squeak of the bathroom door. Her bare feet slapped across the floor and then the door across the hall shut softly. He pictured her sitting in the rocking chair, towel still around her curvy body, and hair pinned up but curls escaping.

He hadn't been able to spend a single night in that room after she was gone. Her anger and disappointment in his actions, all of it was over there among the pictures of the good times they shared. Their married life had been spent in that room and he'd shattered it all.

Nona had dropped her stuffed animal beside the pickup when they got home from Amarillo that evening. Loretta had been eager to get her into the house for her bath and put her to bed. Jackson thought at the time that luck was smiling on him. He'd made an excuse to go out to the barn and accidentally stepped on the toy as he headed in that direction. Dina had waited for him, ready to take the flirting to a whole new level. He'd shaken the dirt from the toy and set it on a hay bale not far from where she lay, draped over a couple of bales in a seductive pose.

He had come to his senses when his conscience screamed at him and pushed her away. She'd said something about never being turned down before and stormed out of the barn. He'd turned to get the toy and it was gone; by the time he got to the house, so were his wife, his child, and his life.

Did Loretta realize that he hadn't touched anything and the room was the same as the day she'd left? Did she relive the moments in the pictures? Did the bed remind her of their love?

He was surprised that she hadn't spent more time in the bath. She'd always liked that big old cast-iron tub so much that he was amazed that she hadn't demanded he tear out the wall and give it to her in the divorce. He would have hauled it the four hundred miles on his back for her in those days if she'd asked, but she hadn't. She hadn't wanted anything, and he still wanted everything.

The front door slammed and he recognized Nona's light step on the stairs. She looked like her grandmother Sullivan and God help her little heart, she had her mother's temper. But she had Jackson's love of the land and that's what made a damn fine rancher.

Nona knocked on her mother's bedroom door. "Mama, can I come in?"

"Door's open," she said.

He could hear the buzz of two voices but couldn't make out a thing they said. He paced the floor and finally went to the kitchen to make a leftover roast beef sandwich.

God, he hated eating alone!

❀ ❀ ❀

The canyon as a whole never changed and yet the setting sun could transform the tall, ocher-colored formation visible from the window into a howling coyote or an Indian doing a rain dance. Loretta and Jackson used to draw the curtains back and make a game out of discovering new images.

A light rap on the door startled her, bringing her from past to present. If it was Jackson, he was not coming into the room. She could withstand his subtle touches out there in neutral ground. In the bedroom, she wasn't so sure she was that strong.

"Mama? Are you sleeping?" Nona asked from the other side.

"Come in," Loretta said.

Nona eased the door open and shut it behind her, slumped down in the rocking chair, and sighed. The scarf was gone and the hickey shined like a brand-new penny, but Loretta decided that mentioning it would probably start another fight.

Nona cocked her head to one side. "You are wearing your old work jeans."

Loretta propped a hip on the footboard of the bed. "That makes you sigh like your world is all askew?"

"No, it's just that you never wear those jeans unless you are serious about yard work," Nona answered.

"I brought one pair in case I got serious about yard work and a couple of pair of cutoff jeans to wear if it's real hot. I'm not leaving, Nona, and one declaration of your love and determination isn't enough to run me off." Loretta smiled.

"I'm not here for that worn-out conversation. I came to see what you think of Travis."

"Does it matter?" Loretta asked.

"Of course it does. I've been dying to get home and talk to you about him, but we promised Waylon we'd go with him to look at the ranch. I think Waylon is going to buy it but Mr. Watson, that's the owner, wanted to tell Waylon about everything from the day that God created red dirt."

Loretta rounded the end of the bed and crawled up in the middle of it, crossing her legs Indian-style. "Explain to me about Waylon."

"He's Travis's cousin and they hired on here at the same time, but Waylon told Daddy up front that he was lookin' to buy a small spread. He's older than Travis by about five or six years and is more like an older brother than a cousin, since they lived right next to each other. I'll introduce you to him next time he's around."

"Why is Oliver Watson selling his ranch?"

"I told you that Dora died a few months ago. None of his family is a bit interested in the ranch. They all got out of the canyon as fast as they could and they barely even come home for holidays. One of his sons does live on a spread somewhere in Pennsylvania. I never imagined farms up north, but then that's where a lot of Amish are located so I shouldn't be surprised about farms. Anyway, they've put in a little single-wide trailer on their land for Mr. Watson to live in. He'll still be on a ranch but they can help take care of him," Nona said.

"Lots of changes going on. Looks like a new generation is stepping up to take care of the land down here in the canyon," Loretta said.

By the emphatic nod and the expression on Nona's face, Loretta knew she'd taken two steps backward instead of one forward.

"And some of us have to learn a lot before we're ready to take the reins, Mama. Waylon is about to turn thirty and ready to have his own spread. He and Travis are excited that they'll still be ranchin' close together. I asked you what you thought of Travis and you didn't answer me."

Loretta tried hard not to focus on the hickey. "I only met him today, but he seems to have manners, charm, and he is a handsome young man."

"I'm going to marry him, Mama. It would sure make things easier for the whole family if you liked him."

Loretta's heart fell to the floor. "Has he asked you to marry him?"

"Not yet, but he will. So?"

Loretta pushed out of the rocking chair and paced the floor. "I've never lied to you, Nona, and I'm not starting today. I want you to graduate from college. It's just one year and it'll go by fast. I could preach at you—"

"Like your sisters do you?" Nona asked.

Loretta nodded and went on. "I'm not going to do that. I'll be here when you are ready to go home, but I won't support your decision to give up on school."

"Why are you so adamant?" Nona asked.

"Experience has taught me that a woman needs to be able to make her own way. Life isn't all roses. You need something to fall back on when you fall in a pile of cow shit. An almost degree won't get the jobs that a finished one will," Loretta said.

Nona stood up and went to the window. "Let me make my own way and make my own mistakes, Mama. You can't understand how I feel when I'm here on the ranch. It's like my soul is at home. I'm going to marry Travis Calhoun and even if I didn't, I'd still want to be a rancher. The heart will have what it wants, Mama. It doesn't change its mind once it's set on something."

"But the heart can change its wants," Loretta said.

Nona shook her head. "No, it doesn't. It might learn to live with a change, but it's never really happy."

"You'll get tired of hay in your hair and underpants and the smell of cow shit everywhere. Just tell me when it happens and we'll be out of here so fast that there won't be anything but a memory of us left behind." Loretta left the bed and joined Nona at the window. "Let's go make a sandwich. I'm starving and this conversation is too deep for the end of my first day here."

Nona grabbed her mother's hand and held it to her cheek. "Mama, I've made up my mind about going back to college. I happen to like the smell of hay in my hair. And I heard Daddy open his bedroom door and head toward the kitchen just now. He hates eating alone. I'll meet you downstairs in a minute. I want to see that chimney-looking formation change as the sun sets. Wait, there it is. If you squint, you can see a coyote howling at the moon." Nona pointed.

"I know, darlin'. I've seen it a couple of times," Loretta whispered.

"So you played this game, too?"

"A few times, and it will still be changing when we're both old women, so let's go slice some leftover roast beef for a sandwich. Mustard or mayo?"

"Mama!" Nona rolled her eyes. "You know I hate mayo."

✿ ✿ ✿

Sundays were pure old unadulterated hell. Rosie went to her house after dinner. The house was too quiet. And Jackson always—every single week—remembered what he'd lost on a Sunday evening.

"Hey, Daddy, don't put the food away," Nona called out from the foyer.

Jackson didn't have to turn around or even glance over his shoulder to know that Loretta was with her. The back of his neck itched, his hands were clammy, and his mouth went as dry as if he'd been sucking on an alum lollipop.

"You can get it all out again. I didn't know y'all were going to join me, but I'm glad you did." He smiled.

God, it was good to have Nona at the ranch, even better to think about her staying and never having to tell her good-bye again. It wasn't easy to think of her all grown-up and twenty-one years old. Where had the time gone? Just yesterday she was a toddler and dragging around that stuffed bull his father had given her the day she was born. And Loretta? Well, things were never boring when she was around.

Nona dropped a kiss on the top of Jackson's head. "Did you take your walk to the creek?"

Jackson downed half a glass of sweet tea before he answered. "I did. Saw Waylon there. I guess he's buying that ranch and leaving us. He's good help. I hate to lose him. I was afraid he'd offer Travis a job as his foreman or make him a partner."

Nona opened the refrigerator and handed a platter of roast to Loretta. "Travis is happy here, Daddy. So am I."

Loretta still filled out a pair of jeans perfectly and, Jesus, what she did to a knit shirt would make any man's eyes refuse to blink. Jackson's mouth went dry and he had to clear his throat before he could say a word.

"Still love the old tub?" He immediately wanted to kick himself for asking such a stupid question when a visual of her appeared in his head: stretched out full-length, the water only slightly distorting her near perfect body, her hair pinned up on the top of her head.

Loretta set the roast on the bar separating the breakfast nook from the kitchen and headed for the pantry to get a loaf of bread. "You know I do. Want to sell it?"

"No, ma'am. It's part of the ranch. Nona used to call it her swimming pool," he said hoarsely.

"It makes a great kid's pool. And Rosie let me take my Barbie doll swimming. Remember how horrible her hair was at the end of that summer?"

Jackson smiled. "I remember you cut it all off and we found little pieces of it for months after you went back to Oklahoma."

Nona opened the refrigerator and brought out the roast. "I'm starving. I'd started to think Waylon and Travis were going to talk to Mr. Watson until midnight. Men talk everything to death before you do a blessed thing about it. I swear, Daddy, y'all will talk until the fall cattle sale about whether to castrate a calf or save him for breeding stock."

"Men! That's what women do," Jackson argued.

Nona pulled out lettuce, tomatoes, cucumbers, and bell peppers. "Not us. If that was me, I'd already have my check written for escrow and asked Mr. Watson when he could be out of the house so I could move into it. It's a cute little house, Daddy. Travis and I should build one about that size out on that back forty acres."

"You will be living in this house, young lady, until you get married. You will not be living with your boyfriend, even if I do think he's a good man. Is that understood?" Jackson said sternly.

Nona clicked her boot heels together and saluted sharply. "Sir, yes, sir. I wasn't talking about next week. I was talking about in the future. He hasn't proposed yet, Daddy."

"Evidently he's got to talk about it some more," Jackson said. "Your mayo is in the pantry, Loretta."

There was always a jar of her favorite brand of mayonnaise in the pantry and when the date on the lid expired, he tossed it and bought a new one. Just in case she ever came home.

"You remembered," she whispered.

"Daddy! Menfolks don't talk about feelings and things of the heart. Maybe if they did, they wouldn't have to talk everything else to death," Nona said.

"You ever been shopping with your mama?" he asked.

"Of course."

Any minute now Loretta would lick the mayo knife before she put it in the dishwasher and he didn't want to miss it. Their eyes caught and locked as her tongue reached out to touch the knife. His heart did one of those flips that according to his daughter, menfolks never talked about. He blinked and looked across the table at Nona.

"And you two waltzed right into the western-wear store, bought the first pair of boots you tried on, paid for them and walked out, right?"

Nona shook her head. "No, but that's because I never went into a western-wear store with Mama. But if you want to discuss any other store, I understand what you are saying. We do talk things to death, but that's because what we are talking about is very important."

"Buying a ranch isn't important?" Jackson asked.

"You might as well hush," Loretta said. "He's got age and experience on you."

"And I lived with that redhead long enough to know how to debate," Jackson said.

Nona exhaled deeply. "Speaking of which, I want to know what happened."

"I jogged to the creek, jogged back, took a bath, and now I'm having dinner. I mean, supper," Loretta said quickly.

"Mama! I'm talking about what happened to split you two up, not what happened today," Nona said.

Jackson almost choked before he could swallow. It took several long gulps of sweet tea before he could speak. "Well, that certainly came out of nowhere. Ask your mother. She's the one who left."

The way Nona's body stiffened left no doubt that she was about to explode. "You caused all this, Mama? Was it another man? Is that why you jerked me away from the ranch when I was a little girl? My very first memory is of you crying and cussing and then we were at Grandma Sullivan's in Oklahoma," Nona said. "Were you seeing someone else?"

"Was there someone else?" Jackson asked.

Loretta jerked her head up and locked gazes with him. "You know better than to even ask a stupid question like that and frankly, I think it's your story to tell, not mine. There was no other man. Jackson, do you remember what your dad used to say about letting sleeping dogs alone? He was right. Dragging up old fights and wounds won't change a damn thing."

Nona looked from Jackson to Loretta and back again. "Okay, if you're both going to go all awkward and be stubborn, we'll wait until another time to have this talk. I'll change the subject now so you can both relax and we won't have to get out the butcher knife to cut through the tension. What do you think, Daddy? Is it going to be a real hot summer like last year?" Nona sat down beside him.

"Get your mama to tell you about the summer we got married." He grinned, but it didn't reach his eyes.

"Mama?" Nona asked.

"It was hot," Loretta said.

"Three words don't tell me much."

"I'll tell you," Jackson said. "We were both eighteen and your mama was pregnant with you. My mother had always been snappy, but by then she had a brain tumor that made her even meaner than a snake, and Loretta couldn't walk in her sickroom without takin' a cussin'. My dad had had his first heart attack and we were barely holding on to the ranch with the medical bills and all. But Loretta took the bull by the horns. She ignored my mother's sharp tongue and worked like a field hand all summer right beside me in the miserable heat. And, honey, we went through about forty days and nights that it didn't drop down below a hundred degrees."

Loretta sat down at the far end of the small table. "I said it was hot."

"Without her help we'd have never pulled back into a profitable ranch. She had a sixth sense about cattle and we did better at the fall sale than we'd done in a decade. The next year she did it again, only that time she did it all with you on her hip. She refused to pay a sitter and drove a tractor with you in one of those bucket things beside her. If you learn half as much as she already knows about ranchin', you'll be all right, young lady," Jackson said.

He wanted to reach across the table and lay his hand on Loretta's, but it was way too early for that.

"She's a damn fine real estate agent too, Daddy," Nona said.

"And all the butterin' up in the whole state of Texas won't make me change my mind. If you still want to live here when you finish college next year, I won't stand in your way. But you need that education."

"Why?"

"Because it could mean a big difference in your life. This love shit dims after awhile, believe me," Loretta said.

Jackson talked to Nona, but looked right into Loretta's green eyes. "It don't always dim, honey. I was there with Oliver Watson when Dora took her last breath. Even though she was in a coma, he held her hand and told her that she'd been a fine woman to ride the river with."

"Ridin' the river is one thing. Living in the Palo Duro is another altogether," Loretta said.

Chapter Six

*N*EITHER THE RAPID MOVEMENT OF A PAPER FAN on a stick nor the steady motion of the rocking chair provided enough wind to cool Loretta. The other five rockers sat as still as the leaves on the scrub oak trees. The first week in June meant that you could not buy, borrow, or steal a breeze in the canyon. Not until the end of the summer, and then it would come sweeping down over the edge and blow red dirt in your eyes until the next June.

The twenty-third psalm was written on one side of the fan. On the other was a picture of Jesus with a little lamb and a child, but it was moving so fast that both were a blur. It was a sin to be almost a hundred degrees at ten o'clock in the morning and a worse sin to have a whole damn day stretching out before her with not one thing to keep her from dying of boredom. She was fast sinking into one of her Jesus moods, as her mother called it, saying that when she got in a grand funk even Jesus couldn't live with her.

"Shit!" she exclaimed under her breath as thoughts of Jesus twisted around to Sunday and probably having to stay another week on the ranch. Rosie wouldn't let her help in the house and she'd wither up and die with nothing to do but sit on the porch and think.

The ringtone on her phone was so welcome that she didn't even care if it was Emmy Lou telling her again that she was a big disappointment to the whole family. But she did check the ID and smiled when she saw Clark Sullivan's name.

"Hello, Daddy. Everything under control at the agency?"

"Yes, honey. We closed out on the Wilson house this morning. You'd left everything in perfect order. Your mama hasn't forgotten how to sell real estate, so don't worry about the job. How are you?" he asked.

"I'm fine," she said.

"You don't sound fine. Your voice says you're aggravated."

"Bored is more like it."

"You need to come home. Nona is old enough to make her own decisions and to live with them. All you are going to do is push her into a fight and she'll set her heels when that happens just to show you that she's grown-up."

"My heart says I need to be here to try, Daddy," she said.

"But is it talking about Nona or you and Jackson? You never did settle that business."

"That all happened a long time ago."

"I know, sugar, but you never talked about what happened. Maybe it's time you did. I figured Jackson cheated on you. If he had abused you, he'd be a dead man. You would never have put up with that kind of thing. Am I right?"

"No need in dragging up past history. What about the Thomas house?"

"Loretta, don't try to change the subject. Talk to someone about it. Jackson. Rosie. A therapist. Someone or it won't ever go away. Here comes your mama with my midmorning coffee. I hope to hell she remembered that I drink decaf. I miss you, sugar," he said.

"Me too, Daddy," Loretta said.

She flipped the phone shut and as if on cue, the door out to the porch swung open. Rosie brought out two glasses of sweet tea and set them on a small round table. "Thought you might be getting thirsty. I've got ten minutes before it's time to make the hot rolls for dinner. Want to talk?"

"About what?"

"Why you left? Why you didn't come back?"

"I figured Jackson would have told you." Mercy, but the cold sweet tea tasted good.

"He didn't. So you can."

"Rosie, you know how Eva was. She told me on her deathbed that I'd robbed him of his youth and there would come a day when he went lookin' for it. She was right," Loretta said.

"No, she was a case from the time Sam married her and brought her here. It was her high-dollar ways that put the ranch in the bind it was in. The best was barely good enough for Eva. She hated the ranch, you know. I asked her once before she got crazy with the tumor why she married Sam. She told me flat out that he was the richest one of her boyfriends and she figured she could talk him into selling Lonesome Canyon. It wasn't until they married that she found out he wouldn't sell it. It's always gone from oldest child to oldest child," Rosie said.

"And a divorce?"

"Eva didn't want a divorce. She knew that she had it good here. Sam never denied her one thing. If he needed a new tractor and she wanted a new Caddy, she got the new car and he made do."

They rocked in comfortable silence for a few minutes and then Loretta asked, "With that kind of attitude, why did she have a child?"

Rosie slowly shook her head. "Accidents happen. Oh, man, did she pitch a fit over being pregnant. It was miserable around here for nine months and the night Jackson was born was anything but a happy occasion. She'd hired a nanny—I don't remember her ever holding that child or rocking him. Only time she paid much attention to him was when her friends came, and then she played the mommy part for a little while then. She couldn't help it, Loretta. She had the temperament of a Doberman bitch. You shouldn't have paid any attention to what she said, much less let it drive you away after you'd already put down roots here."

"She planted the seed. Jackson watered it," Loretta whispered. "I've never talked about it to anyone. I was sure he'd call and we'd fight it out or that he'd come to get me, but he didn't do either one."

"I reckon it's past time to talk, ain't it?" Rosie said.

"You'd already gone to your house that Sunday." Loretta went on to tell the story in a voice that sounded hollow and unfamiliar in her ears.

Rosie slapped the arms of the chair. "That bitch."

"Wasn't all her fault. His hands were all over her too."

"You should have come and got me. We would have straightened this out right then," Rosie said.

Loretta shrugged. "I figured Eva was right. I'd ruined his youth, so I gave back what was left of it. I figured he still had a lot of years to chase women and not be tied down to a wife and a child."

A cloud of dust followed Jackson's truck, barely having time to settle in his wake when he came to a stop right outside the yard fence. He crawled out and shook the legs of his jeans down over the tops of his boots.

Rosie pushed out of the rocking chair and glared at him. "Some men ain't got a lick of sense. Wouldn't know a good thing if it bit them square on the ass."

He sat down in the rocking chair beside Loretta. "What are you talking about, Rosie?"

"Nothing you'd understand," she smarted off and stormed into the house.

"What kind of bee is in her bonnet?" he asked.

Loretta raised one shoulder. "Go ask her."

He reached across the foot of space separating them and touched Loretta's arm. "Are you going to sit out in this heat all day long and fan yourself with that church fan?"

"Maybe." She fanned harder. If he didn't remove his hand pretty soon, Jesus was going to catch on fire. "What are you doing back at the house in the middle of the morning?"

His thumb made lazy little fiery-hot circles on her arm. "Ran out of ear tags and came to get some more. Bored yet?"

"Oh, yeah, but I'll suffer through it. The end result will justify it all," she answered.

"Rosie run you out of the house?"

She nodded. "She says a guest doesn't help clean or cook. Truth is, I don't like to do either one, so it's no big deal."

"You could sit in an air-conditioned tractor and plow up about forty acres and give that fan a rest," he offered.

She eyed him carefully. "What do you pay the hired help?"

"In your case, I don't charge you room and board."

"What does the room and board cost me if I don't drive a tractor?"

He wiggled his eyebrows. "Sex three times a week."

She pushed out of the rocking chair and headed for the front door. "I'll change into my boots and jeans."

He slapped a fist over his heart. "Ouch. You are mean to hurt a hardworking old cowboy like that."

"Life's a bitch, ain't it?"

"I'll wait five minutes. After that you'll walk or drive that fancy van out to the west bank. And you only get paid for the time you're in the tractor seat," he said.

She just smiled and took her time getting into the house. But once inside, she took the steps two at a time and tugged off her clothing the second she was in her bedroom. She'd show him that she could get dressed in five minutes and that she'd damn sure not forgotten how to drive a tractor.

She donned faded jeans and her worn cowboy boots from the closet floor. She quickly braided her red hair into two ropes that hung to her shoulders and made a trip through the kitchen before going back outside.

"Rosie, I'm going to do some plowing to pay for my room and board and I need a . . ." She didn't finish the sentence before Rosie picked an old straw hat from the row of nails beside the back door and handed it to her.

"Keep it on. That sun and heat is hell on a fair complexion and you've still got that same peaches-and-cream skin you had as a kid. Don't ruin it," Rosie said.

"Thank you." Loretta smiled.

"Why are you plowing for room and board, anyway?"

Loretta did something that she hadn't done in years: she blushed scarlet. "Ask Jackson next time you see him and you'll understand I don't have a choice."

Jackson checked his watch. "You've now got four minutes, thirty seconds. I'll drive you out to the field where you'll be working. Sure you don't want to change your mind? The other option is a lot easier. We could make a quick trip to the bedroom right now. That would be number one of the three times this week."

"Looks to me like either one is going to make me sweat," she shot back at him. "I'll drive the tractor. You got plenty of CDs in the glove box?"

"Still listenin' to country or has the big city changed you?" Jackson asked.

"It changed me but not my music preference," she answered.

She reached the truck with him right on her heels and quickly crawled inside before he could play the gentleman. She wasn't his date, his woman, or even his friend. She was a hired hand and the mother of his daughter. She could open her own damn truck door.

The rutted path out across the canyon floor jarred her backbone and could scarcely be called a road. Red dust boiled up all around them and settled so thick on the windshield that he turned on the wipers to brush it away.

Jackson stopped at a corral where half a dozen cowboys were riding horseback and herding cattle into and out of the fenced area. He laid a hand on Loretta's knee and said, "Wait here. I'll drop off this stuff and be right back."

She swung the door open and followed him to the weathered wood fence. She breathed in the dust hanging like smoke in a cheap beer joint. It was every bit as intoxicating as it had always been. Did alcoholics feel like this when they walked into a bar? Did the fumes from the beer and liquor make their mouths water as much as the canyon made her soul want what it couldn't have? Could there be truth in that old song about coming home?

Hell, no, I'm not home, she argued with her thoughts. *Home is my cute little house a few blocks from the real estate agency in Mustang, Oklahoma, not this godforsaken canyon where the red dirt settles on everything whether the wind is blowing or not.*

A dark-haired cowboy tipped his hat toward her. The kid couldn't be a day over eighteen and his whole life would be nothing but backbreaking work from daylight to sundown. She looked at the whole lot of them out there—wiping sweat, wrangling calves—and remembered doing the same thing. She wanted so much more for her child than that. Nona was brilliant; she had finished the first three years of college in the top 10 percent of her class and could be anything she set her head to.

A blonde kid swept off a hat and wiped sweat with a red bandanna as her hair tumbled down her back.

That was Nona?

She'd dressed her in lace and ribbons and there she was, looking like a field hand until she took off her hat. Loretta's heart hurt just looking at her daughter with dirt streaks on her face and a farmer's tan on her arms.

"Mama, what are you doing out here?" Nona came to the fence and crawled up the side like a monkey. "I didn't expect to see you out here in the heat."

"I'm going to plow. Your father says I have to earn my room and board," Loretta said.

Nona slapped him on the arm as he opened the gate. "Daddy!"

Jackson frowned at Loretta. "I told you to wait in the truck."

"I heard you, but, darlin', you didn't tell me what to do before we were divorced. What makes you think you've got any power over me now?"

He shrugged. "You want to work cattle or plow? It all pays the same, room and board—unless you've changed your mind about my former offer."

"What offer is that?" Nona asked.

Loretta patted her beautiful daughter on a dirty shoulder. "It doesn't matter. I'm going to plow, not work cattle. You go on and learn all you can about ranchin', honey. If this kind of work doesn't make you realize the need for an education, then nothing can."

"It's more like play than work." She hopped down from the fence and helped a tall, lanky cowboy herd a bull calf into the calf table.

Poor little bawling fellow didn't know what hit him. One minute he was romping with his Angus buddies, the next he was penned into a contraption that looked like a gate on two sides. Once the calf was herded into it, it hugged him tightly and then with the flick of a cowboy's wrist it could move the animal every which way. Within three minutes he had ear tags, bands on his testicles, and vaccinations and was back out in the pasture with his mama, tattling on all the cowboys.

"She's good," Loretta said.

"Yes, she is. Almost as good as her mother. Give her a few years' experience and she and Travis will be ready to put me out in the pasture. For years we had the system built to clamp a calf inside two panels, but she came up with the idea to make it tilt. Then she designed the pens so that the calves can be brought in one at a time. We are working twice as many calves in half the time. She's smart, Loretta."

Loretta headed toward the truck. "I know she's smart. That's why she needs to get this last year of college done. Let's go to work. I have to pay for room and board, remember."

"Don't get all pissy with me. You can go back to the porch and pass plumb out with boredom or better yet, get in that van and take your feisty little ass right back to your fancy office in Oklahoma. I'm just telling you that Nona is a natural-born rancher and she's not afraid of work," he said.

"You are the one who is all pissy. And just because I'm not interested in sex three times a week. I bet you aren't used to women telling you no, are you?"

Hell, she didn't want it three times a damn week. She wanted it three times a damn night.

He kept in step right beside her. "You are the most exasperating woman on the face of the earth, Loretta Bailey. Which reminds me, why didn't you ask for your maiden name back in the divorce?"

"I didn't want Nona to be confused when she started to school. Tell me what you want plowed and I'll drive your truck." She held out her hand for the keys.

"Yeah, right," he snorted. "I'll take you out there. You might have forgotten how to run a tractor and I haven't got time to fix what you could tear up."

"I could outplow you when we were kids and I haven't forgotten a blessed thing about ranchin', even though I've tried. And honey, if I tear up a truck, you can rest assured I can fix it better than you can," she snapped.

Her mama said that first loves were always difficult to forget. What she should have said was that some cowboys, like Jackson Bailey, were totally and completely unforgettable.

❋ ❋ ❋

Jackson had no doubt that Loretta was telling the gospel truth. She really could run that tractor as well as anyone on the ranch. And she could tear down the engine and repair it if something did go wrong.

They rode from the corral to the back wall of the canyon in silence with the dust trailing along in their wake. Jackson stole long glances at her, wishing that he could reach over and touch all that silky smooth red hair, trace her jawline with his finger, and kiss her. God, he wanted to kiss her lips so badly that he actually ran his tongue over his own in anticipation.

"It snowed last year. Got so deep that they closed the roads," he said. "You used to have nightmares that it would fill up the canyon and we'd be buried alive in snow."

"Must have been an omen for me to get out of this place. Hotter'n hell in the summer. Cold as Siberia in the winter. And I remember the snow. Nona couldn't get out to come home for Christmas Day. It's the first time I ever had Christmas without her," she said.

"It was the first time I ever got to spend Christmas Day with her."

"You got her for a whole week up through Christmas Eve, though, so don't bring that up."

He set his mouth in a firm line and changed the subject. "She is going to keep asking. Do we need to get our story straight?"

She jerked her head around, with eyebrows knit together over those sexy green eyes and a frown on her face.

"You are even more beautiful than you were as a kid," he said in a low voice.

"And wiser," she said.

"I hope we both are. So about Nona? I know you saw me and Dina in the barn. It was the first and only time. I couldn't go through with it, Loretta. Bossy kept popping up in my mind reminding me that I had a wife and a child. But when I went to pick the toy up off the bale, it was gone. She cried for it and you found it, right?"

"It's water under the bridge, Jackson. Can't change it. Is that the tractor? It can't be the same old cantankerous machine that you and I . . ." She stopped.

"No, it's not. But we put in some good hours workin' on her, didn't we? That one has gone on to the big tractor dump in the skies. This is a John Deere like the old one. This one has an air-conditioned cab and a decent radio, but we still don't get good reception down here in the canyon, so there's CDs in the glove box."

She got out of the truck the minute it stopped and in a few long strides was beside the big green machine. She slung the door open and looked over her shoulder at him, a smile on her face. "Remember when we had a race to see who could plow the most ground by suppertime and that old tractor started smokin'?"

He leaned against the tractor. "Oh, yeah! And we knew we had to fix the damn thing before my dad found out that we'd caused the problem. We stayed up almost until breakfast getting it repaired and then had to work all the next day. It's a wonder that you didn't lose the baby the way we carried on that summer."

"God protects the young and foolish," she said.

"Would you redo any of it?" he asked.

"We don't have that option, so there's no use dwelling on it."

Chapter Seven

*L*ORETTA TURNED THE TRACTOR AROUND at the end of the field and started back toward the far side. Jackson waited at the end of that row and waved for her to stop. She parked and watched him crawl up the far side of the big machine and settle into the passenger's seat.

"George Strait or Blake Shelton?" Jackson asked as he joined her inside the cab.

She tilted her head to one side. "I don't need you to ride with me, Jackson. I know what I'm doing. Just because I haven't driven a tractor lately doesn't mean I don't remember how to do it."

"Billy Ray it is, then," Jackson said.

"Whatever you say," she said coldly.

He put the CD into the player.

She turned the machine around and headed toward the other side, her rows as straight as a plumb line. She'd forgotten how driving something as big and powerful as a John Deere tractor made her feel. It was an even bigger adrenaline rush than selling a million-dollar home in Mustang's newest development.

"That's not George or Blake," she said.

"I guess Nona put the CD in the wrong case when she plowed last time," he said.

"That's Miranda Lambert," she said.

"'Hell on Heels,'" he said above the music. "Fitting."

"Oh, honey, you are right about me being hell on heels, but I'm not your sugar daddy like she's singing about. And I'm damn sure not coming to take you for a diamond ring, a Caddy, or even a vacation home on a remote island," she told him. "Now why are you in this tractor with me?"

He let the song finish, removed the CD, and slid another one into the player. This time it really was Blake singing. Jackson pushed a button and nodded when the first chords of "Do You Remember?" started.

Jackson started singing along, keeping time with his thumb on his leg. The scent of his shaving lotion combined with his deep voice in the small tractor cab drove her right up the walls.

He sang that he still felt hope in her kisses and he could feel the sun on her skin and that he didn't know he was holding forever back then. Well, he was the one who'd let go of forever, not her.

"Okay, Jackson, answer me. I know how to run this tractor and insert CDs. What do you want?" she asked when she reached the other side of the field.

"I want to get our stories straight. Nona is not going to let this business alone. She'll be like an old dog with a ham bone. So what do we tell her?" he asked.

"The truth," she answered.

"Are you really ready for that?"

"It wasn't my fault," Loretta snapped at him.

"Wasn't it? Why didn't you snatch that woman bald-headed and then fight with me until morning? Wasn't what we had worth fighting for?"

"You weren't fighting." She reached the other end and turned off the engine.

"No, it was a weak moment, but you were a hellcat, Loretta. Why did you run?"

He slid across the big bench seat, traced her jawline with his knuckles, and tangled his fingers in her hair. She braced herself against the kiss, but still when his lips touched hers, sparks danced around in the cab of the tractor. Her arms were suddenly around his neck, cupping the back of his head as the kiss deepened. Her pulse raced and her breath quickened.

He held her for a moment after the kiss ended. Then he moved over, removed the CD and slid in another one.

"What was that all about?" she asked.

"It was a test. You passed. Did you study for it?" he teased.

"Test for what?"

"To see if you would kiss me back or slap the hell out of me," he answered. "Are we going to plow or sit here? If we're going to sit here, maybe we should try that kiss again. What do you think?"

She started the engine and at the same time Highway 101 started singing "Honky Tonk Heart."

Loretta nodded in agreement with the lead singer when she said that they were drifting apart because she wouldn't play second fiddle to the beat of his honky-tonk heart.

"You got a honky-tonk heart?" Jackson asked.

"Do you?" she fired right back at him.

"I still like to dance. Want to go Saturday night?"

She shook her head.

"Did you forget how to two-step?" he asked.

She glared at him.

"Bet you don't even like a cold beer anymore."

"I can still outdrink you and outdance you too." She wished she could grab the words and shove them back into her mouth.

"Prove it!" he taunted.

It was on the tip of her tongue to tell him to drop dead and go straight to hell, but she nodded and said, "Name the day. We'll celebrate Nona going back to college."

"Or staying here with me and learning to run this big ranch. We'll go to the Sugar Shack." He grinned.

She cocked her head to one side. "That thing should have fallen down years ago."

"But it didn't. And they've got a good little local band that plays there on Saturday nights. Time to park this critter and go to lunch. Rosie don't like it when we're late. Listen to this song. Blake is singin' about the good times. I think he's lived through some of the same experiences that we have."

"So you didn't really want to talk about what we'll tell Nona, but you wanted to trick me into going out with you?"

"Oh, there was that too. I intend to tell her the absolute truth and own up to my sin. You can figure out how to tell her your part however you want to," he said.

She geared down without a single grind and brought the tractor to a stop not far from where he'd parked the truck. She slung open the door and gasped when the heat hit her in the face like a blast from a furnace.

"Makes you glad that you ain't plowing in that old open tractor, don't it?" he asked.

"How did we ever survive?" she asked.

He extended a hand. "We were young and stupid."

She took his hand and hopped from the running board to the ground. All it took was a gentle pull and she was plastered tightly against him, listening to his heartbeat thump against his chest. She started to step back, but he held her closer and looked down into her eyes. She'd always loved that she had to look up to him. There weren't many men in the world like that.

He tipped her face up to meet his and she was looking into the sexiest eyes she'd ever seen, the same ones that she'd fallen in love with all those years ago. Then they slowly shut and dark lashes fanned out on his cheeks as his lips moved closer and closer to hers.

She rolled up slightly on her toes and moistened her dry lips with the tip of her tongue. When his mouth claimed hers, she felt as if she and Jackson were the only two people on earth. For that moment there was only the two of them, and they were in a vacuum where everything stood still and it all felt so right.

He ended the kiss with a brief smack on the tip of her nose.

"Just like I remembered and as good as the last one," he said hoarsely.

Loretta spun around and headed for the truck. One more kiss and she would swoon for sure—and tall, gangly women did not faint prettily.

Chapter Eight

$\mathcal{F}$OUR DAYS HAD PASSED and Loretta wasn't one bit ahead of the game. It was the middle of the week and all she'd heard out of her daughter was Travis Calhoun's name a hundred times a day along with ranching business mixed in the middle. She'd thought after one day of doing hard ranch work that Nona would be more than glad to kiss her dad on the cheek and fly off to Paris or Italy with her for a few weeks. But it damn sure had not worked that way.

And in those four days, Jackson hadn't made a single move to kiss her again. She'd been close enough to him that she could count his thick black eyelashes and smell the morning coffee on his breath. But nothing had happened. Not one thing. Nada. Zilch. On one hand, it absolutely frustrated the hell out of her. But on the other hand, the fact that she wanted him to kiss her again aggravated her even worse.

The smell of the oregano and Italian seasonings in Rosie's lasagna drifted up the staircase as she took a fast shower and darted across the landing with a towel wrapped around her body. Her phone was ringing when she reached her room. She dug it out of her dirty jeans and flipped it open.

"Hello."

"Loretta, darlin', why didn't you call us to tell us you were back? We just heard today. I'm on speakerphone and Maria is right here in the truck with me."

"Is that you, Heather? I tried to call the first night I was here but all I got was a recorded message," Loretta answered.

"Who else has a voice that sounds like she's smoked two packs a day?" Heather laughed. "And, honey, since we last talked, I've probably had three phone numbers. I lose these damn cell phones worse than anyone in the world. We're going to the Sugar Shack Saturday night. You want to go with us or meet us there? We've got a lot of catching up to do. What has it been? Five years since the last time we got together?"

"Try ten years," Maria laughed.

"More like twelve next Christmas since we actually saw each other, even though we do talk on the phone," Loretta said. "I'm here for a little while and I'd love to meet you at the Sugar Shack. But I am not here to stay. Nona thinks . . . Oh, crap, I've got a call from my sister. I'll see you Saturday night," she said.

"Go talk to your sister. Is it Dolly, Emmy Lou, or Tammy?"

"Tammy—this time. I'll tell you all about it Saturday." She poked a couple of buttons and said, "Hello, Tammy."

"I've prayed for four days. Please tell me I wasn't wasting my time and you are on your way home," she said.

"Depends on what you were praying for, but I'm not on my way home yet," Loretta said.

"Emmy Lou says that you're being bullheaded," Tammy said. "Are we going to have to come down there and have an intervention? We can, you know. And while we're at it, we'll have a talk with Nona about school. We are her aunts and she'll listen to us."

"I'm a grown woman who is quite capable of handling herself and Nona is my responsibility, not yours, so y'all best leave her

alone. She damn sure doesn't need you interfering in her business," Loretta said.

"Don't you use ugly language around me. I'm a preacher's wife. If you are a grown woman, prove it and act like one."

"I don't have to prove a damn thing to you. I'll talk like I want and I'll make my own mind up about when I'm going home," Loretta told her sister.

The whole family was interfering. She was beginning to understand why Nona had set her heels and refused to budge. Even if Loretta had packed her bags and was ready to walk out the door to go home, she would have stopped and gone back inside the ranch house. She had one sister demanding, one playing multiple parts, and one praying for her. And that didn't even cover her mother's ultimatums and her father's advice.

"Shall we have a little prayer right now?" Tammy asked.

Leave it to her youngest sister to want to pray over the phone.

"Thank you, but no, thank you. I've got to get dressed for supper. Rosie doesn't wait for anyone and it's almost that time. And, Tammy, stop worrying about me. I'm okay. I appreciate the love, but . . ."

Tammy's voice stopped her before she could finish the sentence. "Dear Lord, please take my sister under your sheltering wings and . . ."

"Amen and good-bye." Loretta hung up. Surely God would understand.

Now the aroma of Rosie's famous hot rolls floated up the stairs, which meant there would be cinnamon rolls for dessert. Her theory was that if she had yeast bread in the bowl then she might as well use it for both rolls and dessert. Loretta liked that theory just fine and didn't intend to count calories or fat grams.

Since she was now working like a field hand, she could well afford to eat like one.

When she sat down at the table, Nona was chatting about a calf that showed promise of becoming the next best breeding bull on the ranch. Rosie was talking about her vacation the next week. Jackson was telling her how much he'd miss her cooking. Loretta could hear the excitement in all their voices: Jackson, because his daughter was so interested in a damn bull; Rosie, because she was going on a weeklong senior citizens' cruise with several of her cousins.

Loretta missed times like this when she sat down to supper all alone in her house in Oklahoma. And as bad as Loretta hated to admit it, her daughter was actually happy here. But that didn't mean the war was over. There was still a lot of summer left and school didn't start until September. Happy could fly right out the window in less time than it took a gnat to blink. She was living proof of that statement.

"Hey, hey, where is everyone? Well, I'll be damned. When did you come back?" Dina Mullins stopped so fast that she had to brace herself on the doorjamb to keep from pitching forward into the dinner table.

Think of the devil and he shall appear, Loretta thought, disguised as a petite blonde who still looked at Jackson with enough heat to cause a nuclear meltdown.

"Hello, Dina," Loretta said.

"I heard you'd come back. You haven't changed much, Loretta."

"You have," Loretta said.

Dina pushed away from the doorjamb. "And that is supposed to mean what?"

Dina had been short, delicate, and blonde—all the things that Loretta had always wanted to be, but time and fast living had taken their toll on Dina. She looked sixty instead of forty and her style sense hadn't progressed since high school. She still wore her hair ratted high, but nowadays it looked more like straw. Too many hours in the sun had aged her once delicate skin. Her eyes were glazed with too much drinking and too little happiness. Dina had sown her wild oats and now she was paying the price.

Loretta wanted to feel sorry for the woman but she just couldn't. She picked up a second hot roll and slathered it with butter. "Are you married?"

"More than once. Presently divorced. You?"

"One time. Learned my lesson."

❋ ❋ ❋

Jackson glanced back and forth from Loretta to Dina. He'd been such a fool to let Dina coerce him into the barn or to listen to her and his mother about Nona's parentage.

"What brings you into the canyon in the middle of the week?" Jackson asked.

Dina drew up a chair next to him and laid a hand on his shoulder. It damn sure did not affect him like brushing Loretta's when they passed dishes at the table or when they both went for the coffeepot at the same time.

"Daddy is having his ranch party next Saturday night. I wondered if you might want to escort the prettiest girl in the canyon to it." Dina talked to Jackson but her eyes were locked with Loretta's. "I'm wearing blue satin, so you can bring me a corsage to match. I'm partial to white roses, as you know."

Nona took a deep breath and let it out slowly. "That is pretty brazen right in front of my mother."

"Darlin', you don't understand our history or the inside story about white roses. Besides, your mama has a history of running away when the going gets tough," Dina said.

"Don't you talk about my mama like that, lady," Nona said.

Jackson picked up Dina's hand and dropped it like a bag of trash. "Sorry, but I already have plans, and I had no idea that you liked white roses."

"Don't play coy with me, Jackson." She tapped him on the shoulder playfully. "Nona is a big girl now. I'd guess she knows what goes on behind closed doors since she's got a big old mouth-sized purple mark on her neck. Don't you remember that night you strung white rose petals all over the bed in that hotel room? Or all those other times out in the barn when you sent me home with one just like it?"

"You are drunk. I can smell whiskey all the way over here," Nona said.

"I don't remember any of those times. I do remember one time in the barn, but that didn't go beyond a few kisses and a lot of anger on your part and guilt on mine," Jackson said. "And it would be wise for you to go now."

Dina stood up, but kept one hand on the back of the chair and one on Jackson's shoulder. "So what *are* you doing here, Loretta?"

"I came back to slap the shit out of you," Loretta said.

Son of a bitch! The catfight had arrived. Jackson wasn't sure whether he should sit still and hope the bullets didn't hit him or to run for the hills.

"I did you a favor. Why would you want to hit me?" Dina asked.

"Well, there is the matter of breaking up my marriage. But we'll take care of that later. Rosie doesn't allow fighting in the house and I haven't had my dessert."

"What's that got to do with anything?" Dina snapped.

"I haven't had one of Rosie's cinnamon rolls in a long time and there's not enough soap in the world to get the filth off my hands from touching you, which would ruin the taste of my cinnamon roll. You ain't worth it. But rest assured, I'm not leaving the canyon until I knock you square on your ass," Loretta said.

"And if she needs any help, I'll be glad to step in beside her," Nona said.

"Now, darlin', I told you when I called you that week after you moved to Oklahoma how it was with me and Jackson all through high school. We tried to keep it a secret, especially after you got pregnant, but he couldn't keep his hands off me." Dina's head wiggled like a twelve-year-old girl slinging insults at her enemy.

"*You* called Loretta?" Jackson asked.

"You said that to my mama?" Nona pushed back her chair and came to a standing position, her eyes glued on Dina.

Dina tilted her chin up toward Nona. "Well, I did need to straighten things out with her, darlin', so she could understand the full meaning of my relationship with your daddy and how long it had been going on. I owed it to Jackson to explain it all to her," Dina said.

"Daddy!" Nona turned her gaze to his end of the table.

"We never had a relationship, not in high school, not in the barn that day or since then," Jackson said.

"You remember it the way you want and I'll remember it the way I want," Dina said. "I've got to run. If you change your mind, remember white roses and pick me up at eight. I want to make an appearance, so we'll have a couple of drinks first before we go down to the sale barn for the party."

Loretta held up a palm. "Don't hold your breath, honey. You look pitiful in that shade of blue. And you'd best make other plans, because Jackson and I have a date."

Dina smiled. "And he'll come get me afterward, like he used to do in high school. The reason I came over is that our housekeeper, Hilda, has retired, so she can't come over here and work for you while Rosie is on vacation. 'Bye now. See you later, Jackson."

The air in the kitchen turned eerily quiet and cold.

Nona finally broke the silence. "Okay, I want some explanations. Everyone knows what happened but me. Daddy, what did go on in the barn? Mama, you were baring your claws in that catfight, but if someone treated me like that I'd have mopped up the floor with her. And what does it matter that Hilda retired? You can still go on vacation, Rosie."

Rosie picked up the cinnamon rolls and handed the platter to Loretta. "Not without some help around here. This is a busy time of year and every one is needed on the ranch. Here, Loretta, you deserve the first one. If you'd knocked her square on her ass in the first place, things would have gone a hell of a lot better around this place."

Nona slapped a hand over her mouth. "Oh. My. Sweet. Jesus."

"Yep," her dad said.

"You had an affair with that slut." Nona's words came from behind her hand as she sank back into her chair.

"I did not!" Jackson bellowed.

"But he wanted to," Loretta said.

"And you didn't kill her?" Nona whipped around to face her mother. "You took me away from Lonesome Canyon because of her? If you don't slap the shit out of her, I will."

"It takes two to tango," Rosie said.

All three women's eyes fastened on Jackson. He threw up his palms defensively. "Hey, Dina was like superglue. I peeled her off the best I could, but evidently your mama had already made up her mind about what she saw and she was gone by the time I got to the house. And your mother wouldn't take my calls or talk to me, so it's not all my fault. And for the record, I never, not one time, cheated. I didn't even go out on a date for two years after the divorce."

Nona's blue eyes narrowed into slits. "I don't want a cinnamon roll. I'm going outside to sit on the swing and think about this, but you two"—she pointed her finger first at Loretta and then at Jackson—"are not out of trouble. We will discuss this later when I've had time to give it some thought. Grown-ups talk about their fears and their worries and what happens. They don't run from their problems. It's time for you both to grow up."

Nona pushed back her chair and stormed out of the house by the back door, cussing and mumbling under her breath the whole way.

"Out of the mouths of babes," Rosie said. "You should listen to her."

"It's complicated," Jackson said.

"Like I told your wife, I hate that word," Rosie said.

"Ex," Loretta and Jackson said at the same time.

"I'll call my cousins and tell them I can't go on the family cruise," Rosie sighed.

"Why?" Loretta asked.

"Because," Rosie sighed, "Hilda always comes over to cook and take care of things while I'm gone a week in the summer. They've got enough extra help up at Dina's daddy's farm that she can do that, but now that she's gone, I'll have to stay home," Rosie explained.

"I expect I can cook, clean, and do laundry for a week," Loretta said.

"I'll let you live in my house and give you my paycheck for the week. I've been looking forward to this cruise for a year. Jackson?" Rosie asked.

"Can you still fry chicken and make decent mashed potatoes?" He looked over at Loretta.

She nodded.

"Then I expect we'll be fine, Rosie. But don't get it in your head to stay gone like Hilda did. Ranch would be lost without you," Jackson said.

"Of course it would," Rosie said.

✹ ✹ ✹

Didn't the word *ex* mean that there had been closure? Back in the beginning of the separation, Loretta's mother had told her there would be seven steps of grieving involved in getting a divorce. She'd listed them: shock, denial, anger, bargaining, guilt, depression, and last, acceptance and hope.

Loretta had gone through the first four fairly rapidly, but when it came to the fifth, she'd gotten stuck. That next step didn't look too inviting and the last one? Hell, no! She wasn't ready to accept any bit of the divorce or trust anyone to bring her hope of a new life. So she'd devoted her life to her daughter and her work and learned to live with the guilt.

Driving a hay-hauling truck that afternoon, she went back over those steps and remembered how she'd felt with each one of them. But somehow all of the first four had attached themselves to that fifth step named guilt and hung on like a hound dog with a ham bone. Seeing Dina and Jackson all tangled up together in the shadows of the barn had been the shock of her life, but guilt was its twin sister. The trauma had sent her into flight mode, but the guilt had reminded her that if she had been prettier, smaller, and not a big ugly duckling, then Jackson wouldn't have let Dina into his life.

Denial only lasts a little while. It's impossible to deny to the heart what the eyes have seen firsthand, but guilt can hold denial's hand. Then give anger a BFF called guilt and one fuels the other.

By the time she reached the actual guilt stage of the divorce, it had taken on a whole new size. Guilt for not giving him a chance to explain. Guilt for not returning any of his hundred calls. Guilt for not staying with him so Nona would have both parents. Guilt for not snatching Dina bald-headed. Guilt for tucking her tail and running like a scared puppy. Like the old hound dog, she'd hung on to the guilt for so long it had taken up residence in her heart and soul.

Guilt took a backseat to anger. Why in the hell hadn't he walked right into the real estate office when he came to Mustang? Why hadn't he put up a fight? She wondered.

Maybe he's been living under a cloud of guilt too, her inner voice said.

"Shit!" she mumbled. "Do I have to go on to the next two steps before I'm truly over this divorce crap?"

"Whoa!" Nona called out from the back of the truck and slapped the top of the cab.

Loretta applied the brakes and stopped long enough to let Waylon and Travis throw the rectangular bales onto the back of the flatbed truck. Nona and another cowboy stacked them. When they were ready, Nona slapped the truck again and Loretta moved ahead slowly until she got another sign to stop.

In her wildest dreams, she'd never thought she'd be sitting in a hay truck again, definitely not with her gorgeous daughter stacking hay on the back of it. While they were sitting still, she pulled her cell phone from the pocket of her shirt and hit the speed dial for the real estate agency.

"Loretta? Is that you? Are you on your way home? I'll call and make reservations for your sisters to come over to Mustang and we'll celebrate at your favorite restaurant tonight," her mother said.

"I'm not on my way home. I just called to see how things were going. Have all my houses been sold?"

"Of course not, but we're closing on another one today. You know you belong here or you wouldn't be worrying about the business. And we need you. Your dad isn't getting any younger and I'm retired, remember. I tried to call Nona twice but it went to voice mail. When I get through talking to my granddaughter, she'll be glad to get her butt back home and in college this fall," Katy said.

"Mama, you aren't retired. You still come in to the office when you want to. Besides, you'd go crazy staying home all day. And Nona is my daughter and my responsibility. Leave her alone or she'll sure enough set her heels and refuse to do what she needs to."

"Why did you call then, if you aren't coming home today? It just gives me false hope," Katy said.

"To tell you that I love you and to talk when we aren't both angry. I miss you, Mama. Do you want me to stop calling?" Loretta asked.

"Of course not. I want to talk to you every day just like I do your sisters. Which reminds me, we've decided that you should have had some therapy all those years ago. You never did tell us why you left Jackson and you need to talk about it so you can get over it. So I've been asking around about a good therapist for you to go to when you get home."

"I'm not seeing a shrink," Loretta said. So much for making the first step toward peace with her mother.

"Yes, you are. That is the first stipulation for coming back to work," Katy said.

"And the second?" Loretta asked.

"If you don't come back when your six weeks are up, I'll give your job to someone else. We run a family-owned business here, and either you work or you don't have a job. I don't like having set hours and getting up early every morning," Katy said.

"Go on," Nona yelled from the back of the truck.

"Who just yelled?" Katy asked.

"I'm driving a flatbed hay truck today. Nona is on the back, stacking the bales. One of the cowboys throwing hay is her boyfriend, Travis." Loretta moved on until she heard Nona yell to stop.

"Why are you driving a hay truck? I thought you were going to the canyon to show Nona the difference in fancy living and hard ranchin'," Katy said.

"Room and board. Jackson says I have to pay my way. Starting Sunday morning I have to take over Rosie's job in the house while she goes on a family cruise. I had a choice, though. I could have had sex with him three times a week instead of working in the field or doing Rosie's job," Loretta said.

"My God! What is going on in that damned canyon? I'm calling your sisters right now. Have you gone crazy or are has Jackson Bailey seduced you again?" Katy asked.

"Maybe a little of both," Loretta answered.

Chapter Nine

THE ONLY BOOTS LORETTA HAD were the ones she'd left in the closet as a statement when she left the canyon. Leaving them behind meant that she'd never, ever need them to work on a dusty old ranch. She had taken her dress boots with her, but they'd long since been relegated to the attic.

She'd only packed one pair of jeans, the old, faded work pants that she washed and dried every night. She swung open her closet doors and there were more than a dozen pairs of designer jeans hanging there. Not what she'd wear to the hayfield or to plow, but any one of them would do just fine for dancing at the Sugar Shack.

She pushed them all aside and pulled out a strapless sundress. She pulled it off the hanger and held it up to her body. It was soft chiffon in a wild splash of bright colors over a lime-green under-skirt of pure silk. The hem stopped at her knees in the front but tapered off to her heels in the back. She swept her curly red hair to an off-center ponytail that flowed over one shoulder, fasted big lime-green hoop earrings in her ears, and added a clunky necklace with brilliant stones in the colors of the overskirt. She'd bought lime-green spike heels to go with the outfit but she shoved them aside and stomped her feet down into the old weathered boots.

"Maybe I should polish them," she muttered and then shook her head. "No. Hell, no! It's been years since I've been to an old honky-tonk, but I do remember that a woman needs good comfortable boots to two-step. I really do need a new pair for special occasions, maybe red ones with pointed toes."

Applying a final bit of blush and lipstick, she heard Jackson's door open and close and the sound of his boots on the hardwood as he headed downstairs. One more check at her reflection and second thoughts flooded over her. She couldn't go, especially not in that getup. With her height and red hair, she'd stand out like an overgrown watermelon in a field of strawberries.

The door swung open and Nona gasped. "Mama, you are gorgeous. I love your hair and the boots with that dress are so in style. Besides, they'll be comfortable when you dance with Daddy."

"Who says I'm dancing with him? Maybe I'm using him to check out the rest of the cowboys." Loretta was grateful for the little bit of self-confidence that Nona gave her.

"The boots don't really go with it, do they?" Loretta whispered.

"You are going to turn every head in the club tonight." Nona reached up, laid her hands on Loretta's shoulders, and turned her away from the mirror. "Go right now and don't look back, and if that Dina bitch is there, slap her once for me."

"Club? Honey, the Sugar Shack barely classifies as a beer joint. It certainly wouldn't be in the yellow pages under clubs," Loretta laughed.

"I've been there. I know what it's like," Nona protested.

Loretta shook her finger at Nona. "You aren't old enough to drink or go to the Sugar Shack."

Nona crossed the room and hugged her mother. "Mommy dearest, I'm twenty-one years old, which means I can buy a drink anywhere in the state of Texas or Oklahoma."

Loretta wasn't about to admit that she and Jackson had tried to get into the Sugar Shack when they were sixteen and had gotten turned away. Or that he'd had beer in a cooler in the back of his truck and they'd gone back to the creek to drink it. She sure wasn't going to tell her daughter that she and Jackson had had sex in the back of his truck that same night and that it hadn't been the first time, either.

"No answer, huh?" Nona laughed. "Daddy is waiting. You'd best get on down stairs before Dina comes around trying to beat your time. After all, she does want white roses tonight. Maybe she's going to pick all the petals off and string them from the door of the hotel room to the big king-sized bed."

Loretta shot a dirty look across the room. "And what are you and Travis doing tonight?"

"Skinny-dippin', but I did tell him that Rosie and Daddy got real upset over the hickey and he promised to put them where y'all can't see them from now on," Nona said.

"Wynona Katherine Bailey!" Loretta's voice got higher and shriller with each syllable.

Nona opened the door and stood to one side. "Go while you've still got that attitude."

Loretta breezed out of the room with an over-the-shoulder glance back at her daughter. Nona was dressed in fancy jeans, boots, and a tight-fitting, lacy sleeveless shirt. Surely to God she'd been teasing about skinny-dipping.

❁ ❁ ❁

Jackson sat down in a wing-back chair at the foot of the stairs. He could hear the changing tones of Nona and Loretta's voices but he couldn't make out the words. Having them both back home together under any circumstances was more than he deserved. If he hadn't been letting his eyes wander all those years ago, if he hadn't flirted, however slightly, after church that Sunday morning with Dina, then she wouldn't have come on to him so brazenly. It was his fault that Loretta left; it was hers that she hadn't fought for their marriage. But this was a second chance, the only one he might ever get, and he damn sure wasn't going to blow it.

Like always, he felt her presence as well as heard her footfalls on the hardwood floor. Did he hear boots or were his ears playing tricks on him? His heart tossed in an extra beat when he caught sight of her floating down the stairs. His mouth went dry as he slowly rose to his feet and hoped that his shaky knees didn't forsake him.

"My God, you are beautiful," he whispered.

"My God, that line is old as the hills," she laughed.

Jackson's face broke into a grin. "Darlin', that is not a line. It's an honest opinion from an awestruck cowboy who now wants to stay home, sit across the room from you, and stare at you all evening."

Loretta blushed. "Now that is a beautiful line. But I'm all dressed up and we're going dancing, Jackson Bailey."

"Promise me the last dance right now." He crooked his arm.

She laced hers into it and asked, "Why?"

"Rules haven't changed in the canyon. You go home with the cowboy that you dance the last dance with and I'm terrified that you'll go home with someone else. I don't have a brand on you anymore, Loretta," he said.

"I'll pencil you into my dance card for the last dance. You look pretty damn fine yourself," she said.

"Thank you, darlin'."

* * *

Loretta's insides fluttered as she stole glances at Jackson's chiseled square jaw, which had been sexy when he was a young man but was even more so on a grown, mature cowboy. His shoulders were wide; his biceps filled out every inch of the sleeves in the light blue shirt that matched his eyes perfectly. Her eyes followed the perfect vee from his shoulders to a laced belt with a big silver buckle and then on down to his boots. He'd worn his old ones too, but he had taken time to dust them off more than she had done hers.

Her breath caught in her chest when she caught a whiff of his shaving lotion, tightening it up while her pulse raced. He opened the truck door for her, settled her into the seat and then reached across her lap, his shoulder grazing hers as he buckled her seat belt. On his way back out, he dropped a lingering kiss across her lips—enough to say that he wasn't trying to seduce her, but more than enough to leave her nerves in a tight, tingling ball.

"So," he said as he crawled in the driver's side of the big black truck and started the engine, "what do you think, Loretta? Has the canyon changed much?"

"I've only seen the church and Lonesome Canyon Ranch since I got there. I don't know if it's changed or not," she said. "But I don't expect that it has. There's still red dirt roads, heat, and bawling cows."

And one damn fine sexy cowboy who still has a big part of my heart in his shirt pocket.

She looked out the side window, trying to calm her nerves, but even shutting her eyes tightly didn't help because his image was burned onto the backs of her eyelids.

Finally, she asked, "Has the Sugar Shack changed any? How about Tiny Lee? Is he still running it or did he move away?"

"Tiny Lee won't ever sell the Sugar Shack. They'll take him out in a hearse one of these days, but he'll work there until he drops. He's just a little grayer in the temples and about twenty pounds heavier," Jackson said.

She jerked her head around so quickly that it made her dizzy. "You are kidding me."

"No, he's up near three hundred pounds. Still has three chins, a handlebar mustache, and a double-barreled shotgun up under the bar. No one knows if it's loaded, but there ain't a canyon cowboy who's takin' chances, believe me. Sometimes he lets his nephew tend bar and I heard that he doesn't card the kids as much as Tiny Lee did us when we were young. Guess with all these fake IDs nowadays, it's useless anyway." Jackson smiled.

"Still got the old jukebox?"

"Oh, yeah. Price is higher. You have to feed it two quarters for three songs now," he answered. "And yes, the beer is ice-cold and the dance floor still has sawdust on it. And line or not, you are beautiful, Loretta."

He turned right onto the highway leading through the canyon and drove several miles in silence before he made a right-hand turn down an old red dirt road.

"If it don't rain soon, we're going to be in deep trouble. This drought is killing the ranchers and don't even get me started on the poor old farmers. More than one has sold out since you've been gone," he said.

"My God!" she said. "Tiny Lee painted it."

"No, he had it covered in vinyl siding," Jackson said.

"That is the ugliest shit I've ever seen. It looks like he sprayed the whole place down with Pepto-Bismol. Please tell me the inside is still the same." Her nose curled up and her perfectly arched eyebrows drew into a solid line above her green eyes.

Jackson's laughter bounced around the cab of the truck like marbles in a tin can. "He said that it's that color because cotton candy is spun out of melted sugar."

"I don't care if it's spun out of bullshit. I liked it better as an old weathered shack with a real screen door, not those double metal doors. He ought to bulldoze the damn thing and start all over."

Jackson hiccupped twice before he got control of the laughter. "Are we going in or going straight to the creek to skinny-dip? I've got a cooler in the back with a six-pack of Coors on ice."

"I expect we'd best go inside and dance, since your daughter is going skinny-dippin' and we wouldn't want to run into her and Travis," Loretta said smoothly.

"I'm going to kill that kid," Jackson said through gritted teeth.

"Want my gun?"

"Hell, no! I'm going to do it with my bare hands."

"We are talking about Travis and not Nona?" she asked.

"You know we are. My precious angel of a daughter wouldn't be doing those things if that wild cowboy hadn't talked her into it. It's all his fault. Let's go get a shot of whiskey to get that out of my head and dance until I'm too tired to be mad at him anymore," Jackson said.

She unfastened her seat belt and swung open the door. "It's tough being a parent."

He quickly jogged around the back of the truck and held out a hand to help her out. "At our age we should have a bunch of little kids, not a grown woman for a daughter."

"But we do." She put her hand in his and stepped out of the truck. But it didn't take her long to grab both her ears with her hands. It was downright amazing that the vinyl siding on the building didn't swell out and fly off into the hot night breezes with the loud music coming from the small bar.

"Holy shit! That is loud. Was it that loud when we used to come here?" she asked.

"Oh, yeah, it was. We were too busy making out to realize it."

"Go in there and get two beers. We can dance out here on the porch," she said.

"Oh, no, you are going in on my arm and I'm going to have trouble keeping the buttons from bustin' right off my shirt because I've got the prettiest girl in the whole canyon with me tonight," Jackson said.

"Jackson, a lot of water has gone under the bridge. We can't take up where we left off even if we were both wrong," she said.

"I don't want to take up where we left off. I want to get to know this new, more gorgeous Loretta. Let's start with tonight and going dancing and proceed from this point."

She set her heels at the door. "Is this a ploy to get me to change my mind about Nona?"

"This is about us. Nona is past eighteen. Hell, she could go to the courthouse tonight and get married and there wouldn't be a damn thing we could do about it. She's legally an adult. She'll make her own decisions." He opened the door.

She walked inside the world she knew when she was a teenager. Nothing had changed. The jukebox still sat in the far left corner and the walls were covered with old car tags dating back fifty years and more. The bar ran from one end of the joint to the other and the stools were mismatched. Tiny Lee waved when he saw her.

"Be still my heart. Folks, Loretta Bailey is in the house and she's more beautiful than ever." His big voice boomed above the loud music and he blew kisses her way.

She caught them and pretended to shove them down the front of her dress. That made all three of Tiny Lee's chins dance in laughter.

99

"Come on over here, pretty darlin'. First beer is on the house tonight because something as stunning as you came through the door. Jackson, you lucky sumbitch, how'd you ever talk her into coming home?" Tiny Lee bellowed.

"It was a tough job," Jackson said.

She scanned the smoke-filled room for her friends but the place was so crowded that she couldn't locate them. Then two high-pitched squeals came from the area where the bathrooms were located and a couple of women ran across the dance floor, weaving in and out of a line dance going on to Blake Shelton's "Boys Round Here."

"Don't you go runnin' off with them cacklin' hens before you sit up here at my bar and show the whole canyon that classy women do come see me," Tiny Lee said.

He set two beers on the bar and motioned for Jackson and Loretta to draw up a couple of stools. She had barely gotten settled when Heather and Maria made it through the crowd and grabbed her in a three-way hug.

"You are a sight for sore eyes, girl. You've got to start texting more or get on Facebook so we can keep up on a regular basis," Heather said.

Loretta shook her head slowly. "Facebook isn't for me. When I get out of the real estate office, I want to go outside and play, not sit in the house and read comments. I will promise to call more often, though, and you can always come to Mustang and stay with me. Or I'll meet you halfway and we'll find a place to grab a drink and catch up. Just name the time and place. And call me when you get a new number, okay?"

"You got it, darlin'. I'm just as bad as Heather about the phone business. They don't survive getting run over by truck tires or being thrown out in the middle of the farm pond in a fit of anger. Are you and Jackson back together after all this time? Dina is going to shit little green apples." Maria tried to whisper but it didn't work too well.

Loretta tipped up the bottle of beer and sipped. It tasted better than anything she'd had in years.

"Well?" Heather asked.

"I missed y'all too. It's too damn noisy to talk in here. Come out to the ranch tomorrow afternoon and we'll catch up and the answer is yes, no, maybe, I don't know, Maria," she winked.

Heather had aged as much or more than Dina. Her blonde hair looked more like straw than hair and fine lines circled her mouth. She smelled like cigarettes and whiskey, but her green eyes were still as full of mischief as ever. Maria came from a Latino background and her black hair was still thick and long, her brown eyes sparkling and her skin as pretty as when she was twenty years old.

"Dina does know, right?" Maria said.

Loretta nodded. "She knows. I'm really glad to see you both."

"Me too. I know what happened but I always figured when you called me on your way out of the canyon that afternoon that you and Jackson would make up after a few weeks," Heather said.

"I told you that it was over for good," Loretta said.

"You were so mad and crying so hard when you called that I wanted to strangle Jackson for you," Maria said.

"We're all guilty of not calling often enough or making the trips to see each other like we should. But standing here right now, it seems like we just saw each other yesterday, don't it?" Heather said.

"I heard that's the way real friends are," Loretta answered.

"And we're going to do a hell of a lot better in the future. I'm going to plan something soon, maybe a road trip for a long weekend to San Antonio. That would be fun," Heather said.

"I'm game," Maria said. "Just give me a few days to set things up with one of my sisters to help out at the farm."

"Let's wait until fall. I don't want to leave until I'm sure Nona has changed her mind about staying in the canyon," Loretta said.

"Darlin', I believe this is our song," Jackson said when George Strait's voice came though the jukebox speakers.

"Oh, that is so sweet," Maria said.

"See you tomorrow. Two o'clock?" Loretta held up two fingers.

"We'll be there," Heather said.

Jackson led her out to the middle of the dance floor and wrapped his arms loosely around her waist, letting them fall to the small of her back. She looped hers around his neck and laid her head on his shoulder. They fit together perfectly and dancing with him created sparks, but that didn't mean they had a future together.

The whine of the fiddle and twang of the guitar, along with George's voice, said that from here on after they should stay the way they were right then. He said that he crossed his heart and promised to give all he had to make all her dreams come true. She wasn't sure that she'd ever trust another man, not even Jackson, to make her dreams come true.

Jackson whispered the words softly in her ear as he executed a smooth two-step around the dance floor. For that minute, in the noisy old Sugar Shack, she trusted him. Come light of day, it might be a different story, but right then it felt right and good to open her heart, even if only a tiny crack, and let Jackson inside for a visit. That did not mean he could take up residence!

Neither of them realized that everyone had left the dance floor and was standing in a circle around them until the fiddle whined its last and left the bar in silence. Then the applause started and Loretta blushed.

Jackson removed his hat and bowed; that brought on more whooping and whistling. Tiny Lee gave them two thumbs up and handed Maria more quarters to plug into the jukebox.

She bit back tears when Conway's voice came through the speakers on the next song, "I'd Love to Lay You Down."

"Listen to the words, Loretta. It's the truth, darlin', but I'm not in a hurry and I won't pressure you," Jackson said.

"You've always been a charmer. I suppose we always were good in bed," she said.

"But?"

"But I'm only here for the summer, Jackson. I've got a life and it's not in this canyon. Neither is Nona's and she'll wake up and see that before long."

"Where's your heart, Loretta? Listen to the words. He's saying that when a whole lot of Decembers are showing in her face, that when her auburn hair is fading, he'll still love her. What does your heart say?"

Someone tapped Jackson on the shoulder and he looked around. "Ezra?"

"May I cut in?" Ezra asked.

Jackson stepped aside and Loretta put her hand in Ezra Malloy's. His fingertips barely closed over hers and the other one rested gently on her waist. "You look right pretty tonight, Miz Loretta. I'm glad that you and Jackson are workin' things out. He's always loved you."

"Ezra, I'm not here for good," she said.

"You should be. This is where you belong. You shouldn't have ever left. If I'd have known what that hussy was doing, I'd have shot her myself. Love like yours and Jackson's needs to be protected. I hear your daughter is back to stay. Y'all could be a family again." The song ended and he stepped back. "Thank you for the dance. Old man like me is mighty lucky to get a dance with the prettiest girl in the Sugar Shack."

"Ezra Malloy, you won't ever be old," she said.

"Wish God saw it that way, but I can't complain. I've had a good, long life. Hey, Jackson, you get over here and claim her before I dance another one with her and you're liable to lose her forever." Ezra cackled at his joke.

Chapter Ten

*T*HAT WAS FUN." Jackson eased down onto the swing set back in the shadows of the porch. He patted the place beside him and motioned toward Loretta. "Sit with me for a while."

The little niggling voice in Loretta's head told her it was a bad idea but her heart pulled her toward the swing. She slid down beside him and he kicked the swing into motion with his boot heel. His arm slid around her bare shoulders and his thumb felt like fire against her skin.

"Jackson," she started and then she looked up at him. His lips were coming closer and closer. She should stand up, put some distance between them, at the very least turn her head away. But she wanted the kiss and wanted to feel his strong arms around her. She barely had time to moisten her lips before his closed over hers in a fiery clash of passion that neither time nor space could erase.

She gave herself to the kiss, sliding her tongue over his lips, tasting the remnants of one shot of whiskey and several beers, letting the heat take over the moment. His fingers tangled in her hair, loosening the clamp that held it to one side and letting it fall around her shoulders. One of her arms wrapped around his neck; the other braced against his chest. She didn't know where the making-out session would lead but she was powerless to stop it.

Neither of them heard the engine of the truck coming up the lane or the long screech as it braked. It was the hard slam of the truck door that brought them back to the present world. By the time Nona stomped her way up the wooden steps and onto the porch, they were sitting on opposite ends of the swing.

Loretta's heart raced. Her lips felt bee-stung and swollen. Her pulse raced. She couldn't think of a single excuse to get up and flee to her bedroom before Nona stomped her way from the middle of the porch to the swing and plopped down between them.

"God, what a night! Daddy, I'm so mad I could eat the hindquarter of a cow and spit out hamburgers." She pulled her knees up and wrapped her arms around them.

"I've been lookin' for a sign from heaven to shoot that boy. I think this might be it," Jackson said. "He didn't even walk you to the door or for that matter open the truck door for you."

"That's my fault. I told him if he got out, I'd put a bullet between his eyes, so don't get trigger-happy yet. You might want to load the gun, though," Nona said.

"What happened? I thought you were in love." Loretta was amazed that her voice sounded normal and not like a high-pitched squeak.

"I am in love. That's what caused this damned problem. If I didn't love him, I wouldn't fight for what's mine, right?" Nona turned to face her mother.

"Maybe you'd best explain." Jackson patted her on the ankle.

"It's like this. We were at a party in Goodnight. He's got a cousin over there and the house was so full we couldn't even hear ourselves think for the noise, so it spread to the yard. Travis and I were sharing a hassock and everything was fine. Then he went in to get us another beer and he was gone for a long time." She paused and wiped tears from her cheeks with the back of her hand.

"Have you learned your lesson? Ready to go home and work at the agency with me and your grandmother this summer?" Loretta asked.

She held her breath waiting for the answer. She needed to run away from the ranch before things heated up with Jackson any further. She should have realized she couldn't help herself when it came to Jackson's sexy charm. She'd clearly gotten past that guilt stage.

"Hell, no! I'm not going anywhere and neither is he," Nona said.

"So what happened when he went in to get two beers?" Jackson asked.

"Some two-bit hussy cornered him in the hallway and when I got there, she was trying to unzip his jeans. He said he was trying to push her off him and that he was drunk but it didn't look like he was pushing her too damn hard to me," Nona said.

"Little jealousy there?" Jackson chuckled.

"Hell of a lot of jealousy and a hussy with a black eye who's threatening to get a restraining order on me. Needless to say after I peeled her off my boyfriend and tried to yank her bald-headed, the party was over. Travis picked me up and carried me to the truck and he's mad at *me* for starting a fight. What's wrong with that picture? I should have thrown a couple of right hooks his way too," she said.

"Didn't she fight back?" Loretta asked.

"Oh, yeah. She got a fistful of blonde hair that hurt like a son of a bitch and she scratched my arm, but I reckon neither one will keep me out of church or chores tomorrow," Nona answered.

"So you broke up with Travis, but you're staying on the ranch? Is that the bottom line?" Loretta asked. One hurdle jumped; a bigger one up ahead.

"Mama! I did not break up with Travis. We had a fight. He'll be texting and calling me as soon as he gets to the bunkhouse. And we'll have a come-to-Jesus understanding and by damn he won't ever look at another woman again. Of course, I'll have to promise to pay for the coffee table and the two lamps, but they were both ugly as a mud fence, so his cousin should thank me that she'll get new ones." Nona pulled her phone from her pocket when it rang, checked the ID, and put it back. "I'll answer when he's called three times. He needs to stew for a little bit. We'll be fine by morning."

Jackson kissed her on the cheek. "Good night, princess."

"Good night, Daddy. You always told me not to take shit off nobody and I didn't. Mama, I forgot to ask. How were things at the Sugar Shack?" Nona asked as she unwound her legs and pushed out of the swing.

"It looks like it's been sprayed down with Pepto-Bismol, but at least the inside is still the same. And I saw two of my old friends, Heather and Maria, who are coming for a visit tomorrow afternoon, and I danced with Ezra Malloy. I've always liked him," Loretta said.

"He sure is strange, though." She started toward the door. "Did you dance with Daddy?"

"A couple of times."

"Good. That's a good start to both of you forgiving the other one for all that shit that Dina caused," she said. "There's the second ring and it's Travis. Time to make up so we can . . ." She chuckled. "You know exactly what I'm talking about, so I won't embarrass you by saying makeup sex."

"Wynona Katherine Bailey!" Loretta raised her voice.

"That's twice that you've used all three of my names. One more and I'll be standing in the corner, right?" She hurried through the door before Loretta could say another word.

"Kind of ripped the Band-Aid off all at once, didn't she?" Jackson whispered.

"She did, but I don't want to talk about that tonight, Jackson. It's late and I've only got one more morning to wake up to coffee and breakfast already cooking. Monday morning I take on Rosie's job, so I'm going to bed," she said. Besides, it wasn't easy to hold on to her determination to convince Nona to leave the canyon when she thought about how sticking around every time Jackson kissed her.

"Alone?"

"Yes, alone," she said. "Good night. See you at breakfast. And, Jackson, she should have to pay for the furniture she destroyed out of her own bank account."

"I agree," he said. "She's got to control that temper she got from you. What I'm wondering right now is why you didn't apply it like she did when you were in the same situation," Jackson asked.

"That's something we might discuss another day. Not now," she answered. Before she could talk about what happened that day, she had to sort it out herself.

She passed Nona's closed door and heard the soft tones of her voice. A cloak of doom settled around Loretta's shoulders as she kicked off her boots and fell back on the big four-poster bed. If a fight that big hadn't made Nona run back to the city life, then nothing would. Loretta was going to lose the war. Yet it could be that a couple more colossal arguments would start to pile up and then one little bitty incident would be the straw that broke the proverbial camel's back. She could always hope that it would work that way. She shut her eyes, but there was far too much adrenaline still rushing through her veins to let her sleep.

❋ ❋ ❋

A hot night wind kicked up across the porch as Jackson continued to swing. His eyes grew heavy and he leaned his head over to the side, bracing it against the chains holding the swing. A whiff of Loretta's perfume floated across the porch and he inhaled deeply. Suddenly she straddled his legs and he reached down to cup her bottom. Then her lips ground into his, demanding, forcing her tongue between his lips.

He tasted the salty remains of margaritas, not beer, and his eyes popped wide open. His hands let go of the jeans-clad butt and he stood up abruptly, dropping Dina onto the porch floor with a thud.

"Well, damn, Jackson! What is the matter with you? You don't come to my party. You throw me around like this. Do you like it rough?" She stood up and dusted off the bottom of her skintight jeans.

Jackson wiped at his mouth but it didn't erase the taste she'd left behind. "What are you doing here?"

"Honey, I've decided that I need you to make a marriage work. None of my others have lasted and I just know we could be good together. You are going to be my lifetime commitment. You've always had a thing for me. I know it. You know it. So let's stop beating around the bush and act like two consenting adults. Which way is your bedroom?" She slurred every other word.

"You are drunk. Go home," he said.

"Lovers don't let lovers drive drunk," she quipped.

"Call your dad. I'm going inside and I'm locking the door. You aren't welcome on Lonesome Canyon anymore, Dina. I refuse to let you ruin anything like you did in the past," he said.

She staggered toward the porch steps, using the rail to steady herself. "You aren't a bit of fun. You flirted, but you didn't come through when I came to collect. And honey, Loretta doesn't deserve or appreciate you."

"Call your dad to come get you, Dina. Or I'll call Paula to come drive you."

"You're mean. Paula will lecture me and Daddy said if he had to come get me one more time he's putting me in rehab, but I'd rather do that as listen to Paula. So I'll call him. My phone is in the car. One last chance. Take me now or lose me, darlin'."

"I'm okay with the loss." He left her weaving her way out to her little sports car. The thing was so small and had such a quiet engine; it was no wonder that he hadn't heard it. He hoped when she woke up the next morning that she remembered enough of what had happened to never come around his ranch again. If not, come Monday morning, he might be the second person in line for a restraining order.

He sat down in a recliner and removed his boots, then threw the lever on the side to lie back and stared at the ceiling. He'd noticed that both Loretta's and Nona's lights were still on. Nona would be making up with Travis. What was Loretta doing? He shut his eyes and envisioned her removing that pretty dress and putting on a faded old nightshirt like the one she used to wear. It had some cartoon character on the front and he could skim it up over her head so fast that it was a blur.

None of those fancy corsets and folderol for Jackson. He wasn't one to take hours to unwrap a present. He liked to get right at what was inside. He went to sleep with a smile on his face.

Chapter Eleven

*L*ORETTA AWOKE BEFORE DAYLIGHT and checked the clock to find that it wasn't quite five. She put a pillow over her head, but that didn't work, so she sat up and realized she'd fallen asleep in her clothes. Her mouth felt like it had been packed with cotton and tasted like stale beer. Her head throbbed and her feet hurt and she could not go back to sleep even though it had been less than five hours since she left Jackson on the porch.

She padded across the hall to the bathroom and turned on the water in the tub. While that ran, she brushed her teeth, groaned at the rat's nest in her hair and the bags under her eyes, and slipped off her clothing. Leaving it lying on the floor in a pile, she sank down into the water and let it work warm miracles on the aches and pains in her body. It had been years since she'd danced that much, drank more than one beer, or made out like a sex-starved sophomore on the front porch, and it had all caught up to her at once.

She shampooed the smell of the Sugar Shack out of her hair, shaved her legs, and leaned back, shutting her eyes and letting the whole evening replay in her head. When the water turned lukewarm, she pulled the plug and wrapped a towel around her head and one around her body. She checked the hallway to make sure the coast was clear and carried her smoky-smelling clothing back to her room.

It was too early to get dressed for church, so after she dried her hair and tamed it down with mousse; she pulled on underwear, her work jeans, and a T-shirt. She made her way to the kitchen, put on a pot of coffee, and stood in front of the cabinet while it perked.

"Okay, okay, a watched pot never boils," she mumbled. Her gaze went to the refrigerator where magnets held up pictures of Nona at all stages of her life and cute little quips or sayings that appealed to Rosie.

She read a Bible verse about vengeance belonging to the Lord and then a round magnet with words written over a bank of beautiful clouds caught her eye. She read it aloud: "Change is never easy. We fight to hold on and we fight to let go."

The coffeepot gurgled one final time and she poured a cup, reread the magnet, and nodded.

"A-damn-men to that. Here stands living proof in the body of Loretta Sullivan Bailey in this kitchen," she whispered.

Nona was fighting to hold on and Loretta was fighting to let go. What was Jackson fighting for? Did he think if he held on to Loretta that she'd relent and be happy that Nona was on the ranch?

She was still thinking about the magnet as she carried her cup of steaming hot coffee to the porch swing. The sun had barely peeked up over the edge of the canyon off to the east and there was a warm breeze fluttering the mimosa tree leaves at the edge of the porch. They were in for another long, hot day if it was already this hot before dawn.

She'd set down and put the swing into motion when she noticed the bright yellow sports car sitting in the driveway. The vanity plate on the front said DINA'S BABY and had a wild sunflower entangled among the words.

The driver's door was wide open and two of the ranch dogs were hiking their legs on the back tires. A barn cat walked up across the hood, over the top, and down the back window before he jumped off and circled back around to the driver's side and hopped inside. Then she heard a squeal and a blonde head of big hair popped up over the steering wheel.

"Damn you, cat! You've ruined the inside of my car. Shit, I smell like tomcat piss. I'll sue Jackson for this," she yelled as she scrambled out of the car and grabbed her head.

Loretta set her coffee on the porch and was standing beside the car in half a dozen long-legged strides. "Good mornin', Dina!" She yelled as loudly as her own headache would allow.

"God Almighty." Dina grabbed her head. "Lower your voice. I spent the night with Jackson and we had too many margaritas."

"I'm not buying that brand of bullshit, Dina Mullins. Jackson hates margaritas. The only things he drinks are whiskey and beer. And, honey, there's not a cowboy in the canyon that'd go to bed with someone who smells like tomcat piss. Besides, I spent most of the night with Jackson, so what are you doing here?" Loretta asked.

Dina stared up at Loretta with bloodshot eyes. "I can take a bath and buy a new car, but you can't get any shorter. And, darlin', he told me that he wouldn't take you back if you begged him. He said that he's messin' with you for payback for leaving him."

Loretta leaned down and whispered, "You want to drive out of here with just a hangover or do you want me to drag your sorry ass out of that car and give you what you deserve?"

Dina slung her legs around and got out of the car. "I'm not afraid of you. You are dumb as hell as well as ugly as sin. I can make Jackson believe anything. Just watch me." She fell down in the grass and rolled up in the fetal position, screaming and holding her knees. "Don't hit me again. I was leaving. I told you I'd leave. Why did you attack me?"

Loretta crossed her arms over her chest and waited. The front door opened and Nona rushed out with Jackson right on her heels.

"Mama, what is going on? What in the devil is Dina doing here? She sounds like a dyin' coyote." Nona stopped so suddenly at the bottom of the steps that Jackson had to grab the banister to keep from knocking her down.

"Looks like Dina is having a seizure to me," Loretta said.

Dina jumped up and limped toward Jackson. "Loretta tried to kick me to death. She pulled me out of my car by the hair, slung me down on the ground, and started kicking me with those cowboy boots. Can't you see what a bitch she is, darlin'?"

Loretta held up a bare foot toward Nona and Jackson. "I guess I put one boot in her ass and the other in her lying mouth. Must be what made her scream so loud."

Dina looked at Loretta's feet and broke into tears. "She had on boots. I swear, Jackson. She got mad when she saw me coming out of the house and went crazy. I thought I could get away from her, but she grabbed me before I could shut the door."

"You said you were calling your dad to come drive you home, Dina. What happened?" Jackson asked.

"I fell asleep," she pouted.

Nona took a couple of steps forward. "That means you passed out, right? Mama, are you going to take care of this or am I? I don't believe her for a minute and you shouldn't either. Daddy wouldn't ever date an alcoholic."

"I'm not an alcoholic," Dina shouted, then grabbed her head again. "And I'm leaving, but I'll be back. Nothing can keep me away from what I want." Dina marched back to the car, slammed the door, and left in a cloud of red dirt.

"Sorry about that," Jackson said.

Nona's hands went on her hips at the same time Loretta's hit hers.

"Talk, Daddy. What was that shrew doing here at daybreak? And is that tomcat piss I smell? And you had to have talked to her if you thought she was calling her dad."

"The smell comes from a big old yellow tomcat that marked his territory while she was still passed out. I could have yelled at him but I didn't want to," Loretta said. "She's always been slightly unbalanced, Nona. But it looks like the drinking has pushed her over the edge. She probably did show up here, but I'd bet dollars to cow patties that she passed out in her car. She was trying to prove to me that she could make your dad feel sorry for her. It didn't work and now she's mad as well as hungover."

Jackson looked past Nona at Loretta. "You are right. She showed up last night and I told her to leave and never come back. She got locked into the high school stage and never grew up. I'm not sure therapy would even help her," he said.

Loretta started toward the house. She should hate Dina. But how could she hate someone so pathetic? Mostly what she felt was pity. Besides, she had bigger things to think about than Dina. She still had to convince Nona to finish college. "She's not worth ruining a lovely Sunday over, is she? Coffee is ready. Y'all want to join me in a cup on the porch before Rosie gets up and around?"

"Yes, ma'am," Jackson said.

❈ ❈ ❈

Bobby Lee took his place behind the pulpit and opened his Bible. "The Lord has laid it upon my heart to talk about forgiveness and revenge this morning. The Good Book says that vengeance is the Lord's and that if we don't forgive, we can't expect to be forgiven."

Loretta only listened with one ear; she wasn't completely ready to turn vengeance over to God or to forgive Dina. Besides, she was a whole lot more interested in the way Nona and Travis behaved across the center aisle from where she and Jackson sat.

Travis kept an arm around Nona and she gazed up at him with big blue puppy dog eyes. Fight like hell, then make up. Loretta had been down that path many times. Was it all worth it?

Jackson shifted his weight until his side was pressed against hers. Sparks danced around the church in living colors so bright that if the rest of the congregation could have seen them, they would have thought the second coming had arrived that June morning.

Was it worth it? Yes, definitely, if Nona didn't let guilt or lack of self-esteem rob her of what she loved. Travis would learn eventually that only a woman who truly loved a man would break two lamps and a coffee table for him.

Dammit! She'd had the perfect opportunity to kick Dina's ass and she'd let it get by her again. The woman might be wise to check herself into rehab, because it wouldn't happen a third time. Not even if Loretta spent a month in county lockup for it.

"So if there is hardness in your hearts," Bobby Lee was saying when she started listening again, "let it go. Peace and bitterness cannot live together in harmony. Now I'm going to ask Flint to deliver the benediction for us."

☀ ☀ ☀

"Great sermon this morning," Rosie said at dinner. "I invited Bobby Lee and his family to dinner, but I was too late. Someone else had already asked."

"Yes, it was and so timely," Nona said. "But I'm still not ready to forgive that hussy for going after my daddy."

"Me either, or your daddy for not stopping," Loretta said.

"Hey, now," Jackson protested. "I might not be innocent, but let's leave the past in the past. It's not good to keep dragging it up and rehashing it."

"Amen," Travis said.

Nona shot a look his way. "You don't really want to go there, darlin'."

He leaned over and kissed her on the cheek. "Neither do you, sweetheart."

"Looks like to me that the preacher's words didn't hit the right mark," Rosie grumbled. "I'm done eating so I'm going to my house. I'll see y'all later."

"You finished?" Travis asked Nona.

She laid her napkin on the table and nodded.

"What are y'all doin' this afternoon?" Nona looked at her parents.

"I'm watching Westerns on television," he said.

"And falling asleep," Nona laughed.

"You know me too well," he grinned.

"I'm going to the creek to meet up with Heather and Maria. Don't wait up for me. I could be late," Loretta said.

"Probably will be," Rosie said on her way out the door.

"Well, have fun." Nona blew them both kisses as she and Travis left.

Loretta was antsy for the next hour. Suddenly, she couldn't wait to see Maria and Heather. She checked the clock every five minutes and kept her cell phone turned on. She tried sitting in the swing, but time seemed to drag by like at a snail's pace. Reading didn't work, so finally she put a six-pack of cold beer in a small cooler and picked the right keys off the rack beside the back door. If she got there earlier than the other two, she'd sit on the tailgate of the truck and reminisce about what fun they'd had in high school.

Her hair was pulled up in a ponytail and she wore her cowboy boots. Long ago she'd walked to the creek in her bare feet, but she'd learned that morning when she faced off with Dina that she'd turned into a tenderfoot after so many years of wearing high heels every day. No way could she walk twenty yards with her soft feet, much less a mile. And that day she didn't want to walk. She wanted to drive the old truck and spend time with her friends.

Chapter Twelve

*H*EATHER AND MARIA WERE STANDING in the knee-deep water waving at her as she parked the old work truck beside one that didn't look a lot better. If rust was integrity and dents were personality, both vehicles were better than a brand-new Silverado right off the show floor.

Loretta's bare thighs made a sucking noise as they came unglued from the fake-leather seats. She picked up the cooler of beer from the truck bed and smiled all the way to the edge of the water. The three of them had been ornery in their youth and they'd shared everything with each other. She wished they'd all worked harder at staying in touch.

"What are you grinnin' about?" Heather asked.

"Is that the same old truck you used to drive when you and Jackson were together?" Maria asked.

Loretta plopped down on the sandbar, pulled off her boots, and joined them in the knee-deep water. "I don't know if Jackson kept the truck for sentimental reasons or if the damn thing just refuses to give up the ghost, but yes, it's the same one. I was grinnin' because comin' here brings back a whole shitload of memories, Heather. I stuck to the seats just like I used to when the truck was new and Jackson and I were dating."

"It's Texas in June, darlin'. Even with air-conditioning, you'd probably stick to the seats," Heather said. "I brought a quilt." She pointed toward the ancient, gnarly scrub oak tree. "Not much shade, but in this kind of heat it beats nothing. Is that beer?"

"Can't have bologna sandwiches without beer," Loretta said.

"Or cookies," Maria laughed.

"Remember that night we got drunk right here and dipped chocolate cookies in our beer?" Heather waded through the water out onto the sand and headed toward the quilt.

Loretta followed her. "What I remember most is that beer spilled all over me and I just knew Mama would catch me sneaking in after hours smelling like beer."

"I did a hell of a lot more stupid things than that up under that old oak tree, darlin'." Maria blushed.

Loretta laughed. "If that tree could talk, we'd all be in a shitload of trouble." She sat down on the quilt and opened the cooler. "Looks like I should've brought two six-packs with all the catchin' up we've got to do."

"Oh, honey, that'll take more than one visit and cases, not six-packs." Heather reached into the cooler and brought out an icy cold can of Coors. She popped the ring top off and handed it to Loretta, then did the same thing for Maria before opening her own.

"To us." Maria held up her can.

The other two clinked their cans against hers.

Loretta nodded at Maria. "You go first. I know you've got a son. What's happened since we talked last time? Did you move back to this area with your family?"

"Caught the husband cheating about a year ago and divorced him. Our son decided to live with his father. He hates anything that gets his hands dirty like farming and Claude, Texas, bores him to tears. He visits often, but he hates this place."

The orange bill of Maria's baseball cap bobbed up and down and the jet-black ponytail stuffed through the hole in the back swung from side to side. "His name is Liam. Can you believe I let my computer geek husband of the time talk me into an Irish name? He should have been Luiz after my dad, but oh, no, Jimmy wanted to name him Liam and in those days I was so damn much in love I would have named my only child Bugs Bunny if Jimmy insisted."

"Is Jimmy Irish or Scottish?" Loretta asked.

"He's Native American, actually. Full-blood Fox Indian, and his mama was not happy that he married a little Latino girl from Texas, let me tell you. I swear"—Maria held up her hand—"I thought of you when we divorced. Now I understand why you took off like a bolt of greased lightning. His mother was the bitch from hell until after Liam was born and then she at least warmed up enough to speak to me. But, darlin', she wasn't as bad as Eva Bailey."

Loretta smiled. "Eva passed on two years before I left, so she doesn't get to carry the blame for that. She never did like me, but she loved Nona and thought the sun came up in the morning to shine on Jackson. Even there at the end when she didn't know her husband anymore, she'd still smile at Jackson and Nona. And with her confined to the house, I could get away from her."

"You should have killed Dina. You always were too nice to that bitch. Remember how she used to treat you at cheerleading practice? She tried six ways to Sunday to break you and Jackson up before you got married," Heather said.

"I remember it all very well and I didn't do a thing to that girl," Loretta said.

"It wasn't what you did, darlin'. It's what you didn't do. She wanted to move in here from that big city in Florida and be the queen bee when her granddaddy died and left her folks that big ranch. You weren't willing to follow her around and pick up whatever scraps she let fall to the ground. Besides, Jackson was the quarterback and she wanted him," Maria answered.

"Dina was the straw that broke the camel's back," Loretta said. "I caught them kissing in the barn and didn't even give him a chance to explain. I didn't want to hear excuses that day. I was wrong, plain and simple. I should've knocked the hell out of her and then started on him."

"Why? We thought you were the match made in heaven," Heather said. "We all wanted to be you and find our knight in shining armor—or at least an old green-and-white pickup truck."

"I read a magnet thing on the refrigerator this morning that said the hardest lesson in life is letting go. The end of the quote said that we fight to hold on and we fight to let go."

"And?" Heather asked.

"I was tired of fighting for either side back then. Jackson's mother was lucid enough to tell me several times a day that he would have never married me if I hadn't been pregnant. I wasn't blind. I could see that he was flirting when we were among a group or after church. Sly little looks. Cute smiles that used to belong to just me. Hey, I couldn't blame him. He'd been saddled with a wife right after high school graduation and a child the next February when he should have been living in a frat house at some fancy college, so I had enough fuel when I saw Dina wrapped around him like an octopus to fire up my temper real good," Loretta said.

"She's saying that you hit her this morning," Maria said.

"How in the hell did you find that out so fast?" Loretta asked.

Maria shrugged. "She called Abigail Proctor and whined about it. Abigail told Tansy at church and Tansy called her sister, who is my friend, and she told me. You don't keep anything secret in the canyon. You know that, Loretta."

Loretta's mascara flowed down her cheeks in big black streaks by the time she finished telling the Dina-of-the-morning story. "I'm sorry for laughing so hard. It's really kind of pitiful, but lookin' back, it is funny too."

"Some people never grow up," Maria said.

"My ex didn't." Heather turned up her beer and drank the last of it. "I'm ready for a sandwich. I slept until noon and had a candy bar for breakfast."

"Speaking of never growing up," Loretta said.

Heather stuck her tongue out at Loretta as she pulled bread, bologna, and mustard from a brown paper bag.

"What, no lettuce and tomatoes and cheese?" Loretta asked.

"Patience, girlfriend. Patience." She brought out a plastic container of sliced tomatoes, one of lettuce, and a third one containing cheese slices. "And for Maria, ta-da." She fished out a fourth container with dill pickle slices.

"A feast fit for three divorced women. Welcome home, Loretta. We're so glad you are here," Maria said.

"It's a feast, but, darlin', I am not home. I wouldn't even be here if Nona hadn't decided to quit college. She's only got one more year and she'll have her degree," Loretta said.

"I hear the words. I don't believe there's much conviction there," Heather laughed.

"Hand me the pickles. I haven't had a sandwich like this in years," Loretta said, ignoring her.

Heather passed the pickles across the quilt. "You are evading the issue."

"Heather is a schoolteacher in Silverton, if you are wondering," Maria said. "And I'm helping Daddy and Mama run the family farm east of Claude. Daddy isn't well and Mama can't do it all herself."

"I'm sorry. What's wrong with Luiz?" Loretta asked.

"Diabetes. He's lost both legs below the knees and he's in a wheelchair. He's still a good boss, but there are a lot of things he flat-out can't do. All of the other kids have roots and families. So the lot fell to me. When the time comes, the farm will be mine, though, so I don't mind," she answered.

"I'm really sorry to hear that, Maria," Loretta said.

Maria nodded. "Thank you. How's your folks?"

"Mad at me for being here. One sister is praying for me. One is ready to string me up. Mama's giving me ultimatums and Daddy, bless his heart, puts guilt trips on me without even trying."

"That's two," Heather said. "What about the other one?"

"Dolly is a drama professor. She plays several roles in one phone call," Loretta answered.

"Well, we hope that you change your mind and stick around. It's great having you here," Maria said.

"Thanks. What's the story about your ex, Heather? Got kids?"

She held up a finger and finished chewing, swallowed, and took a sip of her second beer. "No kids. Six miscarriages and then a doctor said that I needed a hysterectomy at thirty. I can't blame my ex for anything except that we drifted apart. I was teaching and he was in the service. He was on deployment as much as he was at home and one day we both realized we were married but not married, if you know what I mean. We parted friends and still talked up until six months ago, when he remarried. He retired from the service after twenty years, went to work as a postman over in Tucumcari, where his family lives, and reconnected with his high school sweetheart. They seem real happy and she's pregnant. They're happy and I'm happy that they are."

"God! Pregnant at our age," Loretta groaned.

✺ ✺ ✺

125

Loretta waited until Heather and Maria were gone before she checked behind the wide bench seat in the truck. She squealed when she found it. She'd recognize that wedding ring quilt anywhere. It was the one that she and Jackson always used when they made out under that oak tree. It was the one that he'd spread out in the truck bed when they'd had sex for the first time. And they'd wrapped it around Nona that first winter when they took her outside to see her first snowflakes. She pulled it out, let the tailgate down, and spread it out in the truck bed, then stretched out and watched the sun drift slowly toward the western edge of the canyon.

She heard footsteps and whistling and then Jackson's face appeared over the edge of the truck bed. He tilted his hat back and scanned her from head to toe, his gaze turning up the temperature in the truck bed at least twenty degrees.

"I hope you used a ton of sunscreen if you've spent the whole afternoon out here," he said.

She looked up into his eyes. "Mostly the girls and I stayed under the shade tree, but yes, I did."

He moved from the fender to sit on the tailgate, legs stretched from one side to the other. He'd changed from jeans to khaki shorts and a green tank top the same color as his eyes. There was enough of a five o'clock shadow on his face to be damn sexy. Her fingertips itched to play in his dark hair that was long enough to curl up on the back of his neck and cover half his ears.

"You need a haircut," she said.

He left his perch and crawled up to stretch out beside her, being careful not to touch her. "So when are you giving me a haircut? I've hated going to the barbershop. It's not the same as when you took care of it for me. I don't like the way they cut it and I sure don't like that the lady wears clothes."

Loretta felt the heat rising into a full-fledged blush, but there wasn't a thing she could do about it. She'd cut his hair the first time when they were seventeen. They'd been sitting in the back of the truck, both of them just out of the water from skinny-dipping.

"From that crimson in your cheeks, I guess you remember," he chuckled.

She threw her arm up over her eyes. "Does Rosie cut your hair?"

"Why would you ask a fool question like that?"

"I'm Rosie for the next week. If she doesn't cut your hair, then I don't," Loretta said.

"Then I guess it'll have to get long enough to put into a ponytail," he said.

"How long do you intend for that ponytail to get?"

He grinned. "You decide. But I didn't come out here to talk about my hair."

"I know. This is part of your Sunday routine, right?"

"Yes, it is," he answered. "And I can't get that incident with Dina off my mind. Why didn't you stay and fight for us the way that Nona fought for Travis? I would have gladly paid the bail to get you out of jail for assaulting Dina. Looking back, I think I was trying to get a rise out of you," he said.

The arm went down and she popped straight up to a sitting position. "Why in the hell would you do that?"

"I saw the way the guys flirted with you, the way they always left their hand on your shoulder a second too long, and a hundred other little things. I knew that I ruined your dreams of going to college when I got you pregnant. You were valedictorian of our senior class, for God's sake. Your folks were taking you to the University of Oklahoma to enroll you right after graduation, but then you found out you were pregnant. You could have been anything you wanted. Truth is, I felt guilty, so I was trying to make you jealous to make myself feel better. I wanted you to fight for me, to prove that I hadn't ruined your life and your dreams," he said.

"My dreams? We were both young and stupid. I didn't see a single man flirting with me. I only saw you winking and smiling at the women, especially Dina, like y'all had a little inside joke, and then it all came to a head in the barn. You'd even signed to play for Texas A&M and you had to give it up for me. It had to sting, Jackson."

He sighed. "Mama wanted me to go to college. I wanted to ranch. Sound familiar?"

He didn't make a move to scoot closer to her or to say anything else. The rays of the sun at the end of the day warmed their skin. The ever-blowing west Texas wind kicked up dust devils but they didn't see them. The creek kept right on flowing to wherever it dumped into a bigger body of water.

The earth didn't stand still and time kept right on marching. Nothing changed because they'd confessed to past feelings, but Loretta's heart felt lighter than it had since the morning she'd told Jackson that she was pregnant.

"This is nice," he finally mumbled.

"It is, isn't it? Jackson, I'm not your mother, but I do want Nona to finish her education, even if it's in vet tech or business agriculture. And this thing that's between us—" she said and paused.

"Can go at any rate you want it to," he finished for her.

"Thank you."

"I always thought if you came back I'd take delight in kicking your ass off the ranch," he chuckled.

"I always thought if I came back I'd find Dina in my bed," she said.

He propped up on an elbow but didn't let go of her hand. "Honey, there hasn't been a single woman in your bed, not in all these years."

"And in the other beds in the house?"

"You first, darlin'. If you want to drag out the bones of what happened after we divorced, then you get to go first. If you want to leave them all buried, then we will," he said seriously.

"Fight to let go," she mumbled. It meant more than she'd thought at first. If she wanted to have something to fight for, then she had to learn to let go of the past, and that meant all of it. She couldn't pick and choose what she wanted to forget, what she wanted to remember, and what she wanted to store away for future arguments. She needed to write the future on a clean slate.

"What?" he asked.

"Just something I read on the refrigerator this morning that made a lot of sense to me. How do you ever really bury the past?" she asked. "It's what molded us into the people we are today. Let's go wade in the water to cool off."

He pulled his hand free and hopped off the tailgate. "Upstream or down?"

"You choose," she said.

Chapter Thirteen

Ranching in June is very different than ranching in the fall or even in the winter. It all came back to Loretta as she prepared sandwiches to take to the field for the hands that Monday morning. There are always daily chores: feeding, milking, working cattle, plowing. That's year-round work, but summer on a ranch is busy with a capital B. It's a time of planting, harvesting, hay hauling, and praying for rain, then when the storm clouds gather, the work speeds up even faster to get the hay in before it gets soaked in the field.

She wasn't ready for it on a full-time, forever status. How could Nona want this when she had so much more potential? As always, no matter how much she argued with herself, she couldn't find an answer to her questions.

She'd planned to make fried chicken for dinner, but Nona called at midmorning and said that there was no way with the dark clouds overhead that they could leave the hayfield. It was cut, raked, and dry and they needed to get it baled and in the barn before the rain hit.

She set up an assembly line on the bar like Rosie had taught her when she was a teenager. Lay out a whole loaf of bread, smear mayonnaise on half, light on the mustard on the other half. Meat, cheese, tomatoes, lettuce, top it with a plain slice of bread and then gently put them into the ziplock bags. Stack the mayonnaise ones in the blue plastic container in the pantry; mustard in the yellow one. Two containers of each at least—the hired hands would be starving, since they'd gone to work at daybreak.

She loaded it all along with four boxes of individually wrapped chips and several packages of cookies, a plastic garbage bag to put the trash inside, and the green cooler full of ice with two of the big five-gallon containers of sweet tea. They'd eat in shifts and if there were leftovers, she'd leave it all behind for snacks through the afternoon. If they couldn't come in for supper, she'd repeat the process when Nona or Jackson called.

Nona hopped off the back of a hay truck as soon as Loretta parked. Dusty, dirty, and sweaty, Nona wolfed down two sandwiches and two cups of sweet tea. She tossed her trash in the bag that Loretta had hung on the edge of the tailgate and shoved four cookies into her shirt pocket as she headed inside the barn to trade places with Travis.

"Mornin', Miz Loretta." Travis tipped his misshapen straw hat. He ate twice as much and even faster than Nona.

"Feels like rain," she said.

"Feels like a big storm in the making, 'scuse my language. We'll be lucky if we get this all off the ground and in the barn before it starts," he said. "Thanks for dinner. Unless it comes a frog strangler, we'll see you again at suppertime."

Loretta didn't need a *Ranching for Dummies* book to know what he was saying. Unless it started to rain so hard that the frogs were in danger, she would be making more sandwiches that evening. If it did start to pour, then they'd have to stop and take a loss on what was lying in windrows out there in the fields.

Jackson parked a loaded flatbed truck, crawled out, and stretched. His hair was plastered to his head with sweat. Dirt beads circled his neck and bits of hay stuck to his faded jeans. The blue knit shirt that stretched across his arms and broad chest looked as if he'd been a contestant in a wet T-shirt contest.

Loretta's breath caught in her chest. This was the Jackson she remembered best; the cowboy who worked as hard as he loved. Had she really ever been married to him?

"Thanks for bringing us something to the field. Didn't seem right for me and Nona to take a lunch break when the rest have to keep working." He picked up a sandwich and bit into it.

"I'm Rosie. It's my job," she said. "Y'all don't need me to watch you eat, do you?"

He shook his head. "I reckon we can manage on our own."

"I brought my gloves and my hat. I'm going to help this afternoon. I'll quit long enough to go make sandwiches for supper, but right now I'm going to help stack hay."

"Thank you," he said.

"For what?"

"For being you," he said. "You can drive the truck on the way back out to the field."

"I can throw hay on this round and someone else can do the driving. I'm rested. Y'all are beginning to flag."

He chuckled as she walked away.

She whipped around. "What?"

"One week and you're already givin' orders. Welcome home, Loretta," he answered.

Her eyebrows shot up. "Don't read more into it than it is. I'm bored in the house. That's the real story."

"Whatever you say, darlin'."

In a few long strides she was nose to nose with him. "Don't you get sarcastic with me, Jackson."

"Or what? You'll go home?"

"Or I'll stay and make your life miserable," she said.

Nona shot out of the barn. "Mama, are you and Daddy fighting?"

"Yes, we are," Loretta said. "But it's our fight, so you go on and leave us alone."

Nona looked from one to the other. "You want to meet behind the barn at daylight with pistols drawn? Or how about butcher knives in the kitchen? I'd go for the pistols. Or worse yet, Mama, how would you like to sit on the sofa and hold hands with Daddy for an hour?"

Jackson laughed.

Loretta tried not to grin but it didn't work. "Knives or guns—I always hated that holding-hands shit when I was a kid."

"Then my vote is for the holding-hands shit," Jackson said.

"Well, I'll tell you one thing for damn sure. You must not be working as hard as me and Travis, because if you were, you wouldn't have the energy to fight," Nona said.

Loretta's phone buzzed in her hip pocket and she reached for it.

"Saved by the bell," Jackson said.

"It's Emmy Lou," she said.

"Punishment served." Nona smiled.

❋ ❋ ❋

Three bone-tired people came dragging through the kitchen door at two in the morning. The barn was full and the rest of the summer would be spent making the big round bales that stayed out in the fields covered in white plastic.

Lightning flashed through the sky in a long jagged streak, followed immediately by a clap of thunder so loud that it rattled the dishes in the cabinets.

"Holy shit!" Nona grabbed her ears.

She'd scarcely gotten the words out when the clouds opened the floodgates and it started to rain so hard that even with the lightning, visibility out the kitchen window was limited to only a few feet.

Jackson slumped into a kitchen chair and kicked off his boots. "That's calling it too close for comfort."

Nona opened the refrigerator and brought out three beers. "Not a word out of your mouth, Mama. I deserve this after today. That lightning that came close to parting my hair. When I finish this beer, I'm having first dibs on the bathtub and I'm not getting up at the crack of dawn tomorrow. I forgot to ask, what did Aunt Emmy Lou want to talk about?"

"She wanted to call a truce. It's part of her strategy, believe me. She doesn't give up this easy. They're going to start on you any day now." Loretta twisted off the cap from the bottle of beer Nona handed her and sat down at the table beside Jackson.

"Granny already called a couple of times. I let it go to voice mail. I don't want to talk to them. Right now, let's celebrate." She raised her beer bottle in a toast.

Jackson and Loretta both clinked theirs with hers.

"To us," she said, excitement in her tone. "We did it. We got it all in and we didn't lose a single bale. You must be a good luck charm, Mama."

"Well, thank you. Dolly called and wanted to chat while I was driving the hay truck. She was even more pleasant than Emmy Lou. I wonder what they've got up their sleeves." Loretta thought out loud as she sipped her beer.

"You might want to throw your phone in the creek," Nona said. "I don't want to referee your fights with the aunts. It's all I can do to keep you and Daddy from locking up horns. Besides, you don't want to go home yet. Like you said, when Aunt Emmy Lou calls a truce, there's a hidden agenda."

"Your mother and I weren't really fighting. We were just stating opinions," Jackson said.

"If it looks like a bull, is stubborn as a bull, and produces bullshit in the pasture, chances are it's a bull."

"What has that got to do with anything?" Jackson asked.

"And why would you have to referee my fights? I'm big enough and mean enough to take care of three meddling sisters," Loretta said.

"Changing the subject because I'm too tired to talk about the way the aunts try to make me their business all the time. The weatherman says it's going to rain all day tomorrow and maybe even the next, so I reckon I could sleep past five, right, Daddy? Pancakes and sausage for breakfast, Mama?" Nona asked.

"Maybe until seven since you worked a double today." He grinned. "And, Loretta, thanks again."

She nodded. "No thanks necessary, and, Nona, after all the exercise we had today, a breakfast with a million calories will be just fine."

"Darlin', there's never been an inch to spare on your body," Jackson said.

"If you two are going to talk body parts, I'm going to take a bath and fall into bed," Nona said.

"Don't fall asleep and drown." Jackson picked up his beer.

"If I'm not out in fifteen minutes, send in the rescue squad." Nona left half a bottle of beer on the cabinet and disappeared into the darkness of the foyer.

Loretta downed the rest of her beer and reached for what Nona had left behind. "It's raining, Jackson. I'm taking Nona with me tomorrow. We're going to Amarillo to shop. She needs to visit the beauty parlor for a haircut and she needs to do girl things. If she doesn't, she's going to resent this place."

He covered a yawn with his hand. "Hey, I take her shopping and to the beauty shop when she's here. And if I can't, Rosie does. It's not like she's tied to the ranch and never leaves. But I have to admit, shopping is not my favorite way to spend a day, so I'm not arguing with you. If you want to grab a shower in my room, so you don't have to wait for Nona to finish. I don't mind."

She drank the rest of Nona's beer and tossed two bottles into the trash can. "Thank you. I'd love a quick shower. Speaking of your room, I changed sheets this morning and noticed that you still can't hit the hamper with your clothes, can you?"

He crossed his arms on the table and rested his head on them. "If a sock falls in the forest and no one is there to pick it up, does it make a noise? After the day we put in, who gives a shit if my socks didn't make it all the way inside the hamper? You sound like Rosie."

"If a man throws his clothes toward the hamper and he doesn't have a wife, the next closest female will bitch about it," she said. "Breakfast is at eight tomorrow morning. Nona and I'll leave midmorning."

"Yes, ma'am. Have you talked to Nona about it?"

"Not yet. Do I have to promise with one hand raised to God and the other on the Bible that I won't kidnap her and take her to Oklahoma?" Loretta said.

"The Bible is on the table in the foyer. We can do that tomorrow before you leave," he said.

"You're not kidding, are you?"

"No, ma'am."

"Jackson, we're just going shopping. If I turned my van toward Oklahoma, she'd probably jump out and break an arm or a leg."

"Then you'd have to stay on even longer to get her well again."

"Heaven forbid! Give me five minutes and I'll be out of your room," she said.

136

"If I'm not waiting on the top step, you'd best come on back down here and wake me up," he said.

She left her dirty clothes in a pile on the bathroom floor, adjusted the water to the right temperature, and pulled back the shower curtain. She longed to fill the tub with hot water and soak her aching muscles, but five minutes didn't allow for that kind of treat. So she flipped the switch and stepped over the edge to stand under a pulsating showerhead.

Cold air rushed in when the shower curtain was thrown to one side and her eyes popped from half-closed to wide open. There stood Jackson in all his naked glory, one leg already in the shower, the other on the way.

"I was about to fall asleep sitting out there on the step. Turn around I'll wash your hair for you," he said. "Don't bother looking lower than my belly button. Not even you, with all your stunning beauty, could get a rise out of me tonight, as tired as I am."

The shampoo was the same kind she used to buy. It smelled like coconuts and his hands were magic as they massaged her scalp. She'd showered with him hundreds of times. She'd seen him naked. But this night was a whole new experience. She could feel the heat from his body that was only inches from hers. She could smell the sweat of the day washing down the drain.

"Feel good?" he asked.

"There are no words to tell you how good," she murmured.

"I love your voice when it gets like that." He turned her around and adjusted the showerhead so that it pulsed against her hair. He moved a step closer. Their bodies were like magnets, each drawing the other closer and closer until they were inseparable. He picked up a thick washcloth, lathered it with her favorite soap, and ran it over her body, stopping to plant random soft kisses as he worked his way down her entire body.

"Jackson, we shouldn't," she whispered.

"We have to. We were filthy dirty. We can't get in between clean sheets like that, can we?" he chuckled.

"You asked for it," she said. "Turn around."

"Why?"

"I'm going to wash your hair and make sure you are clean enough to go to bed."

He obeyed.

Like he'd done, she used her fingertips to work the same shampoo into his hair.

He groaned. "You are right. Words can't explain this."

When she finished, she bypassed the washcloth and lathered up her hands. Starting at the tense, hard muscles in his shoulders, she washed and dug her fingers into places that had bigger knots in them. When she finished with his calves, he turned without being told.

"Evidently you aren't as tired as you thought." She smiled.

He glanced down and smiled. "I guess not. What are we going to do about that?"

The shiver that danced down her backbone had nothing to do with cold air flowing from the overhead vent and everything to do with humming hormones. She wanted Jackson. Common sense said that she should grab a towel and run, not walk, to her room. Her heart tried to smother common sense. Every sane thought flew out the window to join the storm going on full force.

She raised up to her full height and wrapped her arms around his neck. Her wet lips met his in a blistering-hot kiss that fogged the entire bathroom. With a little hop, her long legs locked around his waist. Neither of them had forgotten how to have shower sex. Her hand slipped between their wet bodies and guided him inside her. He backed her up against the cold tile and they rocked together, their scorching kisses fueling the hunger that could never be totally satisfied between them. Her nails dug into his shoulders and he cupped her butt for better leverage. She moaned through the kisses and the rhythm increased to a speed and fierceness that made her dizzy. Breasts against bare chest, so close to him that light couldn't separate them, they became one passionate being, trying desperately to bring the other one to a cliff-hanging experience.

She arched at the same time he growled her name and they tumbled over the edge together. He slid down until he was sitting in the tub. She shifted slightly so that she was sitting in his lap with her long legs off to one side.

"My knees are weak," he said.

"You have knees?" she whispered.

The closed shower curtain created a small, foggy space. With the water still rushing down on them, Loretta imagined them behind a waterfall on an exotic island. She buried her head in Jackson's chest, listening to his steady heartbeat. That was most likely the single biggest mistake of her entire life, but she still didn't want it to end.

"You can't spend the night," he said.

"I didn't plan on it."

"I've never slept with a woman I'm not married to in this house. Can't start bad habits now." He tucked a strand of wet hair behind her ear and kissed her on the nose.

She knew Jackson. Even after all the years apart, she could tell when he was teasing to cover up. Now everything was suddenly awkward, like the big thing was in the room with them again and neither of them wanted to admit it was there.

Her knees were weak. Her body hummed with contentment. But common sense said that this shouldn't have happened. She was too tired for fighting forces inside her heart and head.

"Jackson, we were tired and the beer and . . ."

He put a finger over her lips. "Not now. Don't spoil this lovely afterglow. We'll analyze the hell out of it later, but not now."

"Okay." She stretched the word out into five syllables. "Then I think maybe I'd best wrap a towel around my body and hurry across the landing to my room."

"First part is good. Second part, not yet. I still have to brush your hair or it'll look like shit in the morning. And you've got to go shopping. You throw things, like hairbrushes, if your hair looks like shit," he said.

"I can brush my own hair."

"Be still for another five minutes. I've always loved to brush your hair. It's silky and I like the way it smells and that cute little sex noise you make because it feels so good to you." He threw back the curtain, eased her out of his lap, and stood up. "You wouldn't deny a dying man his last wish, would you?"

"Jackson Bailey, you are not dying," she said.

"I could be. I hauled hay all day and half the night and now I've made love to you with the last thread of energy in my body. My poor old heart could stop at any moment. I am forty, you know," he said with seriousness.

"Don't give me that old shit, Jackson. Not after what we just did."

He turned off the shower, wrapped a towel around her body and another one around his hips, and pulled a brush from the vanity.

Her eyes widened out. "Is that—?"

He grinned and kissed her on the forehead. "It's your favorite pink brush. The one that doesn't yank your hair out by the roots." He slipped his big hand over hers and led her to the rocking chair beside his bed, where he pulled her down into his lap.

"I missed that brush. You can't buy them anymore," she whispered.

"That's why you have to come back to the ranch. It's mine now and I never let it leave my room."

❁ ❁ ❁

Loretta awoke in her bedroom at seven o'clock to the sound of a slow drizzling rain slapping against her windows. She stared at the clock, afraid to turn over for fear she'd find Jackson beside her. She could practically feel the heat coming from his body and yet no matter how hard she strained her ears, she couldn't hear his soft breathing. Finally, she reached behind her body and gingerly slid her hand in an arc as far as it would go.

"Whew!" She let out a lung full of pent-up air. "At least that part was a dream."

She bailed out of bed, grabbed a pair of underpants from the top dresser drawer and pulled them on. Now she didn't feel nearly so vulnerable. She riffled through the drawer until she found a bra, then went to the closet to pull out a pair of khaki shorts and a dark green knit shirt. Fully dressed except for her sandals, she trusted herself to look in the mirror.

No hickeys shining on her neck. She didn't have a wanton look in her eyes—well, not too much of one. She did need makeup to cover up those dark circles, but she'd only slept four hours. With that in mind, they didn't look too bad at all.

"And my hair is smooth," she said. "It's that pink brush. I'm going to steal the damn thing before I leave at the end of the summer."

Chapter Fourteen

"I REALLY DO NOT WANT TO GO SHOPPING. Travis and I thought we'd work on that old tractor out in the barn this morning," Nona said at the breakfast table.

Loretta didn't want to fight with Nona on the first day they had off the ranch, so she chose her words carefully. "A day apart does any couple good, and, darlin', your hair needs trimming. The ends look like straw."

Jackson looked up over his morning paper. "Your mama is talking good sense. I'll help Travis get that old tractor running this morning."

"I don't know why you still have that paper delivered. That's yesterday's news. You can get today's instantly on the computer," Nona said.

"Don't change the subject." Loretta's voice raised an octave.

"I like a newspaper that smells like a newspaper. And your mama is right, your hair is starting to look like shit," Jackson said.

"Whose side are you on?" Nona asked.

"Travis's side. I wouldn't want to run my hands though hair like that. I'd feel like I was back in the barn stacking hay," he answered.

She drew a strand of hair through her fingertips. "Okay, you win, but I want to be home by six. Is that a problem?"

"No, ma'am. Not if you can be ready to leave in an hour."
Loretta smiled.

❊ ❊ ❊

Loretta eyed the eastbound ramp on Interstate 40 north of Claude. The canyon was behind them and in four hours she'd be in her cute little house in Mustang, Oklahoma. Nona would pitch a pure bitch fit, but what could she do about it? She'd be in a van doing seventy miles an hour on a four-lane highway.

"Don't even think of it," Nona said.

"How do you know what I'm thinking?"

"You aren't real good at hiding things, Mama. Whatever you think is written on your face. I wish you could have seen yourself when that Dina bitch was acting up in our yard," Nona laughed.

"And what am I thinking now?"

"You are wondering what kind of hissy I'd throw if you turned right instead of left."

Loretta took the west ramp and pointed her van toward Amarillo. "Don't always depend on that. I might be just messin' with you, kiddo." She couldn't resist a look in the rearview mirror.

"You promised," Nona said.

"I didn't promise to not look that direction," Loretta said.

"What are we doing first? Beauty shop or shopping?"

"I made an appointment for the full treatment, including a light lunch. Didn't think we'd need much after that breakfast, and then I thought we'd shop for a couple of hours and be home by six. How does that agenda sound to you?"

"Like heaven," Nona moaned. "I'd commit homicide for a massage. If you'd told me this morning a spa was involved, I wouldn't have even mentioned the tractor."

"You can have those things regularly at college," Loretta said.

"I'm not having this conversation, Mama. My mind is made up. So we're talking about something else. I texted Travis and he's bringing pizza and a movie to the house at six. You and Daddy can watch it with us if you promise not to argue," Nona said.

"Well, thank you so much for inviting us to sit in our living room and for reminding me a dozen times that we have to be home at six," Loretta said.

Nona's eyebrows shot up. "*Our* living room."

"Don't you get all sassy with me."

Nona laughed. "Yes, ma'am. Do I need to remember anything? You need work jeans, right? Anything else?"

"The list is in my purse."

Nona smiled. "I should have known."

"Don't make fun of me, either," Loretta said. "When you are the only parent and working a full-time job plus making sure of dental appointments and doing everything alone, you will make lists too."

"Whoa!" Nona said. "I appreciate you being a role model. I really do. And look—" She pulled a list from her purse. "I'm learning to make lists so I don't forget anything. Besides, there isn't a shopping mall four blocks down the road from Lonesome Canyon, so if I forget something I have to do without."

A grin turned up the corners of Loretta's full mouth. "Thank you. I'd begun to think you'd rejected every strand of my DNA."

"Only the parts we aren't going to talk about today," Nona said.

Their phones rang at the same time. Nona dug hers out of her purse and Loretta fished hers from her shirt pocket and put it on speaker.

"Hey, are y'all in Amarillo yet?" Jackson asked.

"We are passing the second Conway exit right now," she said.

"Would you please go by the vet's office while you are there? They'll have the order ready and they'll bill me, so you don't have to pay for anything." His drawl seemed even deeper on the phone.

"Depends on how much room it's going to take up," she said.

"You could put it in your purse. It's a vial of vaccination medicine that we need to finish working one more pen of calves this week. And tell our daughter that the tractor is fixed. It took twenty minutes," Jackson said.

"Then we'll be glad to make a stop at the vet's," Loretta said. "Anything else?"

"Just a minute. I'll ask Flint." He muffled the phone with his hand but it didn't cut out all the noise. In a few seconds he said, "Flint says to tell you thank you, but that's all we need."

"Who all is there?" she asked.

"Flint, Travis, and Waylon, but Travis is on the phone with our daughter. He's whispering and I don't even want to know what they're talking about. See you later. Oh, a reminder while you are shopping, we still do the big Fourth of July thing here at Lonesome Canyon. So you might want to pick up something for that," he said.

"You telling me I look shabby in what I wear every day?" she asked.

Nona put a finger over her lips. "Shh, not so loud."

"Darlin', you look great in anything or nothing," Jackson said.

Nona blushed. "Tell him that I heard that, so everyone in the living room did too."

"Bet that caused our daughter to suck air," Jackson chuckled. "Y'all have fun now."

"What does that mean? Why would he say that?" Nona quickly hung up and looked at the phone lying on the console between them.

"It means that your father still has a sense of humor," Loretta said. "What were you whispering about? I kind of doubt it had anything to do with rain or stops at the vet's or whether you should have the hairdresser cut one or two inches from your hair."

"Private," Nona said.

"Ditto," Loretta told her.

"I never thought I'd be asking this question, but are you and Daddy dating?"

"Private." Loretta smiled.

"My God! You are too old to be dating and you'd be terrible together. You are both bullheaded, stubborn, and you couldn't make it work the first time, so what makes you think you could at your age?" Nona stopped to catch her breath.

"Still private."

Nona inhaled deeply and set her jaw like her father did when he was angry. "I don't want to live in a house with the two of you permanently. I want you to go home, Mama."

"I will when you go with me." Loretta made a show of looking in the rearview mirror.

Nona crossed her arms over her chest. "It ain't about to happen. I'm stayin' on the ranch. It'll be mine someday and I'm not going to lose what my ancestors have built for me."

"And if your dad remarries and has more children?" Loretta asked.

All the color left Nona's face. "You're not pregnant. Not at your age. Good God almighty, tell me you aren't sleeping with him."

"Wouldn't be any worse than being pregnant at eighteen. And if I am sleeping with him, it's private. Are you ready to discuss your sex life with me?"

"Hell, no!"

"Then don't expect me to talk about mine with you. I will answer your question. I am not pregnant. And I wasn't talking remarrying your father. I was talking about other women. Once we decide we never should have been together in the first place and move on, he will probably find someone else and they might have kids," Loretta said.

Nona threw her hand over her forehead and leaned back against the headrest. "What a horrible thought."

"You might need that education after all," Loretta said.

"I'll take my chances," Nona said.

"Okay, have it your way. We'll go to the vet's place first so we don't forget, and then it's on to the spa," Loretta said.

"We aren't through talking about this," Nona said.

"I am definitely finished talking about it. This is our day and we're not going to spoil it with any more arguing. You are beginning to sound like Emmy Lou."

Nona frowned. "Ouch! That's not nice. Okay, then tell me what's going on with you and Daddy. I saw those little flirty glances at the breakfast table this morning."

"I see little flirty glances all the time between you and Travis. We'll talk about what you think you saw this morning right after we talk about what I definitely see between you and your boyfriend." Loretta parked the car in front of the same vet's office they'd used years before. Hot wind rushed into the car when she opened the door and cool air went out just as fast.

"Mama, you are exasperating!" Nona said dramatically.

"Good. It's payback for all the times when you've been the same way, but I'm still not fighting with you today."

"Leave the car running," Nona said.

"I don't hear you complaining about the heat when you're out there hauling hay or working cattle."

"That's different. You aren't going to talk to me about this thing between you, are you? You're really not playing around with me?"

Loretta raised one eyebrow and said, "Of course I'm joking. I'll tell you everything in one word. Private."

Nona frowned. "Well, shit!"

The gesture reminded Loretta so much of her own mother that she grabbed her phone and punched in the office number as she made her way into the vet's office. She had to walk all the way from the back side of the parking lot, since there were four trucks with long cattle trailers taking up 90 percent of the big space.

"Good morning, Loretta. I was about to leave for my lunch break. Wish you were here. We'd grab a salad at that little café around the corner," Katy said.

"Nona reminded me of you, so I called to tell you that I love you," Loretta said.

"Well, thank you, but I'd rather hear those words with you standing beside me right here in the office. Please tell me that Nona has come to her senses and tell me what's going on with you and Jackson." Katy asked.

"Where did that come from? I was talking about you and Nona. How did he get into the conversation?" Loretta slowed down.

"There's something different in your voice. Either you beat him at the game or you've joined his side," Katy said.

"You even sound like her. She demanded that I answer that same question, so I did, with the same word she gave me when I asked her what she was whispering about with Travis."

She could hear Katy sigh. "And what did you tell her?"

"Private. She used that word today and I really like it," Loretta laughed.

"It must be an inside joke. But it's good that you two are talking. That's the first step in getting her home. And Emmy Lou said that she called and you and your sisters made up. I hate it when you fight," Katy said.

"Me too. I'll talk to you later," Loretta said.

A young woman with blonde hair and brown eyes looked up from behind the desk at the vet's office. She wasn't a day older than Nona and her name tag identified her as Kayla, a vet tech. Nona could do that job. With an extra year of college she could be standing in that place wearing makeup and cute little scrubs.

"Good morning, may I help you?"

"I'm Loretta Bailey. I'm here to pick up some medicine for Lonesome Canyon Ranch."

"I've got it all ready. How is Jackson? Haven't seen him in a few weeks. I didn't even know he'd gotten married. How do you like the canyon? It's gorgeous, isn't it?" Kayla pushed a small bag across the counter.

"Yes, it is. Thank you," Loretta said.

"Tell Nona I'll call her in a few days and we'll go do girl things. She and I try to get together a couple of times every summer," Kayla said.

"I will do that. She's out in the van. We're off for a spa day."

"That is so nice. Bonding time, huh?"

"You might call it that." Loretta smiled.

Nona was on the phone and giggling when she reached the van.

"Tall redhead. Yes, Kayla. I swear it's my mother and she and my dad are not married, trust me. I'm pretty tied up right now with the ranchin' business, but how about we catch up at the Fourth of July picnic? Good, I'll see you then."

"Your friend?" Loretta asked.

Nona nodded. "Mama, it's not like I come to the ranch every year and do nothing but work, work, work. I have a life here. You could have told her that you and Daddy weren't married."

Loretta started up the engine. "I didn't want to waste a single minute of my time with you today, and I already had to walk halfway to China just to get the medicine for your dad. We have to be home by six, remember?"

They walked into the spa with five minutes to spare before their appointment. The slim brunette behind the counter looked up and grinned. "Hi, Nona. I heard you were back for the summer. I can't wait for the picnic. I've got a date with Waylon's youngest brother."

"No kidding. First date?" Nona asked. "Mama, this is my friend Gretchen."

"Pleased to meet you, ma'am. Nona has talked a lot about you. I used to be her babysitter too until she outgrew the need for one. I'll take you on back," Gretchen winked.

"Nice to meet you too," Loretta said. "So how long have you been working here?"

"I was raised in this shop. My mama owned it until last year. She promised she'd sell it to me when I finished college. I kept dropping out and working for her, but then I decided I wanted to own the place, so I got serious. Right here are your cubicles. You know the drill," Gretchen said.

Loretta hung her clothing in the closet and donned the white robe, belting it in at the waist. If only Jackson would tell Nona the same thing—finish college or the ranch would never be hers. Nona might find out that she wanted something different than a ranch that wouldn't be hers for another forty years if she had one more year to think about it. She could have her own veterinary-supply company. Hell, with a few more years she might even get into vet school.

"Mama, you ready?" Nona asked.

"Yes, I am," Loretta said.

It had been a wonderful day except for that statement Nona had made about not wanting her mother to stay on at Lonesome Canyon. It stung, but then, she'd taught her daughter to tell the truth.

They'd turned down the lane and gone under the ranch sign when Nona finally sighed. "Okay, Mama, it's been on my mind ever since I said it and I need to explain something. I said I didn't want you on the ranch and I meant it."

Loretta tapped the brakes and slowed the van down to a crawl. "But?"

"But it's like this. I feel safe on the ranch. I feel safe at our home in Oklahoma. Both are peaceful and quiet to my soul. I don't mean quiet as in no noise."

"I understand," Loretta said.

"I love both of my homes, but I want to be a rancher. Get that straight right here before I go any further," Nona said seriously.

"Okay, but that's not a secret."

"No, ma'am, it's not. There's tension in the air when you and Daddy are together. Like I'm waiting for the whole ranch house to explode. That's why I don't want you here on a full-time basis. So please, Mama, if you love me like you say you do, leave me alone. Let me ranch. Let me make my own decisions. And go home."

Loretta would do anything for her daughter. Living on Lonesome Canyon had proven that, hadn't it? And there was an eerie feeling in the house when she and Jackson were both there. It had always been that way between them. Loretta had always thought of it as passion. Maybe other people saw it differently.

"Tell me something, Nona. When you and Travis are together, is there static in the air?"

Nona shook her head. "It's love, not static."

"That's the way you see it. I see it as static. You know what I mean?"

Nona tilted her head to one side. "What are you saying?"

"I see your relationship with Travis as something that keeps you from hearing the music, like with static, or knowing your lines in life," Loretta said.

"Maybe you hear the static because you aren't supposed to hear what our hearts are saying to each other. Maybe static is God's way of letting a couple have something that is totally private," Nona said.

Loretta smiled. "Now you are beginning to understand. Maybe what you are feeling between your father and me is static. Maybe finally our hearts are trying to let go and it's our own private business. Look, there's Travis and your father waiting on the porch for us. And, Nona, I'm not going home until the end of the summer. Until the first day of school has passed, I will have hope that the static will clear up."

Nona groaned.

Loretta parked the van and hit the button to open the back door. "Don't get in such a hurry to see Travis that you forget to unload all those bags."

"We can't leave things like this," Nona said.

"Yes, we can. You face your static. I'll deal with mine." She honked the horn and motioned for the two men.

They both swaggered out toward the van, but Travis was barely a dot in her peripheral vision. Jackson's white T-shirt stretched over his broad chest and big arms. His skin was tan, but by the end of summer, the sun would have him baked to a nice soft brown.

"Are you still in love with Daddy?" Nona whispered.

"What makes you ask that?" Loretta answered.

"It's in your face right now. Tell me it's not true. It would be a match made in hell. I'm surprised you got along long enough to make a baby," she said.

"Who's having a baby?" Jackson picked up half a dozen bags.

"No one that we know about," Loretta said quickly.

"You didn't answer my question," Nona said.

"What question? Did you ask me something?" Jackson asked. "With all these bags, I imagine you are asking for a raise. Well, it isn't happenin', not until the end of the summer when we see if you've learned enough to earn your room and board."

"Mama?" Nona asked.

"Don't look at me. You wanted to be a rancher and he's your boss. I'm not running interference for you," Loretta said.

"You didn't answer my question," Nona said.

"Go get your birth certificate out of the file cabinet and read it." Loretta swung the door open.

"What's that got to do with anything?"

"Read it carefully. If it says that I have to answer any of your questions because I gave birth to you, then I will. You have the right to ask. I have the right to ignore you. I hope you have five daughters and one wants to fly jet airplanes, one wants to go to Africa and work as a missionary, and the youngest grows up to be a real estate agent and lives with me," Loretta said.

"And the other two will be ranchers, right?"

"Oh, no, they'll open up a spa in Oklahoma City and I'll send lots of business their way," Loretta said.

"You two fightin'?" Travis asked as he reached into the van for the rest of the bags.

"No, we're discussing the scientific facts surrounding static." Loretta smiled brightly.

✸ ✸ ✸

"Holy shit, Jackson! Why doesn't someone haul some gravel in here?" Loretta asked.

The old work truck bumped along over the muddy road, hitting enough potholes to make for a rough ride. Loretta held onto the armrest part of the time and had both hands on the dash when the going got really tough.

"It's private land. County ain't responsible for it."

"Well, whoever the hell owns it needs to ante up for a couple of truckloads of gravel. This is horrible," she said.

"I'm glad you came back," Jackson said.

"So you don't like fending for yourself when Rosie is gone?"

He whipped the steering wheel to the left to avoid a huge hole. "I can fend for myself, darlin'. I like having you around, and there is the fact I didn't want to drive to Amarillo today for that Bovi-Shield to vaccinate the six-month-old calves for respiratory virus. But I could have done it. I've run this place all these years without you."

She was plastered against this side when she stopped sliding. If it hadn't been for the steering wheel, she would have wound up in his lap that time. "The potholes are so big you could lose an army tank in them."

"Ezra's lane is like life—it's one hell of a rough ride," Jackson said.

"Don't go all philosophical on me."

"Just talking about life, ma'am." Jackson dodged a hole on the right and only missed the barbed-wire fence by a whisper.

"Tell me again why we're going to Ezra's?" Loretta asked.

"He called while y'all were gone and invited us to come visit with him. He doesn't do that very often, and I learned a long time ago that you don't go if you are not invited. He's rougher than ninety-grit sandpaper and mean as a rattlesnake, but he tells it like it is. I like the old guy," Jackson said.

Jackson slowed down even more for the cattle guard under an archway. A curved metal sign announced that they were entering Malloy Ranch and the ride became smooth sailing.

"What were we on before we got to this place?" Loretta grabbed the hand grip above the door of the truck.

"Lonesome Canyon. Ezra has always had an easement to his property. You used to know that, Loretta."

"Why in the hell don't you keep it up better than that?" she asked.

"Ezra and his one hired hand are the only folks who use the road, and the easement agreement is that if he wants to cross my land to get to his, then he maintains the road," Jackson said.

"What's that? I can't ever remember being back here before." She pointed to the right.

"The Malloy cemetery. His great-grandfather and all his people since are buried there."

"And what will happen to that when he's gone? I only remember him having one daughter and her mother took her away years ago, right?" Loretta asked.

The little cemetery of no more than thirty tombstones was shaded by a central pecan tree and fenced in with white wrought iron. There were no flowers, but it was pristine—mowed grass and no weeds in the fencerow.

Jackson shrugged. "Hopefully whoever winds up with the place will take care of it."

The ranch house was set right up against the wall of the canyon and painted a rich mustard color that blended in with its surroundings. A wide porch surrounded three sides of the rambling one-story structure and when they stopped at the yard gate, Ezra waved and headed their way.

Loretta started to open the door, but Jackson reached across and touched her knee. "He'll pout if a woman opens it. Don't want to spoil the visit because you didn't let him be hospitable and open the gate."

"Are the stories true about him? We didn't really talk at the Sugar Shack," Loretta asked softly.

Jackson nodded. "Every one of them."

"Y'all get out and set a spell," Ezra yelled as he shut the gate behind them.

Loretta reached for the door handle, only to have it swing open and there was Ezra with a hand out to help her. "Welcome to my ranch, Loretta. You probably don't remember, but you were here one time before. Your daddy brought you here once when you were a little girl. He was looking for a lamb so you could show it at the country fair. I didn't have any young enough, so we didn't do business."

"I'm glad to see you again, Ezra, and I remember trying to find a lamb, but you are right, I don't remember coming here." She smiled.

"You remind me of my third wife. She was a redhead and had long legs. Met her up at a café in Canyon where she was a waitress. I took one look at her and figured she'd throw a son for me. They say the third time is the charm. They lied. All I got was a third daughter and by then I was too damn old to try again." As he talked, he led the way to the porch, where he motioned toward four white rocking chairs.

"I remember her," Loretta said. "I was in high school and dating Jackson. I remember seeing y'all at the county fair. She was a pretty woman."

"All my wives were pretty," Ezra chuckled.

A young man with a crop of light brown hair, wire-rimmed glasses that accentuated his green eyes, and a square-cut jaw poked his head out of the door. "Evenin', folks. Can I get y'all a beer or a glass of sweet tea?"

Ezra made introductions. "This is Rusty Dawson. Hired him last year to help me run this place and now he's like an old hound dog. I can't get rid of him. Rusty, you already know Jackson. This is his wife, Loretta."

"Pleased to meet you ma'am," Rusty said. "Don't pay no attention to him. He likes me, but he don't want nobody to know it. He ain't nearly as mean as he wants folks to think he is."

Ezra cackled out loud. "Boy don't have a bit of problem speakin' his mind. That's why I hired him. Wish he was my son instead of my foreman."

"I'd sure like a beer, Rusty. Loretta?" Jackson asked.

"Tea is fine, and thank you."

"Be right out," he said.

"Set yourself down, Loretta. My bones are old and a gentleman wouldn't ever sit before a lady," Ezra said gruffly.

She eased down into the chair on the far end. "Yes, sir. Sorry about that."

Jackson sat beside her. "So how are things on the Malloy spread?"

"Jackson is a fool," Ezra told Loretta. "If I had a long-legged woman like you in my house and I was his age, I'd be making a son with her."

When Ezra rocked forward and winked, she felt the heat rising from her neck to her cheeks and there wasn't a thing she could do about it. She was almighty glad to see the young man bringing a tray out to the porch at that moment. "Thank you so much. It's a warm night, isn't it?"

"Yes, ma'am."

Ezra handed Loretta a tall glass of tea and then took one of the two longneck bottles of beer from the tray. Rusty handed the second one to Jackson and said, "Y'all have a good visit. I'll see you in the morning, Ezra."

"Any time you get tired of working for this old cantankerous shit, jump the fence, Rusty, and I'll give you a job," Jackson said.

Rusty had a cute lopsided grin. "Thank you. If he gets any worse, I might take you up on it."

"Hey, now! I treat you like the son I ain't got, so don't be threatenin' to leave me," Ezra said.

Rusty waved over his shoulder and in a few minutes, Loretta heard an old wooden screen door slam and a pickup engine fire up, and then a bright red truck rounded the house and headed up the lane.

"He's the best damn help I've ever had. I should leave him my ranch, but there's something tellin' me to make him work for it instead of makin' it easy," Ezra said.

"You could sell it to me and I'll let him run it for me," Jackson said.

"No, sir. I called you because I got something to say. I don't want it spread about but I should tell you. I made you the executor of my will, so you need to sign the papers this week. They're at the lawyers' office in Amarillo. Same one you use. Me and your daddy always said Wilbur is the only lawyer we'd ever trust. Rest of them ain't worth the bullet to put them out of their misery."

"Why would you do that?" Jackson asked.

"The cigarettes have caught up to me, but hell, I give it a good run. I'm eighty years old. Rusty will wind up with the ranch because not a one of those girls I begat will want it. Still, I like a good fight, so my will says that they all have to live here together in this house for a year and the last one standing gets the ranch.

They can have my money, all but a few thousand for Rusty to use as startin' cash, but to get the ranch they'll have to live on it. Last one standing at the end of a year gets it. If there ain't one here, then it goes to Rusty. I want you to promise me that you'll see to it that's the way it happens," Ezra said.

"When did you find out about this?" Jackson asked.

"Been a week or two. I ain't told Rusty yet. Don't want to worry him, so keep it under your hat," Ezra said.

"Aren't there treatments you could take?" Loretta asked.

"Maybe, but I ain't interested. I've had a good life and the only thing I regret is them three girls. I wanted a boy to leave my ranch and money to, but life is what it is. You ever want a son, Jackson?" Ezra asked.

"I wanted a whole yard full of kids. I didn't really care if they were boys or girls, as long as there were lots of them. Guess it's because I was an only child. Maybe Nona will give me a whole yard full of grandkids," Jackson answered.

"Too bad you and Loretta didn't stick. Gettin' a start as early as you did, you might have had a big family. Me, I didn't get started until I was fifty. Married a thirty-year-old woman and had my first daughter that next year. All downhill from there. No grandkids yet, so I don't even get to leave the ranch to a grandson."

"You should get a second opinion," Jackson said.

"I ain't spending money on a second opinion. What sent me to the doctor in the first place is that I knew there was something bad wrong in my lungs. I was coughin' up blood. Pardon me for talkin' about that kind of thing in front of you, Loretta," Ezra said.

She laid a hand on his arm. "I'm sorry Ezra. Is there anything else we can do?"

"Dance with me if you go back to the Sugar Shack any time soon." He patted her hand.

159

"You got it." She smiled.

"When are you going to fix that road back to my place?" Ezra changed the subject abruptly. "It's on your property."

"It's in the papers that you have to keep up the road to your place for the easement through my land," Jackson said.

They were like two tomcats, circling each other warily. Loretta expected fur to start flying any minute.

"Well, you could be a good neighbor to a dying man. It'll be a hell of a job for the coroner's wagon to come tote my dead body off the ranch when I'm gone," Ezra said.

"I haven't seen a doctor's report. You might be jerking my rope to get me to fix a road," Jackson told him.

Ezra yawned. "I wish you'd have been my oldest son and Rusty had been your younger brother. We'd have had some good times on the ranch."

"We really should be going, Jackson," Loretta said.

"Mornin' does come early," Ezra said. "Thank y'all for coming over on short notice and thank you, Jackson, for taking care of things for me."

"I'm glad to do it," Jackson said.

Ezra followed them to the truck and opened the door for Loretta. He stood at the gate and waved until Loretta couldn't see him anymore through the side mirror.

"Daddy still does that," she said.

"What?" Jackson asked.

"Waves until his kids are completely out of sight."

"So do I when I have to tell Nona good-bye," Jackson said softly.

Loretta looked up at the moon. It had not been affected one bit by their separation and divorce, or by the mud puddles in the road. It didn't stop doing its job because Ezra was dying with lung cancer or because Nona wanted to quit school. It didn't care who made a mistake and had to live with the consequences of their choices.

"What are you thinking 'bout so hard? I don't think you even heard me," Jackson asked.

"I was looking at the moon and thinking about how time goes on no matter what happens," she said.

"Maybe the pull of the moon is making you slide over here to me." Jackson grinned. "Got to tell you that I like having you close. It's like old times."

"I think it's got more to do with holes in the road than it does with the moon in the sky," she said, but she didn't move back to her side of the seat. "Why isn't his ranch up next to the road, instead of back against the wall of the canyon?"

"Poker." Jackson pulled back out onto the highway, where the ride was a lot smoother. "Somewhere in the distant past, his daddy and my grandpa were playing poker. They both ran out of money, so Mr. Malloy put up half his ranch and Grandpa put up an equal amount of his. Grandpa won the hand and Mr. Malloy handed over the deed to the front half of his ranch with the stipulation that we'd honor an access easement for his generation and all those to come."

"That is crazy. Who would ever put up land for a damned poker game?" Loretta gasped.

"Evidently two old fellows who each thought they had a winning hand. Shall we go skinny-dippin' or go home and have a beer to get that sweet tea out of our mouths?" he asked.

"Well, that was an abrupt change in the subject matter," Loretta answered.

"Just thought I'd ask. You look gorgeous in those new jeans and your hair is all done up pretty, but you'd look even better out of the jeans and with wet hair stringing down your back, maybe in the shower." He grinned.

"Ice cream it is," she said.

"Well, shit! Me and Ezra ain't got no luck at all when it comes to women. But ice cream does sound good."

Loretta pulled a clamp from her purse and twisted her hair up off her neck. "Were you disappointed when Nona was a girl?"

"No, I hated that name you had picked out for a boy," he answered without hesitation.

"Be serious," she said.

"Loretta, when Nona wrapped her tiny fingers around my pinky, my heart melted. I was a father even if I was barely nineteen and didn't know how to be a husband," he said seriously. "So, the answer is no. I was not disappointed."

"Thank you," she said. "Your mother told me that when you married the right woman, you'd have sons and my daughter wouldn't even matter. I know she was sick, but her words worried me."

He made the turn onto Lonesome Canyon and the first star of the evening popped out over the house. "I wish sometimes we would have gone on to college and gotten out of the canyon until Mama was gone. I loved her, but she sure messed with our marriage, didn't she?"

"We have to realize that she was sick, Jackson, and forgive her," Loretta said.

He parked in front of the house. "Let that water get on under the bridge?"

"That's right. Now, about that ice cream?"

"Chocolate or vanilla?" he asked, but he didn't wait for her answer. He circled the truck, opened the door for her, and held out his hand to help her out of the truck. Her hand still in his, suddenly his face came closer and closer. She barely had time to moisten her lips before his mouth covered hers in a long, lingering kiss that had her leaning in for more when he ended it.

He laced his fingers in hers and led her into the house through the back door, flipped on the light and backed her up against the cabinets until their bodies were plastered together. His eyelashes fluttered shut, fanning out on his cheekbones as he moved toward her for another kiss. She braced herself for the shock.

"Hey, is that you, Daddy?" Nona yelled.

"Kids!" Jackson took two steps toward the refrigerator.

"Mama?" Nona entered the kitchen with Travis right behind her, arms around her waist and chin resting on top of her tangled hair. Her plumped-up lips gave testimony that they'd done more making out than movie watching.

Jackson peeked around the refrigerator door. "We're having ice cream."

"Where have you been? We left you in the kitchen and then you were gone," Nona asked.

"We went to see Ezra," Jackson said. "What kind of ice cream do you want, Travis?"

"None for me," Travis said.

Nona shook her head. "Me, either. You should have told me you were going to Ezra's. We could have gone with you. I like that old guy."

Travis left her long enough to pull out a chair and sit down. She plopped down in his lap and wrapped her arms around his neck.

Jackson got out the ice cream. "Chocolate or vanilla, Loretta?"

Loretta got two bowls from the cabinet and handed him the dipper. "A small scoop of each with caramel on both."

"Dammit! That sounds good," Nona said. "Don't give me the eyebrow thing, Mama. I'm old enough to drink a beer and to say a cussword."

"You keep telling me that, but I'm wondering if you're trying to convince me or yourself." Loretta's chest tightened with the first bite, but she figured it was the ice cream. "I'm going up to my room now." Her voice sounded hollow in her own ears.

"It's early," Jackson said.

"I've got some phone calls to make and a good thick romance novel calling my name." She picked up her ice cream dish and started for the sink.

"Leave that. I'll take care of it with mine," Jackson said.

She set it back down and waved, but they were already talking about vaccinations and tagging and plowing the fields for another crop of alfalfa. Her feet felt like lead as she climbed the stairs. For the first time since she'd been at the ranch, she locked her bedroom door behind her. Without turning on a light, she kicked off her boots and called Heather.

"Hey, Loretta, what's going on in your part of the world tonight? We sure had a good time visiting with you," Heather said.

"Got a few minutes?"

"For you, darlin', I've got all the time in the world. You sound horrible. Is everything all right?"

"I don't think so."

"Do I need to come to the ranch?"

"No, just talk to me. I had all the divorce emotions years ago. The guilt, denial, and all that. But I feel like I just hit the bottom of the barrel and I don't even know why," Loretta said.

"Been there. Only difference was it didn't take years. I went through it all in just a few weeks," she said.

"But I thought your divorce was amicable."

"It was divorce all the same, and I did get depressed."

"How long did it last?" Loretta asked.

"A week or two. Maria was worse. It took a whole month to pull her up out of it," Heather said. "You'll have a tougher time, darlin'."

"Why? I don't like this. I want it to end right now."

"What triggered it?" Heather asked. "Tell me every single thing you did today."

"Spa, shopping," Loretta started.

"No, honey. I want to know from the time you woke up. What you ate, what was said, who you saw or met at the spa, your feelings, all of it. I'm turning off the television and I've got a six-pack of diet cola in the fridge. So start talking."

Loretta sighed. "It might take awhile."

"Divorce is hard. I don't have to get up early tomorrow. I'm listening," Heather said.

"Okay, last night Jackson and I had sex," Loretta said.

"That doesn't surprise me. Go on," Heather said.

Loretta gave her a play-by-play of everything that happened from the morning until the ice-cream-in-the-kitchen scene. "Now you talk," she said.

"It's all clear as a bell. You can't see the forest because you are too close to the trees. You're dealing with mixed feelings about the ranch and Jackson. Nona isn't going to leave the ranch and you figured that out today, but you don't want to admit it even to yourself. She has a life here that includes all the things you thought you could use to entice her away with. She has friends and she's happy. Don't mess with that. And Ezra is dying. Don't worry, I won't spread the gossip. So that's got you to thinking about what you'll have when your last days come around," Heather said.

"And what do I do about it?"

"You realize that you can't really do much about Nona's decision and you are still trying to get over the thing with Jackson," Heather answered.

"And if I make the wrong choices?" Loretta asked.

"Listen to your heart. You know that thing you told us about on the refrigerator magnet about hanging on and letting go?"

"What about it?" Loretta asked.

"I knew my husband wasn't happy. I damn sure wasn't, but I hung on long past when it was time to let go. Looks to me like you got one part of your heart saying to hang on to Jackson and another part saying to let go of Nona. That's pretty powerful shit to have going on all at the same time."

Loretta looked at the clock. "My god, we've been talking four hours."

"And we can talk more if you need it," Heather said. "It's not going to go away miraculously, my friend. So if you need me, just call. I'm here for you, twenty-four-seven."

"Thank you. That sounds like so little, but I mean it."

"Come on up out of the canyon to Silverton if it gets to be more than you can bear and we'll get drunk together," Heather laughed.

Chapter Fifteen

ℒORETTA QUIETLY MADE HER WAY down the stairs, grabbed the keys to the old work truck from the row of hooks by the back door, and slipped outside minutes before Rosie got up that Monday morning. It had been a long week, but not even staying busy from daylight to midnight every single day had brought her up out of the horrible funk. Nona had come in every night after dark with her butt dragging, barely swallowed supper, and gone straight to bed. Jackson had done the same, but then, Loretta couldn't fault either of them. She'd been keeping up the kitchen work as well as putting in long hours in the field. She'd thought when Rosie got home that the heavy feeling would lift, but it hadn't changed at all. If anything, she woke up with a worse case on Monday than she'd taken to bed with her the previous night.

Glad that Rosie was home to take over her normal chores, Loretta gave serious thought to leaving, going home to Mustang, and settling back into her life. But something way far down in the pits of her soul said that she could not run away again. No matter the consequences or the outcome of the battle with Nona, she had to fight this through, and now it had as much to do with her own problems as it did with Nona's college issue.

She drove to the creek, where she pulled the quilt from behind the seat and spread it out in the truck bed. Lying back on it with her arms laced under her head, she watched the most glorious sunrise she'd ever seen. Vibrant colors blended from one to the next in an array that no artist on earth could copy. A camera would have trouble capturing the moment, but Loretta tucked it away tightly in her memory bank to revisit when she was old and gray.

"Old and gray with only months to live, like Ezra. That's when I'll remember this sunrise and it will help me make the transition from this life into the next," she whispered. She folded the quilt and drove over bumpy ground to the highway. Heather had said her door was open and to come to Silverton any time.

She needed to get out of the canyon, even if only for a few hours. Like Heather had said, she was too deep inside the forest to see the trees. But it didn't feel right to just drop in that early, so she fished her phone from her purse and called.

"Good morning, Loretta. Have you made any progress this week?" Heather asked.

"Not much. Would it be all right if I just dropped in this morning?"

"How soon can you get here? Maria and I are having breakfast at the café here in Silverton. Her older sister is here for a couple of weeks, so we are planning a road trip to Florida for a week. Want to go with us?" Heather said.

"I can't leave Nona for that long, but I'll be there in fifteen minutes. Order sausage gravy and biscuits for me and a piece of their pecan pie. I haven't eaten there in ages," Loretta said and then tossed the phone onto the passenger seat.

It had scarcely landed before it rang. She picked it up and said, "Hello, Nona."

"Where are you? The van is here. Did you take a walk out to the barn?"

"Tell your Dad I'm taking the day off and I'm driving the old work truck. I'll be home later," she said.

"But, Mama . . ." Nona started.

"The ranch ran without me being there and it doesn't need me now. I'll see y'all later," Loretta said.

"But I need you, Mama. You aren't going back to Mustang, are you?"

"Not in this truck," Loretta laughed. "And thank you, for needing me."

Some of the horrible heaviness left her chest as she drove up out of the canyon and into Silverton. She parked alongside a dozen other trucks that didn't look a lot different than hers. Once she was inside, Heather and Maria waved from the back table.

As soon as she sat down, Heather said, "Okay, I've filled Maria in on what you told me. What's happened since?"

"Nothing happened and I'm still depressed," Loretta said.

"Then after you eat, we're going to my place and getting drunk," Heather said.

"It's not even eight o'clock," Loretta protested.

"Who gives a shit? You need it and we're your friends. We won't let you drink and drive," Maria said.

"What's it going to accomplish?"

"Maybe nothing. Maybe everything. But that's Dr. Heather's medicine. She made me do it and it worked, so I can testify to the fact that it does cure depression. But you can't start on an empty stomach, so eat up," Maria said.

Loretta shoved a forkful of biscuits and gravy into her mouth. "God, this is good. They must use real cream, not that packaged crap."

169

"Oh, yeah, and the pecan pie isn't one of those frozen ones, either. Have you thought about what I said?" Heather asked.

"All week long, and I'm no closer to finding answers than I was when we talked," Loretta answered.

"Some folks think there is one person out there that completes you," Maria said. "I think you and Jackson are soul mates that were floating together real good down the river and then you got lost from each other and now you're having to find your way back."

"Soul mates? I don't think so," Loretta singsonged.

"Sorry, Loretta," Heather said. "I agree with Maria. We saw the way he looked at you at the Sugar Shack. He loves you and you love him, or you wouldn't be sitting here lookin' for answers. How have you been sleeping?"

"What's that got to do with anything?" Loretta asked.

"You've got dark circles under your eyes," she answered.

"Not too well," she whispered.

"Then it's time for a bottle of Jameson," Maria said.

"You've got Irish whiskey?"

"I have a whole bottle, plus a backup bottle of Jack Daniel's if we run out," Heather said. "I bought it after we talked a few days ago. Figured if we didn't use it, then me and Maria would take it to Florida with us. But we can buy some more when we get there."

"Don't doubt her methods," Maria laughed. "She bought me a bottle of moonshine and mixed it up in daiquiri mix. It was fantastic and I didn't even have a headache the next day."

❀ ❀ ❀

Jackson had just finished eating a quick sandwich and was on his way back to the field when his cell phone rang. Hoping that it was Loretta, he answered it on the first ring.

"Jackson," a strange woman giggled.

"Who is this?" he asked.

"It's Heather. We've got a problem, darlin'." Her words were slightly slurred. "I think you better come on to Silverton and bring someone to drive your work truck home."

His voice caught in his throat. "Is Loretta all right?"

"Wellll," Heather said.

"Give me that phone," a voice said in the background, but it didn't sound like Loretta. "Jackson, this is Maria. Loretta is drunk and she can't drive drunk and we're too drunk to drive her home and so you have got to come and get her. She could stay here with us, but you need to talk to her. Did you know that she's an angry drunk? When we were kids and she got tipsy, she was funny, but she's changed."

"Give it back to me," Heather said. "Jackson, y'all need to get this shit settled. Do you hear me?"

"I'll be there in twenty minutes. Do you still live on Loretta Street?"

Heather giggled. "You can rescue Loretta on Loretta Street. That's funny." The phone went dead.

Jackson shook his head, but the words were still there. What in the devil was Loretta doing getting drunk at this time of day, or for that matter, any time of day?

Thank goodness Nona and Travis had already gone to the barn, so he didn't have to explain what he didn't understand. He got into his truck and then remembered that he needed someone to drive the old truck back home since Loretta damn sure couldn't drive if she was even half as drunk as her two friends. He spotted Waylon going from bunkhouse to barn and honked.

Waylon turned around and waited as Jackson drove up beside him. He leaned in the passenger window. "Yes, sir?"

"Get in. I need you to drive the old work truck home from Silverton. Evidently, Loretta took it up there, but she's in no shape to drive home," Jackson said.

Waylon opened the door and settled into the passenger's seat. "Has she been in an accident?"

"No, she's drunk," Jackson drove away from the ranch.

"But, Jackson, it's noon."

"I can tell time, Waylon. And believe me, she can hold her liquor. She could put me under the table any day of the week, so I'm as confused as you are," he said.

"She don't seem the type," Waylon said.

"That's Loretta. She doesn't have a type, but I'm right glad that her friends called me, because she drives like a bat out of hell when she's been drinkin'," Jackson chuckled.

"Really?" Waylon asked.

"Unless she's changed, she has no sense of speed after a couple of drinks." Jackson pulled his phone from his shirt pocket and punched in Loretta's number.

"Hellllo, Jackson," Maria answered. "Where are you?"

"On my way. Y'all are at Heather's. Where's my truck? There or somewhere else?"

"Out in front of Heather's. Keys are in it," she said.

"Is Loretta able to walk?"

"Hell, no! When we do a job, we do it right. And we wouldn't waste good Jameson," Maria said.

"Okay, then. Why did you ladies start drinking this early in the day on a Monday?"

"You and Nona caused it. She loves her daughter and she loves you and she loves the canyon and she loves everyone, but then she was drunk when she said it and you know what they say, Jackson?"

He waited.

"Do you?" she shouted into the phone.

"About what?"

"They say that you can't believe anything a woman says when she's drinkin' or what a man says when he's having sex. So you'll have to talk to her yourself when she gets sober. Jackson, are you still there?" Maria asked.

"I'm still here."

"Don't let Nona see her like this. It'd break her heart if Nona saw her like this. Promise me or I won't let you have her," Maria said.

"I promise."

"Okay then. We'll unlock the door. If you're lyin' to me, I'll kick your ass," Maria said.

"I'll take her to a motel until she sobers up. I promise."

"Then good-bye."

"What do I tell Flint and Nona?" Waylon asked.

"Tell them that Loretta is spending the day with her girlfriends and had some truck trouble. You drove it home and I'm looking for parts to fix it. Or if you've got a better story, tell them that." Jackson parked outside a white frame house with three trucks out front. He nodded toward his vehicle and said, "The keys are in it."

"Yes, sir."

"I don't have to tell you not to tell anyone," Jackson said.

"No, sir, you do not!"

"Good. Thanks, Waylon. I owe you one."

Maria opened the door. Heather was sitting in a rocking chair with a beer in her hands. She pointed to the sofa, where Loretta was laid out like a princess in one of Nona's childhood movies.

"Be gentle with her," Maria said.

"Did she drink this whole damn bottle of Jameson?" Jackson asked.

"No, we helped a little bit," Heather said. "We celebrated her coming home and we toasted her telling her sisters to go to hell."

"She called her sisters?"

"Oh, yeah, right before she passed plumb out. Emmy Lou said they'll have one of them intervention things," Maria said. "God, my head is already hurting. Never mix beer and whiskey, Jackson."

"Did Loretta mix it?"

"No but she did mix Jameson and Jack Daniel's. It's not bad with a little root beer in it," Heather said.

Loretta was limp in his arms when he picked her up. "One of y'all able to open the door? Either of you want to tell me what sparked all this?"

"You caused it, so don't go all self-righteous on us." It took her three tries to get the *self-righteous* pronounced right. "You can thank us later."

※ ※ ※

Jackson bypassed the idea of a motel and took Loretta to the old hunting cabin at the back of Lonesome Canyon. He laid her on the bottom bunk bed and opened the windows and doors to let what little breeze there was flow through. He pulled up a kitchen chair and drank in his fill of Loretta.

How could he have ever, ever been so stupid as to flirt with other women? How could he not have seen that she didn't have as much self-esteem as a gorgeous, long-legged woman should have?

It was near dark when she groaned and rolled from her side to her back. "Jackson? My mouth tastes like . . . Oh. My. God. I was drunk. Dammit, my head hurts. What happened? Did I wreck the truck?"

He leaned over and kissed her.

"Is this the hunting cabin? What am I doing here? I was at Heather's and . . . Shit! Jackson, I think I talked to all three of my sisters."

"I think that you told them to go to hell and I do believe there was talk of an intervention." He grinned. "What caused all this?"

She frowned. "Heather is a genius."

"For getting you fall-down drunk?"

"It's gone. I guess I just need to talk it to death and tell my sisters where to go, but it's gone."

"What is gone?"

"That feeling that I had all week like everything was unsettled. Do you have some gum or is there toothpaste in this place? There's a horrible taste in my mouth."

He pointed to the cabinet above the sink.

She slung her legs over the side of the bunk and stood up. Without wavering, she made it to the sink and brushed her teeth. "That's much better. Let's go home now."

"Are you hungry? Do you want to go up to Claude for a hamburger?" Jackson asked.

She shook her head. "I want to go home. I want a long soaking bath," she said. "I'm not hungry."

"Then we'll go home. You want to tell me what this was all about? Heather says I caused it. Is that true?" he asked.

"You did. We had sex and then Ezra talked about dying and Nona is probably going to stay on the ranch no matter what I say. And it seemed like my world was twirling off the axis, but it's better now," she said.

"Where do we go from here? We need to talk about this some more."

"Hell if I know where we are going, but I'm all talked out. Remember when Nona told you that men talked things to death?

175

Well, sometimes us womenfolks need the same thing even if it is about something different than buying a damn ranch or which field to plow up next. Evidently I needed my two old friends to listen and I needed to get drunk so I would talk. It was the best damn therapy in the whole world." She smiled.

Jackson leaned across the seat and kissed her again. "Welcome home, Loretta."

"We'll see about that," she said.

He was whistling "Deeper Than the Holler" when he helped her stand up. "Do I need to carry you to the truck or can you make it on your own two feet?"

"Honey, I could walk all the way to Oklahoma right now if I wanted to."

Chapter Sixteen

$\mathcal{A}$FTER SUPPER ROSIE BROUGHT a thick three-ring binder to the table and laid it down with a thud. "Two things are happening this summer. Number one, I'm training a replacement and retiring. I'm not leaving the ranch. I will still live in my little house out at the base of the canyon, but I won't be coming in here every day to cook and clean. So you'll start interviewing my replacement by the end of this week. My last day on the job will be September first."

"Oh, no!" Nona gasped.

"Oh, yes," Rosie nodded. "I'm eighty years old. It's time for me to step down."

"And the second thing?" Jackson asked.

"Loretta is planning the Fourth of July party." She slid the book across the table. "It's your baby. Have fun."

"Oh, no!" It was Loretta's turn to suck air.

Loretta had come to the ranch focused on a mission. It damn sure wasn't planning a party for the whole canyon, but the notebook was in front of her and Rosie's expression said she meant business.

"Rosie, you know how you love planning for the party," Jackson said.

She pointed her finger at him and her dark eyes flashed. "Don't turn on that charm with me, Jackson Bailey. I'll be at the party, but I'm not lifting a single finger to plan it, to keep it going, or to play nice with all the people. I'm going to eat good food, sit in my lawn chair, and visit with the folks and then watch the fireworks show."

"Will you help us pick out someone to take care of cooking and cleaning?" Jackson asked.

Rosie shook her head. "I'll help train if the new person needs it. I won't do any picking or choosing. That's y'all's job. You're the ones who'll have to live with her, not me."

"And where is this new person going to live?" Nona asked.

"That's your business, long as you don't expect her to share my house. I'm too damned old and set in my ways to have to worry with someone else's coming and going. And besides, my youngest sister is coming for a long visit this fall and you know my kids come for Christmas every year, so don't go puttin' some stranger in my house," Rosie answered.

Jackson nodded. "I've been expecting this for the past five years. Just promise me you won't leave the ranch."

"Wouldn't dream of it. The ranch will need a granny someday." She grinned.

※ ※ ※

Loretta wasn't worried about the party. She had a book with all the past caterers, party supply rentals, phone numbers, and everything she needed to get it all together. She laid the binder on the coffee table. Her phone rang at the same time she flipped the book open.

"Mama, I've been tricked by Rosie," she said.

"She's always been a sneaky one, but after what your sisters told me, you deserve it. What's she done now?" Katy asked.

"Tricked me into staying until after the big July blowout on the ranch and turned the whole party over to me to plan. I'm sitting here looking at an old picture of me and Jackson the first year I came to the ranch party. I bet that cruise she went on was planned at the last minute too, just to keep me here for that week," Loretta said.

"Well, darlin' daughter, their time is limited. We have decided that we're coming to the canyon for the Fourth of July party," Katy said. "I swear to God. That Heather and Maria were wild when y'all were teenagers and evidently they haven't grown up yet. Drinking at eleven o'clock in the morning? What were you thinking?"

"That it tasted damn fine. We started two hours before that and I was tossing back whiskey like it was water by eleven," Loretta said.

"Lord, love a duck! What has happened to my sweet daughter?"

Loretta laughed. "We all have a devil inside us, don't we, Mama?"

"Yes, and yours is Jackson Bailey."

Loretta really laughed then. "Mama, think about what you just said."

"Oh, hush! That canyon brings out the worst in you. I'll see you on the Fourth and between your sisters and me, we will straighten you out."

"You too busy to take a ride?" Jackson yelled from the foyer.

"I'm plannin' a party for the next two weeks," Loretta shouted back.

He swaggered into the living room in faded jeans, a plaid work shirt, an old straw hat, and cowboy boots that had seen lots of wear. Her chest tightened and her pulse jacked up into high gear.

"Is that Jackson I hear?" Katy asked.

"Yes, ma'am," she said.

"Your voice changes when he's in the room. I don't like it, never did."

"I'll call you later," she said.

He stopped inside the door. "Tell your mother hello for me."

"I hear him. Get your bags packed. Your vacation is over the day after your Fourth of July party," Katy said.

The line went dead.

She looked up at Jackson. "Take a ride where?"

"Wherever you want to go long as it's in Silverton. I need to pick up a tractor part for Flint up there," he said.

"I want a snow cone. A rainbow one with cherry, grape, and banana," she said.

"Silverton it is. They've got a little stand set up across from the courthouse that makes the kind like we had in high school. Even put them in a cone-shaped container." He smiled.

"I'll get my boots on," she said.

❀ ❀ ❀

Jackson sniffed the air when she came down the stairs. Was that perfume?

Loretta had changed into denim shorts and tied her long red hair to one side. He longed to bury his face in her soft neck and kiss his way around to her full lips. And yes, that was perfume, he decided when he got a better whiff of it. It was the same scent she'd used in high school and it took him back to those days.

He quickly shook his head. He was a grown man. A woman's perfume shouldn't turn him inside out.

But the heart doesn't have eyes or ears and it doesn't give a damn about time or age, his conscience reminded him.

"Ready?" he asked hoarsely.

She nodded. "Do they stay open this late? Don't get my hopes up for a rainbow snow cone and then disappoint me, cowboy."

"They're open until nine every night, and believe me, you won't be disappointed." He laid a hand on the small of her back and guided her through the house to the back door.

He started the engine and pulled around the house to the lane. "Why didn't you tell me you were stressing out? It's a wonder you didn't die of alcohol poisoning."

"Guess I'm a tough old broad. I came out on the other side with only a little scorch on my wings," Loretta said.

"I don't smell smoke. I smell that perfume you've always worn. The kind that I bought you for Christmas when we were about sixteen."

"I was fifteen. And I still wear it. Now what?"

"I could buy it for you again this Christmas if you'll put it on your list." He grinned.

"You know what I'm talking about, Jackson. It's been too long. We can't take up where we left off all those years ago." She turned toward him, their gazes meeting.

"You are right. We've changed and we're two different people now. Crazy thing is"—he looked back at the road—"my heart still feels the same. It didn't get the memo about us growing up."

"So what now?" she asked again.

"I'm as attracted to you as I was in the fifth grade, Loretta, and ever' bit as much as I was in high school. I've measured every woman I've gone out with by your yardstick and they came up lacking. So I vote that we start with right now, leave the past alone and move forward. Loretta, would you go to dinner and dancing with me on Saturday night after work?"

"Well?" Jackson finally asked when she didn't answer right away.

"The Sugar Shack?" she asked. Somehow that didn't seem like a real date.

You've slept with him. What does a real date matter anyway? that irritating voice in her head asked.

It means another step in a direction I don't know if I'm ready to take, she argued.

"Wherever you want to go. I'll pick you up at seven and you choose the place," he said.

"What if I want to go to Mustang and eat at my favorite restaurant?"

"Then I guess we'll knock off work at noon," he grinned.

"Why are you being nice? You wasted a whole afternoon sitting with me in a cabin with no air-conditioning and it was hot as hell in there," she asked.

He raised a dark eyebrow as they came up out of the canyon into land so flat and far-reaching that cotton fields met the sky out there in the distance.

"Did you miss our beautiful sunsets when you left? Do the ones in your part of Oklahoma compare to that?" he asked.

"Yes, I miss them very much. And no, Oklahoma sunsets are gorgeous, but they damn sure aren't as pretty as that," she said.

"Where are we going to dinner Saturday night?" he asked.

"The creek with a picnic." She said the first thing that came to her mind.

He drove down the wide Main Street in Silverton. "That sounds like fun, but I want to take you to a nice place with maybe a live band and good food."

"Then you choose," she said. It was all moot anyway, since her mother had said that Friday was the end of her vacation time. On Saturday she had to be ready to go back to her job or forfeit it forever—yet another decision to be made in a swirling sea of craziness.

He parked in front of the courthouse and hand in hand they walked across the street to the snow-cone stand, where he ordered two with cherry on one side, grape on the other, and a strip of banana right down the middle. They carried them back to the pickup, where they sat on the tailgate to eat them as they watched the occasional pickup or car go by.

"Things haven't changed much around here. I am surprised that there aren't more teenagers in pickup trucks out this time of evening," she said.

"They all go to Amarillo on the weekends nowadays," he said.

Some things do change, she thought.

"Do you remember Cooper Wilson?" Jackson asked.

"Of course. He was a little shit. Is he in prison?"

"No." Jackson grinned. "He's the sheriff and that's him coming out of the courthouse right now."

"Are you joking? Bobby Lee is preaching and Cooper is in law enforcement? Holy shit!" Loretta exclaimed.

"Hey, Cooper," Jackson yelled and waved.

The officer waved back and headed toward them.

"That's not Cooper. He's just a little kid," she said.

"He's about thirty now," Jackson said.

"He does look like a grown-up version of the little kid who used to sing that kissing song in the church parking lot," she said.

Jackson laughed. "Hey, you want a snow cone, Coop? I'm buying if you do," Jackson asked. "You remember Loretta, right?"

He leaned on the side of the truck. "Naw, I done had two snow cones today, but thank you all the same. Good to see that you're back home, Loretta. I probably owe both of you an apology the way I picked on you when I was a little kid. But I thought you was the prettiest girl in the world and I was jealous of Jackson. That might be the reason I got this thing for red-haired women."

"I can't believe you are the sheriff," Loretta said.

"I only got elected because I didn't draw an opponent. Still do some ranchin' down in the canyon on the side. It's an elected position, so I have to have something to fall back on in case someone goes up against me next time around," Cooper said. "I got a little spread next to Ezra's place. I'd love to buy him out, but I hear that Ezra is leaving it to his three daughters."

His radio made a fuzzy noise and he touched a button. The grainy voice said he'd left behind some papers and needed to come back to the sheriff's station before he left town.

"Guess I'll be going. Y'all enjoy your snow cones. You havin' the big party on the Fourth, Jackson?"

"Like always. Bring your lawn chair or a blanket and a big appetite. Waylon and Travis are in charge of the barbecue this year. We'll see what they can produce," Jackson said.

"I'll be there, and, Miz Loretta, you see any redheads, you herd them up in a corral for me." He tipped his hat and headed off into the dusk.

"I can't believe little Cooper Wilson is old enough to be a sheriff," Loretta whispered.

Jackson slowly shook his head from side to side. "It's a lot harder to believe that our daughter is as old as she is. She should still be four years old and lugging around that old stuffed cow toy. We should have known then that she was a rancher. She always liked that old cow better than dolls."

"She did, didn't she?" Loretta said. "Speakin' of little kids, I want to do something different at the ranch party this summer. I'm thinking a bounce house and maybe a small carnival."

He set his jaw and almost shot the rest of his snow cone out into his lap when he squeezed the paper too tightly.

"You got a problem with that?" she asked.

He hesitated a couple of seconds before he answered. "No, but I had one back when Nona was little. She loved it, but the clowns made her cry."

"Well, then scratch that. I don't want crying kids. We'll just have a bounce house and lots of games."

He grabbed her around the waist and before she could even shut her eyes, his lips were on hers in a kiss that rivaled the hot summer wind. His tongue slipped inside her mouth and did a mating dance with hers, causing her to forget all about carnivals, parties, and even her daughter.

"Holy shit!" she murmured when he broke away.

"Point proven."

She touched her lips to see if they were as hot as they felt. "What point?"

"That we don't have to argue to have passion, darlin'. Now let's go get a beer and put a few quarters in the jukebox at the Sugar Shack. I've got enough energy left to do some serious dancin' with this redhead I've had my eye on for a while."

"Am I going to be jealous?"

"I don't know. I fell in love with her back in the fifth grade and she's pretty damn sexy," he teased.

☀ ☀ ☀

Loretta wanted more than a couple of beers and a dance or two. She wanted to fall backward into a bed with Jackson, not dance around the floor of a smoky, noisy honky-tonk with him. Sex, in today's world, didn't mean they were on any kind of road to reconciliation. It didn't mean commitment or even a relationship.

She wanted to feel Jackson's body next to hers, to cuddle up with him in the afterglow, to have those moments of pillow talk. The heart wants what it wants, as her daughter so aptly said.

She touched him on the leg. "I don't want to go to the Sugar Shack. I want to go back to the hunting cabin."

His face searched hers. "Are you sure, Loretta?"

She nodded and inhaled deeply. "I'm sure."

The ruts in the overgrown path were barely visible even in the moonlight, but Jackson kept going, sometimes at less than ten miles an hour as he kept time to the country music with his thumbs on the steering wheel. Even if there had been deep mud holes, she couldn't have slid across to sit beside him, not with bucket seats and a wide console between them.

Folks said the new trucks were the best thing since sliced bread with their comfortable seats and fancy bells and whistles. For Loretta's part, she'd rather have the old work truck with a wide bench seat.

The cabin appeared like a small brown blob at first, then slowly it became more visible, each stone that had been laid so carefully taking on a personality of its own to make a small house right up against the wall of the west bank of the canyon.

"I bet Ezra's place isn't two miles away over in that direction." She pointed.

"Probably about three as the crow flies. One of my great-grandpas built this when he first got his chunk of the canyon. I hear there's a similar one somewhere over there on Ezra's place, but I've never seen it. Are we getting out or just sitting here and looking at the stars?" Jackson asked.

"I want to go inside." She opened the door and started that way without waiting for him. She was already about to lose her nerve, and she wanted to see if that shower sex had really been that damn good or if it was a fluke.

The door wasn't locked and when she opened it, the smell of cold ashes and coffee grounds floated out. Jackson stepped in behind her, found a box of matches in the dark, and lit a hurricane lamp. It hadn't changed since the last time she'd been there. She lowered herself onto a bottom bunkbed covered with an old patch work quilt. "This smells like it was just brought in off the line," she said. "Did you plan this, Jackson?"

"Guilty of premeditation. I'd like to make a deal. Three years of confinement in this cabin with you," he teased.

"How did you know I'd want to come back here?" she asked.

"I didn't, but I could always hope you might," he answered.

A wood table with four mismatched chairs sat beside make-shift cabinets with curtains in place of doors and a big bearskin rug in front of a cold fireplace. The last time they'd come back here, they'd made love on that rug in front of a blazing fireplace.

"Want some coffee? There's a gas-powered little hot plate. We wouldn't have to heat up the place with a fire," he asked.

She walked right into his chest, put her arms around his neck, and rolled up on her toes until her lips were even with his. "I want you, Jackson Bailey. No questions. No future plans. I want you right now in this moment."

"Those're the sweetest words I've heard in years." He scooped her up and carried her to the bed, where he sat down with her in his lap and, without breaking a string of kisses, began to unfasten one button at a time on her shirt. His big rough hands gently pushed the shirt back and caressed her ribs, her back and slipped even higher, past her bra, to massage her neck as he laid her on the bed and stretched out beside her.

"I want to take my time and savor every moment of this night," he whispered.

She didn't care if he took all night. Not when every touch and every word proved that what happened in the shower hadn't been a flash in the pan, but the real thing.

He peeled her bra off an inch at a time, his eyes getting softer and softer with each bit of revealed skin. "You take my breath away, just like you always have."

She did hear him talking, but as she felt his hands moving over her body, taking off her boots, kissing the arches of her feet, removing her jeans, the words blurred in the passion of the moment.

How he went from dressed to naked was a complete mystery, but there he was poised over her, his face so close that she could see single whiskers in his five o'clock shadow. Her long legs wound their way around his waist and one hand slipped between them to guide him inside her body. Then nothing mattered but satisfying the rising hot need they shared.

She rocked with him, arching against him in that final moment and crying out his name in a muffled scream. Her legs relaxed and slipped back to the bed. He rolled to one side with her tight in his arms. The warm afterglow wrapped them in the sweet arms of pure unadulterated satisfaction.

"My God, Loretta," he said, hoarsely.

"I know, Jackson," she whispered.

And then they slept.

Chapter Seventeen

$\mathcal{T}$HE WEATHERMAN CALLED FOR A HEAT WAVE that would cause the temperatures to rise to the triple digits and not drop below ninety even at night. For once, that fellow knew exactly what he was talking about. The sun came up like an orange ball of fire over the eastern horizon of the canyon and with it came the stuff that truly made a long, hot Texas summer.

No rain in sight for at least two weeks and no relief from the scorching heat wasn't anything new to the canyon folks, but it made for short tempers and long days. Even Rosie was grumpy that evening after supper.

"I'm going home. I'll be here to cook breakfast tomorrow morning and I'll take care of dinner, but I'm going home as soon as it's over. I'm getting too damned old to be going back and forth between houses. So, Loretta, you're going to take on supper from now on until you can get someone hired. I told you two weeks ago today that I was quitting, so consider this my half retirement," she said.

Loretta poured a glass of sweet tea and took a sip. When Rosie spoke it was law, but maybe this one time Loretta could sweet talk her out of her decision. "Rosie, you can't do this. I'm supposed to plow all day tomorrow."

"Too damn bad." Rosie hung her apron on a hook beside the door. "Besides, you've got a party to take care of this coming weekend. Have you got all your ducks in a row? You will need your afternoons for the rest of the week to take care of last-minute stuff. The hired hands can plow. Maybe it'll get you and Jackson on the ball and you'll get serious about interviews. I mean it, Loretta. I'm retiring."

"Hiring someone else is between you and Jackson. I'm only here for a visit, remember," Loretta snapped. And besides, she was having sex at least three times a week even if it wasn't in the house, so by damn, she shouldn't have to cook and clean for her room and board.

Rosie's finger came up so quick that it almost popped Loretta right on the nose. "Don't you sass me, girl. And anyone who sleeps in this house, eats in this house, and uses that big bathtub damn sure lives in this house."

"You said I was only visiting a few weeks ago."

"That's when I thought you'd lost your backbone and you'd be gone in forty-eight hours. You proved me wrong, so now you get to take over the house in the afternoons. Good luck with that and the party." Rosie slammed the door on her way outside.

Jackson meandered through the kitchen, empty tea glass in his hand. "I came for a refill and heard voices. Nona and Travis at it again?"

Loretta gave him a look and shrugged.

"The back door slammed. I figured she followed him outside," he explained.

"It was Rosie," Loretta said. "I think she means it about retiring, Jackson. She says I have to take over supper from now on and she's going home right after she puts the noon meal on the table. I wouldn't be a bit surprised if she makes me take on dinner and supper entirely after the party is done. You'd best get real serious about hiring someone."

Jackson slumped down in a kitchen chair. "Well, shit, Loretta! I haven't got time for interviews in the middle of a summer like we've got. Will you take care of it for me?"

She nodded. It might be a good thing. She could pick out someone who would be good to her daughter if Nona won their fight after all.

"But one thing at a time. She says that the first of September is her last day, so we'll have a few weeks to get serious about hiring someone after the big ranch party. I'll interview and pick out the top two folks for the job. But you have to make the final decision, Jackson. Nona's tuition is due by the end of July. If she still won't go back to college and there's no hope left, I'm going home. So you'll sure need to have someone hired."

He filled his empty glass with ice cubes and more tea. "We still have a date for Saturday night?"

"Of course, but what has that got to do with hiring someone? She's dead serious, Jackson."

"Like you said before, one thing at a time, Loretta. After the party on Friday and the cleanup on Saturday, we deserve a night out. Plus, your folks are coming, so after they leave, you'll be ready for a night away from the ranch. On Monday we'll start working on hiring someone. I promise."

"You win. Instead of a picnic at the creek, let's go to a hotel in Amarillo that has a pool and a restaurant attached to it that offers room service. Why didn't you ever put in a pool?" She wrung water out of a dishrag and wiped down the sticky counter.

"I was afraid Nona would drown. If anything happened to her on my watch, I would have died, Loretta."

His tone was so serious that she stopped what she was doing and laid a hand on his arm. "But she's an excellent swimmer."

"Losing you about killed me, so it was hard for me to even let her out of my sight," he admitted. "And then my dad died before I could face myself for what I'd done. If anything would have happened to Nona, I'd be an alcoholic far worse than Dina is."

She laid a hand on his shoulder. "I'm sorry, Jackson."

Before Jackson could say another word, Nona and Travis wandered through the kitchen and Nona asked, "Y'all want to play a game of Monopoly or watch a movie? It's too hot to sit outside."

"Not me. I vowed that when you grew up I'd never play Monopoly again," Loretta said. "Besides, I've got a party to plan, and believe me, I'm thinking simple is good in this heat. The kids would smother in a bouncy house."

"Carnival?" Nona asked.

Loretta shook her head. "Not that either. Plain old horseshoes and croquet, and I'm delegating the job of buying prizes to you two. You know what kids like these days."

Nona's eyes glittered. "Snow-cone gift cards and movie DVDs. Oh, and maybe some matinee tickets. What's our budget? I love it, Mama."

"Whatever a bounce house and a carnival would have cost," Loretta answered. "And I love you too."

Her phone rang so she stepped out on the porch and answered it. "Hi, Maria. Are you in Florida yet?"

"We just took each other's pictures in front of the Disney World sign. Check your phone when we get finished talking. Maria's inside buying souvenirs for all her relatives," Heather said. "I wanted to be sure you are okay."

"I've never been better, but I can't believe I said those things to my sisters," Loretta said.

"You really did, and it's about time you put them in their place. We had to take the phone from you and hide it before you called your mother," Heather laughed. "Shit fire, girl! Miss Katy didn't like us real good when we were kids. She'd string us up if you talked to her like you did your sisters."

"Hey, they needed a good dressing-down. Believe me, they've done the same to me in the past. Maybe not with the same language, but still, I think they might have gotten the message. Thank y'all both for letting me talk it out and for crying and laughing with me."

"You're welcome," Heather said.

"And if either of you need anything, call me. Keep me posted on the trip."

"You could still join us. You could fly down to Florida and we'll come pick you up at the airport. We're finished here in Orlando and on our way to Laguna Beach for a few days of sun and fun and half-naked men," Heather teased.

"Maybe another time," Loretta said.

"Okay, darlin'. We're rootin' for you. Got to go. It's my turn to drive. Big hugs," Heather said.

Loretta put the phone back in her pocket. She had friends in Mustang. Good friends whom she went to church with, out to eat with, and to the movies with. But no one knew her like Heather and Maria.

❋ ❋ ❋

Rosie was humming in the kitchen when Loretta poured her first cup of coffee. "I'm making a ham for dinner today. You can slice the leftovers for supper and make potato salad if there are leftover mashed potatoes."

"I thought maybe you'd got over your snit," Loretta said.

"Ain't a snit. It's a fact."

"Rosie, are you playing matchmaker?" Loretta asked.

"Hell, no! I don't give a rat's ass what you and Jackson do about this thing between the two of you. You can't jump over it. You can't slide under it. It's too damn wide to go around and too long to ever see the end of it. But it's your business if you want to ignore it another blasted seventeen years. I think you are both acting like kids. Worse than Nona and Travis. When they fight, they keep at it until they figure out what was wrong and make up. They don't run for the hills and pout for nigh on to two decades," Rosie said.

"Looks like another hot one." Nona pulled her blonde pony-tail through the hole in a baseball cap as she crossed the kitchen floor and poured a cup of coffee. "I'm glad the tractors have air-conditioned cabs. What are you doing today, Mama?"

"Until noon, I'm disking that forty acres over beside Ezra's place, getting it ready for a new crop of alfalfa," she said. "After that I'll be in the house, because Rosie is damned and determined that she's semiretired."

Nona set her mug on the cabinet and hugged Rosie. "Thank you."

Rosie's big eyes widened. "For retiring?"

"No, for making Mama stay in the house. I hate cleaning, cooking, and housework. I was afraid you'd make me do all that when you retired," Nona answered.

Rosie clucked like an old hen gathering in her chickens. "And here you are thinking of getting married? A married woman should know how to do all that."

"Oh, believe me, Mama saw to it I had a real good education in that department, but it don't mean I like it one bit. I'd do the work of a field hand and use my paycheck to pay someone to clean for me."

Loretta shrugged. "My mama made me learn, and I didn't like it either. I figured Nona needed to know how, even if it brought the same result."

"Like mother, like daughter," Rosie said.

Nona picked up her coffee. "Amen and hallelujah for that. I'm going out to the porch and enjoying some semidecent weather. You know, Mama, the porch is my one memory when we were all here together. You and Daddy would sit in the swing and I'd play with my stuffed cow."

"Good morning," Jackson said from the doorway.

Loretta could count the muscles leading down to his belt buckle through the snug shirt. Faded jeans hugged his hips and thighs and he already had his boots on, ready for the day's work.

"Can't get around it or over it or under it," Rosie mumbled.

"Looks like we'll have to irrigate twice as much as usual. Flint and I are getting the equipment ready to start watering this morning," Jackson said.

"According to the weather report, the heat wave will move on out in two weeks," Loretta said.

Rosie had been absolutely right about the words on the magnet. She couldn't fight it, but joining it meant giving up a life that she'd carefully built. Joining it would mean she'd given up trying to convince Nona to finish college. She wasn't ready to run the white flag up the pole—not yet.

"Two weeks of this is thirteen days too many. What's for breakfast, Rosie?" Jackson asked.

Rosie cracked a dozen eggs into a bowl and whipped them up with a whisk. "Bacon and eggs. Ranchers got to eat good at breakfast. You will remember that, right, Loretta?"

"Yes, ma'am." Loretta smiled.

"You bringing that coffee to the porch with me and Nona?" Jackson asked.

Nona met them in the hallway on her way back into the house for a refill. "Travis called. He's joining us for breakfast."

Jackson held the door for Loretta and followed her to the swing. "What's Rosie in a stew about?" he whispered.

"She still doesn't think we're taking her serious about retirement."

Jackson threw an arm over the back of the swing, letting his hand rest on Loretta's shoulder. "It's not easy getting old and stepping down."

"I love that old girl even when she's cantankerous and bossy," Loretta said.

❊ ❊ ❊

Loretta turned off the music in the tractor and let her mind wander. It might have been the monotony of driving back and forth from one side of the pasture to the other, but everything seemed to bring her back to what Rosie had said about there not being a way to get over the feelings she had for Jackson.

The question was whether she wanted to get over it or whether she wanted to see where the pathway led. Either way, she didn't want to answer the question, not even to herself, so she picked up a CD from the passenger seat and slid it into the player. The first song on it was "I Won't Let Go."

You don't seem to want to let go, so why are you fighting against a good thing? the voice in her heart asked.

"Because I'm as afraid as Jackson was of putting in a pool. What if I lose her? She's all I've got," Loretta whispered.

The cell phone ringtone jarred her for a second. It wasn't until the third ring that she fished it out of her pocket. She checked the caller ID and answered on the fourth ring. "Hello, Jackson."

"I'm thinkin' about Saturday night and a big old Jacuzzi tub in a fancy hotel room with a king-sized bed. Would you be thinkin' the same thing?" Jackson asked.

"Which hotel?"

"It's a surprise. Pick you up at seven. What's for supper tonight?" he asked.

"Something cold. We may have ice cream sundaes," she answered.

"Sounds good right now. Another hour and it'll be quittin' time. What CD do you have playing?"

"I don't know. It doesn't have a cover, so it could be something Travis made for Nona. It's a mixed tape with love songs," she answered.

"Well, they definitely are in love," Jackson said.

"No shit, Sherlock. What gave you the first clue? That hickey on her neck the first night I got here or the way he looks at her or their fights?"

"All of the above. And thanks for helping with the ranch work, Loretta."

"I'm doing it at this point because I like it. I'm paying for my room and board with sex. Guess that tells you what I am, right?" she told him.

His laughter echoed off the sides of the tractor cab even after she hung up.

Chapter Eighteen

*N*ona held a worn old stuffed animal in one hand and poured a cup of coffee with the other one. She looked over her shoulder at Rosie and her mother. "If you can't find me, I'll be in the barn. I've built a fort for me and Bossy. We are going to hide out there until everyone goes home. Travis says he'll look in on me on his breaks and he's promised to bring me beer and bologna sandwiches."

Loretta's brow drew down as she squinted. Sure enough, that was Nona's old stuffed animal. How had it gotten to the ranch? She'd put it on the attic years ago in the house in Mustang.

One minute Rosie was cracking eggs into a bowl. The next her finger was an inch from Nona's nose. "Young lady, you say you want to be a rancher, well, by damn, this is part of the job. You don't get to spend every day getting sweaty and working. Sometimes you have to dress up and go to a party. It's when you show the hired hands how much you appreciate all their hard work and let the people in the canyon know that you are one of them."

"So"—Loretta could feel her nose curling in disgust at the idea of beer and bologna—"what's got a burr stickin' in your ass anyway, Nona? You love parties. You love the canyon folks, even old Ezra. I thought Bossy was in the attic in Oklahoma."

What was the matter with her? The mere thought of bologna or mayonnaise turned her stomach and the smell of beer gagged her.

Nona blushed. "Bossy was in the attic. You put him up there with the rest of my stuffed toys that year when I gave up my Barbie dolls and toys. It was the worst night of my life. I couldn't sleep without him, but I didn't want you to think I was still a little kid, so I waited until you went to work and rescued him. He goes everywhere with me." She pushed away from the cabinet and came to military attention. "My name is Wynona Katherine Bailey. I am a grown woman. I am addicted to a stuffed black-and-white bull named Bossy."

Rosie laughed. "You are a comedienne, Wynona Katherine. Take your coffee to the table and sit down. I'd rather you were addicted to a stuffed animal than booze, like Dina, or drugs or tobacco."

"What are you afraid of, anyway? These people love you," Loretta asked.

"It's not the canyon folks, Mama. Or the ranchers from Claude, Silverton, Turkey, or Goodnight. It's not any of them. It's our Sullivan relatives. Are you aware that they are coming for the whole weekend? They'll be here by the middle of the afternoon and they're convoying with all three of your sisters and their families in their motor homes."

"I know," Loretta sighed. "They were supposed to come for the day and leave, but they've decided to stay for the whole weekend. I think they might be bringing an intervention with them."

Nona sat down beside Loretta. "From what my sweet cousin Faith tells me, they are coming to back you up on the Nona/college issue and to convince us both to go back to Oklahoma. That's why me and Bossy are heading for the hills. We'll watch the fireworks from the hayloft," Nona said.

"Bullshit!" Rosie exclaimed. "You are both strong women. Nona, you are going to be your mama's right arm today. And, Loretta, you are going to be the perfect hostess. Now stop your whining and get a backbone. I know you've both got one. Hell, I been puttin' up with your bitchin' for a month now. Ain't neither one of you willin' to give an inch to me, so buck up and find that strength, even if you have to support one another for a weekend."

Loretta chuckled down deep in her chest. "You'll get your share of lecturing about college. After all, I didn't get a college degree and I wound up divorced. Your aunts did get their education and they have stayed married, so that could be their argument. But don't think for one second you are the main target. Mama is coming to the canyon, which she hates, for one reason. And she's bringing reinforcements with her for the cause."

"And what's that?" Nona asked.

"They are planning an intervention. The black sheep of the whole family is about to get her comeuppance. I haven't been real nice when my sisters called this summer and they're out for revenge. They've got some notion that I'm thinking of staying in the canyon."

"Are you?" Nona's eyes widened.

"Right now I just want to get through this party. I'm not as quick at making decisions as you are," Loretta said.

"Hey, I told you, I've thought this through, but me and Bossy don't want to fight with you today. We got to do what Rosie said. We got to make a stand together."

Rosie tapped the sign on the refrigerator. "See this. Read it carefully. You got to fight to hang on. So double up your fists and get after whatever it is you want."

❋ ❋ ❋

Before noon the whole ranch seemed to be alive with activity. The tent folks arrived in their big trucks promptly at nine. Flint and Paula were busy unloading ponies from a long horse trailer and getting the corral decorated for the pony rides. Travis and Waylon waved from the enormous black barrel-shaped smoker parked out under a pecan copse. The smell of smoked briskets, turkeys, and pork loins filled the whole canyon.

"That won't harm the pecan crop this year, will it?" Loretta asked Jackson.

"It shouldn't. Might produce a whole new breed that tastes a little like brisket." He drove a stake into the ground for the first tent. "Still thinking about tomorrow night?"

"Hell, no! That's off. My folks, all of them, sisters and families as well as Mama and Daddy, are coming for the whole weekend." She shaded her eyes with her hand and watched the convoy kick up a red dirt cloud. "Looks like Nona gets the surprise. She wasn't expecting them until midafternoon, but there they are and it's not even lunchtime."

"Dinner, darlin'." He grinned.

"You know what I mean. The whole family. Dolly, Emmy Lou, and Tammy, plus husbands and kids."

"It's been years since I've seen the family. Let's go welcome them to the ranch." He waved with his hat, grabbed her hand, and started across the pasture in a long-legged jog.

She was totally breathless by the time they rounded the end of the house. Four big motor homes had lined up single file. The doors opened as if on cue and people poured out like ants. Her sisters all converged upon her in a group hug and Clark Sullivan, her father, shook Jackson's hand like he was truly glad to see him.

Not much shorter than Jackson, Clark was a tall man. His brown hair flashed touches of auburn in the bright sunlight and wire-rimmed glasses made his green eyes appear even larger than they were.

"Been a long time," Clark said. "Ranch looks good and that brisket smells wonderful."

"That's Nona's boyfriend and his cousin's job today. I don't think we'll have too many complaints on what they're cookin'. Want to welcome all y'all"—he motioned with his hand—"to Lonesome Canyon. Make yourselves at home. There's plenty of room in the backyard for you to pull those trailers around under the shade trees."

"Aunt 'Retta, tell them boys that we get to stay in the house with Nona and they have to go to the bunkhouse. We haven't seen our cousin all summer," LeAnn said.

Her twin, Deanna, piped up right behind her, "And if she stays on the ranch, it might be a year before we see her again."

"You six girls unload your things in the house. Faith gets to stay in Nona's room. LeAnn and Mindy can share the room across the hall from her. Lorrie and Paulette, you two can have the room with twin beds right next to her room," Loretta said.

"Thank God, you made the decision. We've listened to them whine for four hours," Dolly said.

"And thank God you didn't put Deanna and LeAnn in the same room. They are constantly fighting. Must be what fifteen-year-old girls do," Emmy Lou said.

"I remember when four other girls used to fight a lot worse than Deanna and LeAnn do. And don't think it will end when they grow up, Emmy Lou. At least it hasn't with my girls." Katy stepped forward for her turn to hug Loretta.

Loretta had to bend for the embrace. Her mother's blonde hair smelled like coconut shampoo and hairspray and for a split second Loretta was homesick for Mustang. For the order in her life, her office at the real estate agency. She missed getting her father's midmorning coffee at the little shop around the corner and listening to him sing off-key when he worked up a sale.

"Can all us boys go to the bunkhouse? We was teasin' them girls about stayin' in the house. We really want to see what it's like to be cowboys for the weekend," Garth asked.

No one even noticed the pickup driving across the pasture. But when the door slammed and Nona crawled out, settled her straw hat firmly above her blonde braids, and waved, they all stopped talking at once.

"Is that Nona?" Emmy Lou asked.

Loretta nodded.

"She's dead serious about this ranchin' shit, isn't she?" Deanna said.

"Young lady," Katy scolded.

"You say it all the time, Granny," Deanna pouted.

"That doesn't mean you can," Emmy Lou said.

Nona started across the yard with her hand firmly in Travis's. "Hello, all my relatives. I want you to meet Travis Calhoun before you split and scatter. Girl cousins can stay in the house with me. Boy cousins can take their bedrolls to the bunkhouse. Travis will bring you in the back of his truck," she said.

"We've already settled that." Tammy grinned.

Nona started with her favorite aunt, Dolly, and passed out hugs and made introductions. "Well, then I'm reinforcing the settlement. I hope to hell you didn't come to sit on your cans and be entertained. This isn't a dude ranch. It's a working ranch, so you can all pitch in and help make this party a success for me and Mama."

Garth and Collin were both fifteen, Billy Ray was fourteen, and Vince was twelve. They looked at Travis in awe.

"You guys are under this cowboy's supervision. Take a deep breath and get a whiff of that barbecue cookin' out there under the shade trees. That's what he and Waylon are doing today and they can sure use some help with setting up games and other things." She pointed and narrowed her eyes. "If I catch you tryin' to sneak a beer, I'll make you muck horseshit out of stables all afternoon and you won't get to eat a bit of supper."

"Granny, she said *shit* and you didn't yell at her," Deanna said.

"She's twenty-one," Katy said. "You can say bad words when you are twenty-one, but I still won't like it."

"You're still bossy as hell, Loretta," Garth told her.

"Garth! You aren't twenty-one either," his mother, Dolly, fussed.

"She is, Mama. She's always bossed us boys around and she let the girls do it too," Garth said.

"Travis, darlin', please take these cowboys to the bunkhouse and then put them to work." Nona kissed him right there in front of aunts, cousins, and even her granny, who shot a glaring look that way.

The boys dashed inside the motor homes and were back out in record time, each holding a bedroll and a duffel bag. They scrambled over the side of the truck like monkeys climbing trees.

"Right nice to meet all of you," Travis said.

The brothers-in-law nodded at the same time—Isaac, Stephen, and Terrance, the best husbands Loretta's sisters could have ever found. Loretta had approved of the three hardworking men from the day she met them. But she did feel sorry for them. Living with her sisters couldn't be easy by any stretch of the imagination.

"Enough jawin' for now. Get back in your wagons and we'll line 'em up in the backyard and then we'll see what we can do to help," Clark chuckled.

"Well, done," Loretta whispered to Nona as they loaded back up. "And you did it without Bossy to help you."

Nona smiled up at Loretta and said softly, "They don't scare me nearly as bad as Rosie does, and she said we both had to get a backbone. I could understand her telling me that, but you've always made Superman seem like a wimp."

"Thank you for that. I needed it today. Take the girls on into the house. I told them which rooms they are staying in this weekend," Loretta said.

"I'll help get the electricity run to the motor homes and then we'll grab a beer and go help get the tents set up. I haven't seen y'all since Emmy Lou's wedding." Jackson followed Clark to the lead motor home.

"Seventeen years is a long time," Clark said.

"Too long." Jackson smiled.

❋ ❋ ❋

Loretta crawled up the ladder to the hayloft and chose her spot carefully—far enough back that no one could spot her from below, close enough that she could see everyone working like ants getting ready for the party. Ezra and several of the older folks had already arrived and were sitting inside a tent with big fans on either end. The thermometer already registered three digits, but at least the cool air kept the elderly from heatstroke.

Rosie had stepped up, God love her soul, and hauled Katy and the sisters off to the kitchen to help her bake chocolate sheet cakes all afternoon. And after she'd sworn that she wouldn't do a damn thing to help with the party. Loretta owed her big-time.

All the phone calls and hard work looked to be coming together out there. Tents were up. Baskets of those little cardboard church fans with bright-colored fireworks pictured on one side and the Lonesome Canyon logo on the other were ready for use. The boy cousins were busy setting up two croquet games, badminton, and a baseball diamond. Flint and Paula had the pony rides ready. Now all they needed was people to come help them celebrate.

She heard someone coming up the ladder, but wasn't surprised when Nona poked her head through the hole in the floor.

"Hey, got room for me and Bossy? I rescued him out of my bedroom. He's not real fond of all those people. I may let him sleep up here tonight," Nona said.

"There's always room for you and Bossy. I bet he'll be real happy sitting on that hay bale over there in the corner tonight. Where's everyone else?" Loretta asked.

"Right now we've set up a beauty shop in the dining room. All the little girls and women who want to visit can have their nails done and/or faces painted with red, white, and blue bursts like sparklers," Nona said. "Faith is in charge and Deanna and Paulette are helping her. LeAnn and Mindy are taking care of refreshments—sweet tea, coffee, and soft drinks and cookies. The others are in the kitchen with the aunts. Delegate. That's the secret."

"Have you gotten the talk yet?" Loretta asked.

Nona sat down beside her mother, leaving a foot of space between them. "I'd sit closer, but I smell like a locker room. I'm a lost cause. They've given up on me, Mama. You were right. They're here to make sure you go home to Oklahoma. Aunt Emmy Lou was whispering to Granny, but she shut up in a hurry when I went in the kitchen. But believe me, Faith was willing to tell all for an introduction to one or two cowboys."

"And you? Are you on their side?" Loretta asked.

Nona shook her head. "Not anymore. I like having you here. It's like we are a family again. Now you, Mama? Are you going to stop pressuring me to go back to college in the fall?"

"Never. Please finish. If not in Oklahoma, you can take classes here. There's a college in Amarillo. I don't care if you have an OU degree. I just want you to finish," Loretta answered.

"Well, I'd say that's negotiable." Nona smiled. "We'll talk more about that idea when we get through this weekend. I hear someone on the ladder."

"Hey, do I hear voices in my attic?" Jackson's voice preceded him up to the loft. "I figured I might find you here. The caterers have arrived and they'll be setting up in the food tent. Rosie has bullied the brothers-in-law into carrying the sheet cakes to the dessert tent. It's already filling up with cobblers, cakes, cookies, and I even saw two freezers of homemade ice cream."

"That's what I like about the canyon. Folks don't ever come to a party empty-handed. I'm going to be first in line for ice cream," Nona said.

Travis yelled from below, "Hey, the hayloft."

Nona scooted over and dangled her legs over the edge. "Hey, just look at that sexy cook!"

Travis struck a pose, muscles bulging and a grin on his face. "One hour and we'll be ready to take the briskets out of the smoker and cut them up. Your older cousins are now valets. They're parking cars out in the north pasture. Glad we moved the cattle to make more room. Place is filling up and folks are asking for you and your mama," he said.

"Catch me," Nona said.

"No!" Loretta gasped.

Travis stepped back and shook his head emphatically. "Don't you dare. If you break a leg, Jackson will shoot me for sure. I'll wait for you at the bottom of the ladder."

She scrambled backward and disappeared through the hole in the floor.

"Alone at last," Jackson sighed.

"But only for a minute or two. We've got to go play host and hostess. And we do have a chaperone." She pointed to Bossy, sitting in the corner.

"My God! Is that what I think it is?" Jackson asked.

"Yes, it is. It appears he's not happy in her room right now with all the people in the house, so he's going to stay out here. I'd bet dollars to cow patties that she takes him in before bedtime, though."

"I won't tell a soul that he's out here," Jackson said, "but I am going to take a picture of him with my phone."

"I didn't think of that. Send it to me when you get time."

He quickly took the photograph and then sat down beside her, tilted his hat back, and tipped her chin up with his fist. The kiss was long, lingering, hungry, and hot. It blocked out friends, family, enemies, and even the thought of homemade ice cream. When it ended he continued to hold her close to his chest, their hearts beating in unison.

"I needed that to get me through the rest of the afternoon and evening," he said.

"I might need a booster shot over the weekend." She smiled.

"You get to feelin' weak, honey, you just wink at me and I'll be glad to take care of that for you," he teased. "It's kind of amazing how that Clark and I fell right back into our old friendship like we'd only talked yesterday. I thought it might be awkward, but it wasn't."

"I'm sorry about tomorrow," she whispered.

"Me too. But I changed the reservations to next week, so it's not canceled. It's only postponed. Meet you up here tomorrow evening at eleven o'clock?" he asked.

She leaned back and smiled. "It's a date."

"Does that mean we are dating?" he asked.

"Nona asked me the same thing when we went to the spa. What do I tell her?" Loretta asked.

"You decide and then let me know. Right now I don't have to break up with anyone. Do you?"

"I wouldn't be sleeping with you if I had a boyfriend," she said.

"Well, that's good news," he chuckled. "Should I write you another note and send it by Bobby Lee? Will you check the yes box again, Loretta?"

She remembered that day when they were ten and he'd sent Bobby Lee to bring her the note. "Why don't you try it and see?" She wondered what checking yes would entail at their age now. Back when they were ten years old, it meant that she liked him and she was his girlfriend, but they'd grown past that, fallen in love, gotten a divorce, and now—what were they?

☀ ☀ ☀

Her hand felt small in Jackson's as they made their way from barn to the party, spread out over ten acres of ground with folks from Ezra's age and older to tiny babies in strollers and infant carriers. Travis held up a fist from the smoker area and Jackson nodded.

"I guess that means they'll start cutting up the brisket now," Loretta said. "I never realized how much work there is in this party. How are we ever going to make it without Rosie?"

"I'll hire you to come back every year, or else you'd best teach Nona all the ropes," Jackson said.

"What does it pay?" Loretta asked.

"Sex three times a week as long as you are here," he teased.

"I can get that anywhere in the world without planning a party," she whispered.

"But it won't be like what we have, will it, darlin'?"

Ezra waved from inside the tent. Jackson waved back and Ezra shook his head. When he pointed at Loretta, she pulled her hand free. She touched her chest with a finger and Ezra nodded.

Jackson dropped a kiss on the tip of her nose. "I'll see you later."

"If you can't find me, check the loft. It's my sanctuary," she said.

"Loretta!" Heather and Maria yelled from the backyard.

She waved back and pointed to the open-front tent where Ezra was sitting. They nodded and ducked into the tent, where appetizers and drinks were set up.

Ezra patted the empty chair beside his. "Sit with me a few minutes. This is one hell of a party you've put together."

"Can I get you something? Another beer? Some sweet tea?"

"Hell, no! I'm hungry, not thirsty. When's the dinner bell going to ring?" Ezra asked.

Loretta checked her watch. "Twenty-seven minutes. Wait right here and don't let anyone have my chair." She hurried over to the dessert table and picked up two brownies. She put them in his hand. "This might hold you until they ring the dinner bell."

"Maybe, but I'm not here for the brisket. I'm here for the pork loin. Doctor told me my 'lesterol was too high and to stay away from pork and bacon. I don't give a shit what that little young feller says. I've got six months and I'm going to eat and drink what I want and die when I'm supposed to. Hmm, these are Ellen Baker's brownies. She gives them a little extra kick by using whiskey instead of vanilla." He polished off one but held the other in his hand.

"You cool enough?" Loretta asked.

One thick gray eyebrow wiggled. "Fans are doin' a fine job. And these brownies hit the spot. I heard tell that you like fine Irish whiskey."

Loretta blushed. "I can't deny that."

"Well, thing is, I make a little moonshine and I figure it's ever' bit as good as Jameson. I was thinking that if you married Jackson again before I died, I might give you a jar for a weddin' gift," he said.

"Ezra, you old coot. Why would you want me to remarry a man I couldn't live with the first time around?"

"Because you two belong together. You make him happy. If he was my son, I'd want to see him happy. Now go on and get out of here. When Jackson rings the bell to start dinnertime, you need to be right beside him."

"Why's that?"

"So all these other hussies, includin' them two who is your friends, won't be leadin' him off to the barn for some hanky-panky. These old eyes might be dyin', but by damn, they can see what's goin' on right now," he chuckled.

"I'm not too worried," Loretta said.

"You should be. That would be Dina Mullins sidling up to him right now."

Loretta's head whipped around and, sure enough, there was Dina, pressed up against Jackson's side with one arm around his waist and the other on his chest.

"Shit fire!" Loretta mumbled.

"Protect it or lose it," Ezra said.

Heather grabbed Loretta by the arm before she'd taken two steps. "You better go take care of that right now. She's probably drunk." She gave her a gentle shove in that direction.

It took several long strides before Loretta was standing in front of Jackson and Dina. Dina wasn't just drunk; she was sloppy and could hardly stand up.

Loretta draped an arm around Dina's shoulders. "It's time for you to leave. You are making a fool out of yourself."

Dina shrugged off Loretta's arm and fell against Jackson's chest. "We were meant to be together, Jackson. I knew it from the time I saw you on the football field when we were seniors in high school. This bitch can't keep us apart forever. I'm pregnant and you are the father."

Loretta peeled her away from Jackson and ushered her into the house. "What you are is drunk as hell. You better hope you're not pregnant."

The clock on the stove said that it was five minutes until time to ring the dinner bell when she got Dina into the kitchen and into a chair. Then the tears started and Dina began to blubber. "All I ever wanted was what you had. I hate being short. I hate blonde hair. I hate my eyes. I want to be a tall redhead that all the boys like and I want Jackson Bailey."

Rosie set a cup of coffee in front of Dina. "Right now, you are going to get this coffee. Loretta, you get out of here and go ring the dinner bell with Jackson. I've got this under control."

"But . . ." Loretta started.

"I called her father and he's on the way from Silverton to get her. Go or I'll retire right now this minute," Rosie threatened.

It only took a few long strides and she was at the back door. Her father opened it for her and Jackson motioned her to his side.

"Everything all right in there?" he asked.

"Rosie is taking care of it," she answered. "I don't even like Dina, but I feel sorry for her. She needs help."

Jackson nodded, reached up, and clanged the old dinner bell several times. The noise settled immediately. He picked up a microphone from the porch railing, turned it on, and said, "Welcome to our annual Fourth of July picnic, fireworks, and dance here on Lonesome Canyon Ranch. We're glad that you could all attend and want you to make yourselves at home. Bobby

Lee will say grace for us and then the feasting will begin. Oh, and one more thing. Thank you to all the ladies who've filled up the dessert tent and to Loretta's sisters, who spent the afternoon making chocolate sheet cakes."

He handed the microphone off to the preacher beside him.

Bobby Lee made a thankfully short grace and then said, "If you leave hungry, it's your own fault. See you all in church Sunday morning!" He turned around and slipped something into Loretta's back pocket. He whispered in her ear, "I'm not playing with your butt. There is something in your pocket for you."

Clark took his place beside her as Bobby Lee moved away. They were an equal height and he smelled like Stetson aftershave, a scent that would always bring up memories of him breezing into the office first thing in the morning, always with a smile and never fussing at her like her mother did.

"This is nice, honey. It's like a family reunion with benefits. Plenty of room for the kids to stay out of each other's hair and lots for them to do that don't involve cell phones."

"Thank you, Daddy."

"Is that Dina's father?" Jackson nodded toward a big black truck pulling up in front of the house.

"Yes, it is. She's too drunk to drive," Loretta said.

Jackson chuckled.

Loretta cut her eyes around at him. "That was only one time and there were circumstances. It doesn't happen on a regular basis."

"Yes, it was." Heather appeared out of the crowd. "Hello, Mr. Sullivan. It's sure good to see you again. I'm Heather, in case you don't remember."

"Of course I remember you. And this is Maria, right?" Clark said.

"Yes, sir," Maria said. "It's been fun to have Loretta back in the canyon."

"Is nice to see y'all again, but Katy is motioning for me to join her in the food line. Maybe we'll run into each other again this afternoon, girls," Clark said.

Loretta caught the look her mother shot her, but she didn't flinch or move away. Jackson's arm felt right and natural around her waist, and she was forty by damn years old, not twenty-one. She could make her own decisions about whom she chose to have sex with, whom to drink with or ring the dinner bell with.

"Do you believe that sometimes what a drunk person says is really the underlying truth of all their problems?" Loretta asked.

"Are we talkin' about Dina or are you thinkin' about spikin' your mother's drink?" Jackson asked.

"Both."

"What did Dina say in there?" he asked.

"That she wanted to be like me and have what I had and have," Loretta answered.

"I'm sure she does, but in order to do that she has to be selfless, not selfish. I don't see it happening, not even with lots of therapy."

Chapter Nineteen

LORETTA THOUGHT MAYBE GOD had granted her a big favor since she'd exercised patience and not murdered Dina right there in front of a cloud of witnesses the day before. Her sisters had all three danced until after midnight and not a one of them had brought up the fact she was living in the same house with Jackson or mentioned anything about Nona, college, or the intervention idea.

It wasn't until she woke on Saturday morning that she sat straight up in bed and realized that she was due a walk across the coals of hell. That no one had mentioned anything meant the whole bunch of them were busy hoarding ammunition for the war. She crawled out of bed and dressed in her oldest pair of jeans, a hot-pink tank top, and boots. Her plans were to sneak down to the kitchen and take a cup of coffee to the front porch. She'd need that much fortification before they all arrived in the house that morning.

But the light was on in the kitchen and the look on Emmy Lou's face told Loretta that the battle lines had been drawn. Emmy Lou set two cups of coffee on the table and pulled out a chair. No one would ever believe the dark-haired, brown-eyed smaller woman was Loretta's sister. Emmy Lou was the bossiest one of the four sisters. She expected her to cut right to the chase.

"What are you doing up this early?" Loretta asked.

"I'm always up at five o'clock. Not all of us can eat like a pregnant horse and never gain an ounce or sleep until the sun comes up like you do, Loretta. I run on the treadmill until five thirty, cook breakfast, and pack the girls' lunches when school is going on or plan my day when it's not. Isaac and I leave for the hospital at seven for rounds," she said. "Have you talked any sense into Nona?"

"We're working on that."

"So she's going back to Oklahoma with you?" Emmy Lou asked.

"Probably not."

"Then you've failed," Emmy Lou said bluntly.

"No, I regrouped and reorganized. I've realized it's not her going back to Oklahoma that I'm adamant about. It's her finishing college."

Dolly came through the kitchen door. She carried a cup to the table and sat down at the far end. The bright-colored cotton caftan looked like she'd dragged it right out of the laundry basket that morning. She ran a hand through her tangled hair and shielded the light from her bloodshot eyes with the back of her hand. "My head hurts. I shouldn't have drunk so damn much and that bed in the trailer is hard as hell. Thank God Terrance was too drunk to want sex, or I'd have bruises on my butt."

Emmy Lou waved her hand. "Too much information, Dolly."

"You mean drinking doesn't make you all hot like it did when you and Terrance were dating?" Loretta asked.

"Not after three kids. Speaking of kids, is yours going back to Oklahoma to finish college or not? It looks to me like Nona's in love with that cowboy," Dolly asked.

The door opened again, letting in a rush of hot air even though the sun was barely up. "Don't start without me. Ah, coffee!" Tammy said.

Always the perfect sister, Tammy didn't have a single blonde hair out of place. Her cute little cotton sweater even bore the proof, by the lines in the sleeves, that it had had a close encounter with an iron. Her clear blue eyes settled on each sister and for a minute Loretta thought she'd start praying for all of them.

"Now"—she sat down across the table from Emmy Lou—"I'm here. Shall we pray before we begin?"

"Hell, no!" Loretta said. "Why do we need to pray? We were discussing Nona going to school, not saving souls."

"Is she coming home?" Tammy asked.

"She is home whether I like it or not," Loretta said. "But she could also finish college here. I want her to get her degree. That's been my main worry and we're going to talk about where and how she's going to do that sometime next week."

"Compromise is good," Dolly said.

"One more year away from the ranch would be good for her and Travis," Tammy said. "If it's real, it'll make it stronger. If it's not, then it's better to find out before she winds up like you, Loretta—divorced and regretting it."

Katy poked her head inside the house and carried in a bottle of diet root beer. "Good morning, all my daughters. It's good to see you gathered around the table together and not hear anyone screaming. I'm sure I've missed something, but first, Loretta, what about Nona? College or not?"

"College, most likely, but not OU. Probably in Amarillo. I don't think I'm going to get her off the ranch," Loretta said. "Now that we've got that settled, I understand y'all are here for intervention, not on Nona's behalf, but on mine. Before you get started—"

Emmy Lou held up a hand and butted in, "Before you say another word, we did intend to have an intervention. We had the full intention of pulling out all the plugs and making you go home to Oklahoma, but Daddy set us all down before we left on Saturday morning and . . ."

Dolly jumped in when Emmy Lou hesitated. "He said that you are a grown woman who can make your own decisions and we are to keep our mouths shut."

Before Tammy could add her two cents into the mix, Nona breezed across the floor and headed for the coffeepot. "Good morning, aunts, Granny, and Mama. I thought we were all sleeping until noon," she said. "Aunt Emmy Lou, did you know that Faith snores and talks in her sleep at the same time?"

"We're having a private conversation here with your mother. Just get a cup of coffee and go back to your room," Emmy Lou said.

"Well, I would, but this is my house and this is my mama, so I don't think I will. Faith told me about the intervention shit. I'm twenty-one, the age all three of you were when you got married"—she waved to include her aunts—"and the way I see it is this. You made your decisions. I'm going to make mine. Mama is older than any of you, and I reckon if she wants to screw my daddy, that's her business. If they want to live together in sin, that's her business. If they want to get remarried, that's her business. So my suggestion is that you all take that coffee and root beer back to *your* trailers and come back about nine. Me and Mama will have a hell of a breakfast ready for you and the intervention? I love you all, but it ain't happenin'." She shook her head. "Not on my watch. Come on, Mama. Let's go grab a couple of more hours of rest in your room. I can't hear Faith snore-talking that far away."

"You are sleeping with Jackson—again!" Katy gasped.

"Right here in the house with Nona here and you not married?" Tammy asked.

"Holy shit," Dolly exclaimed.

"What did I tell the whole bunch of you before we left Mustang?" Clark appeared from the living room and leaned on the doorjamb.

"How long have you been in there, Grandpa?" Nona asked.

"Awhile. Looks like the bunch of you still need a referee." He grinned. "Nona, it's time you tell your mother your plans and stop this tug-of-war. It's only fair."

"Yes, sir," Nona said. "Mama, I'm going to finish my last year with online courses from Oklahoma University. My first-semester tuition is due by the end of July. I'm already enrolled for both semesters and I'll be graduating with my class next May."

"Daddy?" Loretta looked up at him.

"I talked to her last night. She's not being fair with you any more than your sisters are. But then you haven't been fair, either. Nona is twenty-one and you need to cut the apron strings. That doesn't mean you stop loving her," he answered.

"I could never do that," Loretta whispered.

"You sisters were here to apologize for the way they've talked to you, but I understand that you raked them over the coals pretty bad the day you had way too much whiskey, so I reckon you all need to kiss and make up. What you do or don't do is your business as far as Jackson is concerned. Now, I'm going out to the backyard so I can see one of these Texas sunrises, which is the only thing I ever missed about this whole place," Clark said.

Emmy Lou blew a kiss toward her sister. "I'm sorry," she said.

"Me too," Dolly said.

"I'll ask Jesus to forgive me, Loretta," Tammy said.

"You weren't mean to Jesus," Nona said.

Tammy frowned at her for a moment. "Okay, I'm sorry, Loretta."

"I guess we might as well start breakfast," Nona said. "Mama?"

"I apologize for calling each of you and especially for the language I used when I was drunk," she said.

"Drunk?" Nona asked.

"Sometimes daughters can drive a mother to drinking," Katy said. "I'm glad you are going to finish your education, Nona. It will make your mama happy and you will have finished something that you started. Speaking of which, we'll talk about your job later, Loretta."

※ ※ ※

Jackson sat down beside Loretta and draped an arm across the back of the sofa, letting only his fingertips touch her bare arm. "You and your sisters seemed to be getting along really well by suppertime. We still got a hayloft date in about thirty minutes?"

"I don't think we should go to the hayloft. Nona and Travis are most likely hiding out there this evening. They snuck out across the yard about thirty minutes ago," she said.

"And?"

"Nona is going to finish college with online courses from the University and graduate with her class next May. It looks like we both win. She stays here and yet she finishes school. I'm going to miss her, Jackson."

"But she lived in the dorm, Loretta. She only came home on weekends."

"But I knew she was only an hour away," Loretta sighed. "Let's go to the old huntin' cabin."

"And what happens in an old cabin?" he asked.

"Just like Vegas," she said, "it stays in the cabin. You worried that it'll get around the canyon that you're a loose-legged cowboy?"

"Might be. You want to take a ride instead?"

"Let's go to the creek."

"It's pretty low with this heat. Got enough water in it to keep the cattle happy, but not enough to skinny-dip," he said.

She leaned on his shoulder. "I wasn't thinking of skinny-dippin'. Is the quilt still behind the seat in our old truck?"

"You're the only person I've ever taken that quilt out for." He grinned.

"Then let's go count the stars," she said.

"Sure you don't want to talk about what's happened? It's got to bother you more than you are admitting. I'll be a good listener even if I don't have a bottle of Jameson."

"I'll tell you all about it on the way. But what I really need has more to do with stars and a quilt than with listening ears and a bottle of whiskey."

He pushed himself out of the swing and held out a hand. She took it, no longer surprised at how his slightest touch affected her senses. It had always been that way with Jackson, from a time when she was too young to understand the attraction between them. She liked the way she felt with Jackson. She loved the way her heart skipped a beat when he walked into a room.

So why do you fight it? He's sure let you know that he wants a future. You need to make up your mind what you want and then don't look back, she thought.

The note was in her pocket and the time had come to either give it to him or tear it up.

Jackson parked the truck beside the creek and took out the quilt. He spread it out smoothly in the back of the truck and they stretched out beside each other, only holding hands.

"Are you willing to give us another chance?" he whispered.

"Are you?" She reached in her hip pocket and touched the note that Bobby Lee had put there the day before. The handwriting hadn't changed much since Jackson had written the first one when they were ten years old. The wording was different this time, though: *Will you give me a second chance? Please check yes if you will.*

She had read it quickly on her way inside the house to deal with Dina. It had a spot on the upper left-hand corner where a tear had landed it on that afternoon when she'd snuck it out of her pocket and read it for the twentieth or thirtieth time. She'd thought about it a lot longer than she had before she checked the box back in the fifth grade, but when she handed it to Jackson now, there was a mark in the box. Yes, she loved him.

"Do I want to open it?" he asked.

"I hope so," she said.

"Thank you, Loretta. That makes this next question a lot easier. I know you've got at least two more weeks of vacation. Will you please stay here on the ranch and give us a chance to really work at this thing? I have no doubt that we can manage a long-distance relationship, but I really want some more time with you."

She nodded and said, "I can do that."

He cupped her face in his hands and lowered his lips to hers in a kiss that held the promise of a future. "I love you," he said softly, then laid his finger across her warm lips. "Don't say anything right now. Knowing that I have a chance and that I can say those three words to you again is enough for tonight."

She wanted to say the words, but she couldn't. So many things ran through her mind. Practical things, like how on earth they would ever make a long-distance relationship work and if they would be any better at a second chance than the first time around.

The man just asked for a second chance and told you he loves you, her inner voice said. *Actions speak louder than words. What are you waiting for?*

She rolled over, threw one long leg over his waist, and settled onto his body like it was a comfortable old saddle. Leaning forward, her lips met his in a searing kiss that burned every thought of anything other than making love with Jackson out of her mind.

His hands went to her back to unhook her bra and slowly pull the straps from her shoulders. She pulled his blue knit shirt over his head and tossed it toward the side.

"You are going to get all sweaty," he said.

"I know where there is a real nice shower, even if the cowboy on that side of the hallway won't let women stay overnight. Or we could always cool off in the creek." She undid his belt and slid his tight jeans down to his boots.

He started to sit up to help get his boots off, but she shook her head. "Darlin', I still know how to do this job. You lay back tonight and enjoy the ride."

He obeyed right up until he could take no more, then flipped her over. "Tonight we are going to make love."

"We haven't before?" she whispered.

"We've had lots of wonderful sex, but tonight is special, so we're making love." His breath was hot in her ear as his hands wandered over her body. Whoever said that whatever a man said anything a woman wanted to hear when he was having sex had to be wrong, because Loretta believed every single one of the sweet things Jackson said.

This was what she wanted at the end of a day. He was the only one who could satisfy her in and out of bed, even after disappointments. And, yes, she loved him, always had. Jackson took her to the pinnacle of the biggest climax she'd ever known. Nothing mattered but satisfaction and the moment, not tomorrow or next week, just right now.

"Intense," she panted when he rolled to one side.

"Wild," he said hoarsely.

They woke as the first rays of sun peeked over the horizon. She cuddled up next to him for a few seconds then sat straight up. "Oh, my God! Daylight is almost here. Rosie will be in the house in a few minutes to start breakfast and we've got church and my family is still there."

He pulled her back down. "And we are grown adults who do not owe anyone an explanation for anything. But I *am* hungry. How about you?"

"Starving." She smiled up at him.

"Then let's go home."

She put her hand in his. "Soon as I find my britches and bra, I'll be ready."

Chapter Twenty

$\mathcal{L}$ORETTA RAPPED ON THE METAL TRAILER DOOR. The lights were on, and even over the noisy generator, she could hear people inside. She waited a few seconds and knocked again, harder that time.

Her mother's voice made its way through the door. "Come in, Loretta."

The door swung open, but before her hand made it to the knob, her father stepped outside. She could tell by the way his jaw worked and by the look in his green eyes that he wasn't happy with the women inside the trailer.

"I kept them from one of them intervention things, honey. But this one is between you and your mama about your work, so you'll have to face the music with it. Seems to me like you've got a new lease on life since you come down here, so I expect you can hold your own." Clark kissed her on the cheek.

"Throwin' me to the lions, are you?" Loretta said.

"I reckon you can tame them."

Loretta hugged her father tightly. "Thank you, Daddy."

"Love you, kitten."

His use of her childhood nickname brought a tear to her eye, but she refused to let it fall. There wasn't room for another person around the booth-type table, so she pulled a tall stool from beside the cabinets and sat down. The aroma of the coffee they were drinking turned her stomach. Beer, bologna, her beloved mayonnaise, and now coffee? There had only been one other time that coffee smelled like shit.

It couldn't be happening again.

She wasn't eighteen.

She was forty; she could not be pregnant!

"Are you going home with us?" Katy asked. "Now that the issue with Nona has been solved, your job here is done."

"I've got two more weeks of vacation time left. I've worked at the family agency for seventeen years and I haven't had a vacation since Nona was fifteen. Don't be giving me ultimatums, Mama," Loretta said.

Katy crossed her arms over her chest. "It's not an ultimatum. Either your van is leading the way out of this canyon after church or else I'm hiring someone next week. I have a whole stack of applicants, good ones with real estate licenses who are eager to work with our firm."

Tammy held up a finger. "Think long and hard before you speak in anger. That comes from Scripture, not from me."

"I'm not angry. Mama, I realize it was a sacrifice to take me and Nona in when you still had Tammy to get through her final year of high school and Dolly still in college. So thank you," Loretta said and paused.

"I did it because I believed you had made the right decision," Katy said.

"If you want to fire me, that's fine. I understand, but I'm staying for two more weeks. My heart says it's the right thing. Nothing any of you can say will change my mind."

❋ ❋ ❋

"I'm so glad this weekend is over," Loretta said as the motor homes pulled away from the ranch.

Jackson slipped an arm around her waist. "Me too. I'd like to show you something. How quick can you change into boots and jean shorts?"

"Ten minutes," she laughed.

"I'll load a cooler up with beer and drive the truck to the front yard," he said.

"No beer for me. A couple of cans of cola will be fine," she said.

"Never did know you to turn down a beer," Jackson said.

"Since that morning with the whiskey, just the smell of anything alcoholic makes me queasy. And you're not going to believe this, but so does mayonnaise and bologna," she said.

"But not barbecued ribs? Remember when you got past that first three months with Nona and you hated the smell of barbecue, eggs, and bacon?" Jackson said.

She smiled. "I'll never forget those days. I was so glad when the second trimester started and I could eat anything I wanted."

He was sitting in the front seat of the old truck when she came out of the kitchen door, holding a brown paper bag in the other. His smile lit up the whole canyon.

They bumped along the pathway back toward the cabin. But before they reached it, he made a hard left and left any sign of a trail behind as they cut a swath through the weeds with the old truck. Grasshoppers flew every which way and a rabbit didn't look too happy that his Sunday nap had been disturbed.

"We're headed toward Ezra's place, aren't we?" she asked.

"Yes, we are, but we won't cross over on his land. Did you see Rusty dancing with your oldest niece last night?" Jackson asked.

"Emmy Lou would have a coronary if Faith settled down on a ranch. She already has all three of her girls' futures planned down to the second that they graduate from medical school," Loretta said. "She can tell me how to go about raising Nona, but she's got control issues worse than I ever had or will have."

"I like what Nona has planned," Jackson said.

"So do I. I don't know why I didn't think of online courses. We raised a pretty smart kid, didn't we, Jackson?"

"We sure did," he said.

Loretta pointed to a small white house with peeling paint. "What is that?"

"If you'll bring the quilt, I'll get the supper and the drinks."

"And explain what this is and how it got here?"

"Yes, ma'am," he agreed.

He pulled a key from his pocket and opened the door. In spite of the heat, it was fairly cool inside. The air-conditioning unit hummed away, sending cold air through the big silver vents already attached to the ceiling trusses. There was no drywall or cabinets, but the studs were up, marking where the rooms would be someday.

"I drove out early this morning and adjusted the thermometer," he explained. "This is the living room. This part and the kitchen are built on the old stones put down by my grandparents when they took over the ranch from his parents. The rest has a new foundation but it all blends together," he said.

She thought it would make a fine home for Travis and Nona.

"Now bring the quilt in here," he said.

He led the way down what would be a hallway someday, even if the bare studs and no drywall gave it a skeletal look right then. "Spread it out. This is the master bedroom and that is the bathroom over there. A walk-in closet right here, and look at the view."

The room faced the west, with a bank of floor-to-ceiling windows that looked out over an array of cactus, scrub oaks, and desert wildflowers. She could easily imagine going to bed at night to a big moon and millions of stars peeking through the window. It would be every bit as wonderful as sleeping outside, without the chiggers and the heat.

Memories flooded through her mind. Even in the beginning stages she recognized the house now. It was the one that they'd laid out on paper that first year they were married. They'd called it their dream house. It was to be the one they'd build someday when they could afford to leave the big ranch house.

"Jackson, is this going to be your present to the kids when they get married?" she asked.

He hugged her close to his side and said, "No, darlin', this has always been and will always be just for us. No one else is ever going to live in it. I started building it the year before you left, intending to surprise you with it when it was all finished. Remember, we wanted something small of our own. I haven't touched it since you left."

"I love it," she whispered.

"Sit down on the bed. I'm not doing one thing to it until you say so and there is no hurry. You tell me when the time is right."

She settled close to him and leaned on his shoulder. "And what's to become of the big house, Jackson?"

"We'll live in it until Nona gets married. I don't know if that will be in a year or ten years, but someday when she does, we'll move out here and give her the big house. We'll pick out our own furniture, our own flooring, and our own sheets and towels. And our bed will be right here, where I can see the sunset every evening in your gorgeous green eyes." He pulled her down beside him.

"Why, Jackson Bailey, is this a proposal?" she asked.

"No, ma'am. Not yet. For starters in this relationship, I just want to know when to call the contractors to finish this place."

"And build my porch and put up a yard fence?" she asked.

"Yes, ma'am. Both of those things. You just stake out where you want that yard fence."

She should tell him about the pregnancy fear, but somehow she couldn't say the words. Maybe, just maybe, it was the earliest signs of menopause. Until she knew for absolutely sure, she wasn't telling anyone.

"Jackson, you told Ezra you wanted a whole yard full of kids," she said.

He hugged her tighter. "Honey, I'm content just to have you on the ranch. To tell the truth, that was a big dose of teenagers this weekend," he chuckled.

A baby deer pressed his nose to the glass and stared in at them. "Would you look at that?" Loretta whispered.

"Pretty amazing, isn't it? I forgot about pillows for our bed, but you can lie on my arm like you do in the back of the truck. Let's take a nap in our very own bedroom," he said.

"Sounds wonderful to me." She curled up next to his side and shut her eyes. Peace, wonderful peace surrounded her like an old worn denim coat on a bitter cold night.

"Jackson," she said.

"Hmm," he mumbled.

"I love you."

He kissed the top of her head. "I love you, Loretta. Always have."

Chapter Twenty-One

*H*OURS MELTED INTO DAYS and the whole ranch settled down to a steady diet of hard work and little play except on Sunday afternoons. The house out there with the fawn outside the window stayed on Loretta's mind, but neither she nor Jackson mentioned it again. They grabbed an hour or two now and then to go to the cabin, but even that only happened on Sunday afternoons.

Loretta knew that she should use that pregnancy kit up there in her bedroom, but to know and have to do something about it was worse than not knowing at all. Until it became a fact, she wouldn't have to do anything about it. She had been sick with Nona and she wasn't now, although her list of foods that made her snarl her nose was getting longer with each passing day.

Nona reached for platter of cinnamon rolls. "Are you ever going to teach me how to make these, Rosie?"

"No, I'm not. You can learn on your own," Rosie said.

"Shit!" Nona said.

"Y'all are on your own for the rest of the day. I'm not making dinner." Rosie hung her apron on a nail and headed out the back door.

"Shit!" Loretta said.

"Like mother, like daughter." Rosie's laughter stayed behind long after she'd left.

Nona leaned over and kissed Travis on the cheek. "Mama. Daddy. I've got an announcement. Travis asked me to marry him last night. We're engaged."

"Congratulations," Loretta said without hesitation.

"You're not angry?" Nona asked.

"Not as long as you keep your word and finish college," Loretta said.

"Daddy?" Nona said.

"I think I'm going to cry. But big old cowboys aren't supposed to get like that. I knew this was going to happen soon, because Travis and I had a talk at the party," Jackson said.

Nona left Travis's side and hugged both her parents. "I love y'all so much. Mama, we've got a wedding to plan and, Daddy, we've got a ranch to run."

※ ※ ※

Loretta took the kit to the bathroom and opened it. They'd come a long way in the years since she'd taken the first one and found out she was pregnant with Nona. This new fancy item could even tell a woman approximately how far along she was.

She opened it up and laid it on the counter, stared at it for a full minute before she could bring herself to read the directions. Not much different there than the first one she'd bought. Her hands shook as she did exactly what it said. She laid it on the countertop and shut her eyes.

She couldn't look. She'd throw it away and never look at it.

But she had to know before they went to the house, before they put out the stakes. Jackson might not want to start all over at their age and he had a right to know that day.

She opened one eye and slowly put the lid down on the potty before she plopped down. She didn't know if she was disappointed or scared senseless but at least she had her answer.

※ ※ ※

Jackson turned the radio to the country music station. Two DJs were talking about bologna sandwiches. "You'll never believe what they're talking about," he said when she crawled into the truck.

"So what do you think, folks? Do you like bologna better than ham or turkey sandwiches?" one DJ asked.

Loretta raised one eyebrow at Jackson. She should tell him right now, but she had to decide what she would do first.

"And do you like your bologna fried or cold?" the DJ asked.

"Bologna is good no matter how you serve it. Cold or fried, with white bread or on wheat, with mustard or mayonnaise," Jackson answered.

"Speaking of bologna, we'll have a contest. Tell us what year this next song came out and what album it was on and when it ends the seventh caller will get two tickets to the Alan Jackson concert nearest your hometown this fall," the DJ said.

The first strains of a steel guitar started and before Alan sang the first words, Loretta said, "That would be Alan's *Good Time* CD in, let's see, 2009 . . . no, 2008, because that was the year Nona was fourteen and she was not into country music that year. The name of the song is 'I Still Like Bologna.'"

Jackson kept time to the beat with his thumbs on the steering wheel. "We never had to worry about things having enough money to buy food or pay rent, did we?"

"No, Rosie made sure there was plenty of food and we didn't have to pay your folks a dime to live at the ranch," she said.

It took five callers before one got the name of the CD and the year right. The lady who won the two tickets was squealing when Jackson parked the truck in the backyard. "You should have called. You would have won on the first try."

Half an hour later they were at the house, sitting in the kitchen on two lawn chairs that Jackson had brought along at the last minute. Their knees touched, making a table of their laps, and a bag of barbecue chips lay open between them. Loretta nibbled on a few chips but she couldn't force anything else past the lump in her throat.

She loved the peace inside the house and wished to hell that she had the same peace inside her heart right then. She was jittery just thinking about what she had to say to Jackson and scared about what he would say.

He finally moved the chips to the floor, pushed back his chair, and kneeled on one knee in front of her. "I've been waiting and hoping and dreaming for this day, Loretta. Will you please marry me? We can wait however long you need to. We can go to the courthouse tomorrow or you can have the wedding you never got to have the first time. I'm willing for whatever makes you happy."

She laid a hand on each shoulder. "You make me happy. Even more so now that we are wise enough to appreciate what we have in each other. Yes, I will marry you, but, darlin', I don't need a big wedding. We'll be busy planning one for the kids, so I'd just as soon go on to the courthouse tomorrow morning. Besides…" She paused.

He picked her up and swung her around in circles until they were both breathless. "I'm the happiest man alive today."

"You might not be when you hear my besides," she said.

"I don't care what it is. If you want to sell real estate, I'll build you an office right here in the canyon. If you want to go to Claude or Silverton or Canyon or even Amarillo to work, that's fine. Just come home to me every night." He set her down and tipped her chin up for another kiss.

Her stomach drew up into knots even worse than when she smelled beer. "I'm pregnant," she blurted out.

She was afraid to look at his face, terrified that she'd see disappointment and entrapment there. So she shut her eyes and said, "I wasn't careless, Jackson. I was on the pill but I must be that point-nine percent that fell between the cracks. And according to the test I took a few minutes ago, I probably got pregnant right after that stunt with the whiskey. I had my suspicious but I just couldn't make myself find out for sure. I won't trap you a second time, but I'm scared out of my mind to face this without you."

"Look at me, Loretta," he whispered.

She opened her eyes slowly, tears streaming down her cheeks.

"I love you and I'll love however many more children we are blessed with at our age. You didn't trap me the first time and you're damn sure not this time. We can add on to the house and make the yard bigger. I want to marry you. I want to share the rest of our lives with you. I want this child. And like I told you before, forty is the new thirty."

It was more than words. His eyes said that he was telling the absolute truth.

"But you're going to tell Nona," he whispered.

She chuckled and then laughter filled the whole house.

"Think she'll give Bossy to her baby sister or brother?"

"I wouldn't count on it," Jackson said.

"I have a white dress to wear but I want to buy a brand-new pair of bright red boots, so we'll need to make a stop at the western-wear store."

Jackson kissed her on the nose and said, "I love you, Loretta, and you will be gorgeous in your white dress and red boots."

Epilogue

Four Months Later

Loretta set the veil on Nona's head, being very careful not to mess up a single blonde curl in the upswept hairdo. "You are the most beautiful bride in the world," she whispered.

"Mama, I'm scared," Nona said.

"Of what?"

"What if Travis decides in five years that he got married too soon? What if I do?"

"We don't get to look down the road five years or even five days. All we get is today and we have to work with what we've got this day," Loretta answered.

"It's a big house and you'll be gone when I come home from the islands. That's scary," Nona said.

"Yes, I will, but the new housekeeper, Dotty, is there and I'll be in and out. She's been a good replacement for Rosie. And you'll be busy with your last semester of classes and with the ranch. I'm so proud of you, Nona, for all you've taken on. You and Travis have proved to be two fine ranchers."

"You're going to make me cry yet." Nona dabbed under her eyes with a tissue.

"Then let's talk about something else."

"When are you and Daddy going to spend the first night in your house?" Nona fluffed her white velvet wedding dress out over the hoopskirt.

"Tonight. It's all ready and set up. The yard still looks like shit, but come spring we'll have some sod laid and keep it watered."

"It'll be ready for my sisters to play on it by the time they can walk." She smiled.

"I remember the first time you got to put your bare feet in soft green grass. The way you giggled, I should have known that you were going to love the land," Loretta said. "Are you really going to be all right with this idea of twin sisters that are twenty-two years younger than you are?"

"I'm fine with it. Hell, Mama—oops, we're in church, aren't we? I'm just happy you and Daddy are together," Nona said. "Now hug me one more time and get out of here before I really start bawling and mess up my makeup."

Loretta opened the door to find Jackson waiting outside with Waylon and Cooper. Jackson crooked his arm and she slipped hers into it. "You are prettier than any woman in this place," he whispered as he escorted her down the center aisle.

"You could have a biased opinion," she said.

"No, ma'am. In that dress and with your hair all done up like that you look like a pregnant runway model." He kissed her on the cheek when she took her place on the front pew.

She turned slightly in her seat so that she could watch him swagger back up the aisle. His next job would be to bring his daughter halfway down and stop, where Travis would come to claim her as his and walk the rest of the way with her. It wasn't the traditional way, but Nona was a free spirit who wanted things done her way. And it was her wedding, after all.

Instead of the usual wedding music, six of Nona's cousins, all wearing crimson velvet dresses, strolled to their places to the tinkling piano sounds of "The Rose" in true Floyd Cramer style. Then Bobby Lee made a motion with his hands and the whole congregation rose when the doors at the back of the church opened and there was Nona on Jackson's arm. Immediately the recording of Randy Travis singing "Deeper Than the Holler" started.

That's when Loretta reached for a tissue. She'd conceived that gorgeous child when that song was playing and now she was watching her come down the aisle toward her groom to the same music.

She was still dabbing away the tears when Jackson joined her.

"It's okay," he whispered. "I'm not so old that I won't be able to walk the twins down the aisle."

"You always could read my mind." She smiled.

Acknowledgments

$\mathcal{D}$EAR READER,

Welcome to the Palo Duro Canyon, with all its interesting formations and earthy colors. I hope that you've enjoyed meeting Loretta and Jackson and that you'll come back and visit in the wintertime when the second book is published in a few months.

Husband and I made several trips to the canyon before this book was written. I wanted to see it in every season—with an icing of snow, with heat bearing down in the summer, with wild-flowers blooming in the spring, and with a hint of cool air on an early-fall morning. It was a desolate area in every season, but it still called out to me, telling me that people who lived there had a story to tell.

As I stood inside a fenced area on a ledge and looked out over the canyon, I could see why Loretta didn't want to come back, and at the same time why she didn't want to leave once she was there. It was eerily peaceful with the wind blowing against my face and the distant sounds of cattle. It was then that I was sure that two people really could find a second chance at love in a place dotted with red dirt roads, wildflowers, and shallow streams.

Special thanks goes to the awesome Montlake staff for their dedication and work on this book. To all those behind-the-scenes folks, from editors to artists, whose names I don't even know—thank you. To my awesome agent, Erin Niumata, and of course to my husband, Charles Brown, who is always ready to drop everything and go with me on research trips. It takes a special person to live with a writer who talks to the voices in her head.

To all of you who continue to read my books, tell your neighbors and friends about them, review them in your book clubs and pass your used copies on to your best friend, please know that you are appreciated.

Happy reading!

Carolyn Brown

About the Author

Carolyn Brown is a *New York Times* and *USA Today* bestselling author and a RITA finalist. Her books include historical, contemporary, cowboy, and country music mass-market paperbacks. She and her husband live in Davis, Oklahoma. They have three grown children and enough grandchildren to keep them young.